WING WIFE

How To Be Married To A Marine Fighter Pilot

MARCIA J. SARGENT

ISBN: 1-4538-0926-0
ISBN-13: 9781453809266

Dedication

This book is dedicated to all the military spouses, past and present. Bless you for all you have done and do for others, to raise the children and to keep home a haven.

Table of Contents

Who's Who

(Some names have been changed to protect the guilty)

Marcia and Andy "Snatch" Sargent

Family
    Mom: Mary Jean Jones
    Dad: Stuart Jones
    Brother: Don "Bullet" and Kathy
    Timothy, Kellen and Toburn—children
    Rheta Lyn: married to brother Charly and Matron
        of Honor at wedding

Training Squadron 22, Kingsville, Texas
    1st Lt. Skip "Pipperburn"

VMFA 314 The Black Knights and their Ladies
    "Trigger" Bobby, a RIO, and Sundy Rodgers
    "Bird" *Jake*, pilot, and *Julie*
    Budman , RIO, and his date Candy "Mounds"
    Cindy and "Agile" Jon Morrow, pilot
    Kelly and Greg—children
    Willie "Donut" Duncan, RIO, and wife Marilyn
    Randi Noelle Duncan—child

Kate and Warrant Officer "Duff" Alger
Michael—child
"Waldo" Walsh, pilot, and *Debby*
"Jaime" Messerschmidt, RIO
Harley Chapman (CO 1975) and Fran
Hanley (XO) and *Margaret*
"Pops" Morrow RIO
"Unsafe at Any Speed" *Bill Jackson* and *Mikki*
Mike Wadsworth (CO starting July 1975) and Ernie
Captain Samuels and *Linda*
Bob Jacobs
Merle
"Groove" Chuck and *Janey*
Phil Lahlum
Mike Maher and Diane
Dwayne "Bash" Wills (XO) and Patty
Lt. Jim Bassett
"OJ" Oren Riddell and Sherry
"Terrible Ted" (call sign Scorpion) Berwald (CO) and Sarah
"Hombre" and Susan

Other people and military personnel
"Toad"
Father Vince Germano
"Jimbo"
"Col. Profane"
Leo "the RIO" Kraus
"Worm" Lieutenant in VMFA 232

"JC" John Kauffman
Fran Brinkley—Cindy's friend
Jack Hartman
Randy Brinkley

Mission Viejo
Mary, a neighbor

Twentynine Palms
Ken and Sue Flanders
Lt. Col. Jim Sparks and Ann, next door neighbors
and their daughter Susan
Stella Betelmann, Battalion CO's wife
Ray Rideout
Millie, a lieutenant colonel's wife
Nurse Dayrit
Lt Col John Ressmeyer
"Yucca Man" Bob Haber
Beau Wiley
Lt. Col. Bob Liston-Wakefield

Beaufort, South Carolina
Dave and Donna Seder
"Slug" Jim Forney
Ray Sanford
Robbie Barkley
Val, Kathy's sister

VMFA 531 The Grey Ghosts and their Ladies
"Burner" Mitchell

"Swizzle" Chwaliscz
"Fog" Macy and Diane
"Spud"
"Soupy"
"Flokker"

VMFA 323 The Death Rattlers and their Ladies
  Gary "Gazelle" Van Gysel and Bev
  "Taco" Calderon and Cis

The truth? I never flew in a military high performance aircraft. Not even once. But I married a Marine fighter pilot. In the testosterone-heavy atmosphere of jet jockeys, Peter Pan and his boys soared high above reality, believing they'd all live forever in Never Neverland.

Chapter 1
Wedding the Corps

My brother loomed over both of us but stared at Andy. "Curfew's at ten o-clock," Don said. He'd just escorted us to the door of his Mission Viejo house on our way to New Year's Eve and our first date after our official engagement.

I smiled up at all six foot two, two-hundred and ten pounds of my older brother. He was joking, right?

Andy laughed. "Hey, Don. This is your buddy Andy you're talking to." They'd been roommates through four and a half years of Marine flight training and during their first overseas deployment.

My brother didn't smile. "I don't care who you are, this is my kid sister. Curfew's at ten o-clock."

The whole time out the door and across my brother's lawn, my guy shook his head.

I shook my head, too. Silly silly big brother.

Andy said, "It's never going to work."

He might as well have thrown a lead weight down my throat. I couldn't swallow. I couldn't speak in dread of what would come next. He was going to call the whole thing off. No engagement, no wedding, no marrying my beautiful Marine captain. I knew Andy loving me had been too good to be true.

"It's not?" I managed to respond.

"No. We're going to have to get married as soon as my parents can get out here for the wedding. Don would never forgive me if I shacked up with his sister."

Shacking up had been the plan. Liberated 70's and all. We hardly knew each other—well, we knew each other in the Biblical sense and I knew that Andy was someone my very particular brother liked—but we hadn't spent all that much time together. The plan had been I'd move into Andy's house for four or five months and we'd see how it went before we took the leap.

The weight in my stomach lightened. Not only did he still want to marry me, he wanted to marry me sooner.

Mom had three weeks to put it all together.

———

Now, two weeks after the wedding, Andy and I were off to our first social function as captain and wife: a potluck at Bird's house.

Whoever felt up to it, or wanted to, held the squadron parties. Potlucks and BYOBs—Bring Your Own Booze—allowed the entertainment of large numbers of hungry, thirsty people on a small budget.

Large numbers of people—people I did not know. My brothers had often called me Dork or named me Dweeb when I first lost my way in the mists of puberty. Names held power, power that said I'd no business going to a gathering of strangers. My gut felt like a garter snake had taken up residence.

I rubbed my tummy and reminded myself I knew about the men I'd be partying with. Andy had told me various stories of squadron life, work, and reputation that included his squadron-mates' call signs. Odd to know men by such names as Trigger, Agile, and Donut. Agile and Bird had been at our wedding reception, but I didn't remember meeting them or their wives in the swarm of uniformed attendees. Not that I would have been able to tag faces, civilian names, call signs and spouses together.

"Do I look okay?"

"You look great. I have the cutest wife in the squadron."

He always said things like that—and meant them.

I knew I was the youngest—a twenty-two year old wife newly married to a thirty year old senior Captain. Most of the wives were in their early thirties and had kids. I was used to partying with people my own age.

I touched Andy on the arm. "Will they like me?"

He patted my hand and smiled down at me. "Of course they'll like you."

Doubt slithered deeper in my abdomen. No "of course" about it. I didn't even know if *I* liked me. Why should anyone else enjoy having me around?

"Will I know anyone?"

"Some of the guys and their wives were at the wedding. And Bullet will be there. Not Kathy, though— their babysitter backed out at the last minute and she's the designated stay-at-home."

Bullet. The blunt-nosed shape of my brother Don's head in the cockpit melded into his shoulders, mimicking the live ammo F-4 Phantoms carried. Was that the reason for his call sign, or was it because Don often took aim at a target—usually a member of the group he

3

called 'the idiots of the world'—and shot it down? He didn't tolerate fools and worked to make them suffer.

It would be good to have him at the party. His pride in my bachelor's degree had been amplified by my marrying his best friend and bringing Andy permanently into the family. Besides, Bullet livened up any gathering with his charisma.

I wished I'd inherited some of Bullet's confidence. Damp hands wiped on my new Ditto bell-bottoms. A wide leather belt with a large brass buckle, a tie-dyed t-shirt, and an aren't-these-men-too-wonderful-for-words attitude completed my outfit. I needed them to like me.

I turned the corner into the host's living room— and my first question about squadron parties popped right out at me.

"Marcia, Candy. Candy, Marcia."

My question: if a woman has fifty-four double deltas, should she wear a skintight t-shirt with the picture of a Mounds bar silk-screened across them—especially if her given name is Candace?

The look on the fighter pilots and RIOs' faces answered, "Yes. Absolutely." For the squadron wives, the answer involved whapping their husbands on the shoulder and telling them to wipe the drool off their chins.

Besides 'Mounds' and her boyfriend, a bulky mustached RIO with the call sign 'Budman,' two distinct groups and a couple of outliers populated the living room. One group consisted entirely of women. The other group held only men—men who either flew their hands through the air to demonstrate tactical maneuvers, or watched those who flew their hands through the air.

Warmth against my side. I looked up, startled, into a wide grin. The host, lanky and dark-haired.

My husband said, "You remember Bird?"

"Bird? Because you fly so well?"

"No, for my command presence in the plane." His tone predicted a future including the rank of full colonel, bird colonel.

"Hah!" Andy said. "Bird—because he has skinny legs with knobby knees."

"Can I get you a drink?" Bird asked.

"A beer for me," Andy answered.

"I didn't ask you, Snatch. I asked the pretty one here."

Snatch. Andy said his call sign meant 'to grab fast' and came from his ability to snatch victory from defeat in a dogfight. He never explained the inevitable laughter.

Andy said, "Quit schmoozing up to her. She's already taken."

"So am I. What's your point?" Bird grinned.

A protective arm. "I'll get her drink." Andy steered me to the bar that took up one corner of the room. "Bird is one of the few people I could call at four in the morning who would get out of bed and come help me with anything I needed. A very good friend, but—" He filled my glass from the gallon jug of Almaden at one end.

The flashing neon Coors light behind the bar competed with the illuminated plastic screen showing a trout on the fly before flipping to a red Miller logo on a gold field. The black Naugahyde surface of the eight-foot-long bar matched a couple of Naugahyde-covered barstools, inhabited by a lieutenant and his date.

The lieutenant's date looked too old and hard for him, like she'd been around the O-Club a few times with a variety of officers. Andy often laughed about lieutenants following their little heads around, willing and eager to take sexual favors over beauty or brains.

I took the plastic glass of white wine and smiled into Andy's sherry eyes. "Thanks." I snuggled against his hip.

"So," I asked. "Where'd Budman's call sign come from?"

"He's a very loyal customer."

I nodded, remembering Mounds' date had been holding a distinctive red and white can. Hard to imagine being in a relationship with a 'Budman'. My guy drank one beer a night—and then only on the weekend.

My brother waved at us from the men's corner.

"Don!" I hurried over to him for a hug. He felt good. Big. Strong. Safe. I stood next to him and asked about Kathy and the kids. I could hang out with him and Andy all night. Then I wouldn't have to try to talk to people I didn't know, who might not want to talk to me.

Don and my husband were joined by a guy named Toad. Toad looked normal. Tall enough, a pleasant smile, he didn't have warts or the build to justify his call sign. They spoke about something called MAWTS and the move to Yuma.

Military minds love acronyms. As a civilian, decoding strings of capital letters pronounced as words was an exercise in frustration.

"What's MAWTS?" I'd never know if I didn't ask.

"Marine Air Weapons Training Squadron." Andy's hand in the small of my back urged me away. "Hey, honey. Go mingle. You know Cindy and Julie." He pointed to the women's group.

I knew Cindy and Julie about as well as I knew the guy who washed my windows at the gas station while he filled the tank. All I knew about Cindy and Julie was that they were squadron wives and we had exchanged some sort of conversation at my wedding reception.

Groups of women made me nervous. My mother loved social organizations such as Junior Women's League (I did wonder where all the Senior Women were), Assistance League, and Girl Scout Leadership Council. She believed that if I would wear the clothes she wore (a generation out of date—but the *workmanship*), if I belonged where she belonged (or at least if I *tried* to belong), smiled at the right people (but who I never saw do anything worth smiling about), then I would be happy. The few times I tried reminded me I wore the wrong clothes, spoke the wrong code words, laughed at all the wrong things. I wasn't my mother and didn't want to be like her. In the deepest part of me, I knew my mother wasn't happy.

But boys—they knew how to be happy and how to deal with things that caused unhappiness. When my brothers and their friends had a problem with me when we were growing up, they'd ignore me or make a straightforward assault with threats or fists. Girls struck from behind with gossip, innuendo, and you-can-be-my-friend or you-can't-be-my-friend edicts. Wanting to fit in with my older brothers, avoiding my mother's dictates, I never learned how to fit in with my female peers. I grew up reminded at every turn I was *other*—not one of the girls.

Now Andy wanted me to fit in. I loved Andy. Although I wanted to step away and hide in a corner, I edged closer to the women.

Murmurs about Christmas Eve. Talk of *the accident*, quickly hushed. They spoke of babies, children, and childbirth.

What accident?

They saw me at the edge of the group. Ten pairs of curious eyes. Ten officer's wives. Silence. A long silence.

"Here's the new bride." Julie, brown hair softly falling to her shoulders, a kind voice with an educated, southern drawl. I remembered her from the wedding reception. Andy had known her and her husband in the Training Command. I remembered her because Andy liked her.

She introduced me around.

I barely heard for the nerves buzzing in my ears. So many names but no connections. Who was Julie's husband? I couldn't remember. Wives didn't have call signs.

Call signs were military nicknames used in air-to-air combat to avoid revealing an aviator's identity to the enemy. In the world of friendlies they identified members of the fraternity of airmen.

Given names were common fodder for call sign generation: Swizzle's last name Cwaliscz, properly pronounced "Fah-leash"—impossible to see and say—so the guys gave him an easier version; Bolt's last name of Leitner; Soupy's last name of Campbell. J.C.'s first name and middle initial was John C., but he built his reputation doing stunts in and out of airplanes that made others say, "Jesus Christ!"

An ideal name like Burner incorporated an aviation term so those not in the know would think it came from afterburner—a part of a jet airplane that when lit makes the plane very loud and very fast. The way the name game was played, he could be very slow, very quiet, or have a tendency to pass gas with explosive consequences. Like Andy, Burner never explained.

Who wouldn't remember these characters?

My recall connected to my funnybone.

Women I'd known had rarely been funny so most of the wives' names or to whom they were married had gone directly to my I-can't-keep-them-straight-so-I'll-throw-them-in-the-kitchen-drawer memory file. The drawer had been stirred too many times—names and callsigns, stories and wives jumbled together. Now I couldn't connect anyone to anyone.

The wives smiled. They murmured, "Oh yes. Snatch's wife."

"How's married life treating you?" A thirty-ish brunette, matronly. She reminded me of my cousins in Wisconsin.

"Good. It's good."

"Look at the stars in her eyes." A statuesque blonde.

"That won't last." This from a heavyset woman with a gravelly voice, smoking a cigarette—its smoke curling up to the ceiling in a thin line like a dissipating rocket trail.

"Hey, Kate. Let her have her honeymoon. Snatch is worth mooning over."

I smiled. I agreed with the blonde.

Kate shrugged and blew out a cloud of haze.

"We heard about the moon at your wedding," the blonde said. "Cindy, you were there. Tell us."

"Sorry, Debby." Cindy, the matronly, Midwest one frowned. "We missed it. We never found the church and went straight to the reception."

Eyes turned to me. I blushed as I remembered what Cindy had missed.

I'd wanted a fairytale wedding: flowers, moonlight, laughter and magic. My wedding entwined all of those, but not at all in the ways I'd imagined.

I remember I'd paced the cramped back room of the chapel dressed in my retro medieval white gown, snood and all—the dress more beautiful than the bride. My gardenia, rose and stephanotis bouquet twisted in dampening hands.

My matron of honor, Rheta, had burst in the door. "Don't worry, Marcia. I think I've convinced them not to moon the congregation."

Them. The Navy and Marine Corps pilots who flew out from Andy's Training Command Squadron in Texas.

"Why'd you do that?" The display of thirty-one naked rear-ends sounded like fun to me. Only twenty-two,

I wanted some fun. A wedding involved too many details and too little time with my guy, even in the short time I gave my folks to put one together.

Mendlessohn's Wedding March, played by the ancient organist, sounded like a dirge. My dad held out his arm.

Rheta in the lead, I proceeded past the risers on my left filled with aviators and turned toward the altar of the Mt. Baldy Chapel in the San Gabriel Mountains of California. My bouquet could have been a stand-in for those feathered gourds Tahitian dancers shake. The baby's breath threatened to break loose from its fragile stems and shower the audience with bridal nerves confetti.

I heard a collective gasp, a few snickers, and then, outright laughter.

Were they laughing at me?

Don't think about it. Don't faint. Reach my handsome husband-to-be.

I focused instead on moving, one slow step at a time, down the aisle. Through the strains of "Here Comes the Bride," I still heard titters.

I found out later they laughed at First Lieutenant 'Pipperburn' making my bridal processional special by turning around, dropping his trousers, and showing his very fine ass to the assembled guests.

Rheta had the best view of the lieutenant's ham and eggs. She was supposed to look toward *me*, smiling encouragement as I progressed down the aisle, not toward Pipperburn bent-over, in the back risers at the back of the chapel.

Every flier I'd ever met wanted to look good at the field—the airfield of life. Pilots and RIOs—Radar Intercept Officers—were allowed, even encouraged, to do wild and crazy things in the air and on the ground, but if they didn't show to advantage, they'd get a ration of shit and lose the respect of the fliers who heard the story.

Rheta Lyn told me Pipperburn had looked good. In fact, she said he definitely put his best face forward.

Too bad I didn't see his display. The double scotch-on-the-rocks my mother had given me two hours before had worn off, and I could've used a distraction.

My childhood had been spent with the unhappily married—my parents and their friends. I escaped into books when family mayhem and my father's anger threatened, believing in the promise of fairytales: if I were good and true and honest and brave, a prince— also good and true and honest and brave—would come along, love me, and we would live happily ever after.

Legal and religious union never occurred to me.

I didn't believe in marriage, but my big brother, Don, didn't believe in me living in sin. Andy recognized his friend Don's protective instincts. Caught between the rock of my brother's morals and wanting a place for my heart, I chose to marry.

I walked down the aisle, past the chapel rows of cousins I barely knew and friends of my parents. If I'd had an ejection handle, I'd have pulled it.

My brother Don's wide, white smile gleamed in front of the night dark, stained glass windows.

I was in love, scared, and elated to almost be part of the best club, my brother's flyboys' club, Andy's club.

I looked up, and the sight of Andy drew me toward the altar. My prince had come. If I could face this scary marriage part, maybe we'd live happily ever after.

Step, feet together, step.

Andy stood straight, strong-nosed, and grinning in his formal Marine Corps mess dress: red cummerbund and all. Next to him, his brother stood in Air Force dress uniform, all muted blues and black. Step, feet together, step. I concentrated on reaching Andy, on getting to the altar. Heaven forbid I trip. I gripped my father's arm in a death hold.

Finally, I stood next to my husband-to-be before the altar.

Father Vince Germano, the Navy chaplain who had flown out from Kingsville, Texas in the backseat of one of the sixteen jet trainers, leaned toward me.

I leaned toward him. Every rose, gardenia, and stephanotis shook with my pulse of a hundred and sixty beats a minute. This was it. Now a Catholic priest—a priest with a clerical collar and a white surplice covering *his* Marine blues—would marry me to my Marine Corps beauty of a captain.

I waited breathlessly. Stars started spinning in from the outer reaches of my vision. My knees wibble-wobbled.

Andy's arm dragged me upright.

Still leaning toward me, Father Germano whispered, "If you don't relax, I'll have to tell you a dirty joke."

The priest said what? I looked up, too startled to keep shaking.

He had winked.

I had giggled. In a totally silent chapel in the mountains in the winter with snow falling outside, I giggled.

No one—except myself and my husband-to-be—could have heard the padre. Everyone heard my nervous laugh. Laughter again rolled through the pews.

So began my marriage and life in the fraternity of pilots—with a moon over a quivering baby's breath bouquet, and a giggle over the threat of an off-color joke.

After the ceremony and photos, we ran to the car. Snow, like pixie dust, sprinkled on us and ice slicked the path beneath our feet. Fair warning of what was ahead—if only I'd paid attention.

———

The sound of women chuckling reminded me I wasn't in the Mt. Baldy chapel anymore. The wives were laughing—at me? No. Someone had told a joke. I'd missed it, but they hadn't noticed.

I stood in Bird's living room in front of the officer's wives who still expected the salacious details. "I never saw Pipperburn bare his assets. I'd turned toward the front of the church while he was at the backend."

Pipperburn's call sign referred to something called the pipper. The pipper—predicted impact point—was the location where a bomb, missile, or bullet was expected to strike if fired. When an electronic aiming device was locked on an opponent, but not fired, it burned an imaginary hole in the opponent—and accomplished nothing. Pipperburn's youth, inexperience, and tendency to consume copious amounts of alcoholic beverages all precluded him from ever actually firing on any target—whether an adversarial airplane or a female. He'd be expected to aim often, but never shoot.

I wondered what he'd aimed for when I walked down the aisle.

Many Johns, Jims and Roberts existed in the world, but I knew only one Pipperburn, only one Snatch.

I mentally matched names to women. Debby was the statuesque blonde; Kate smoked and sounded like it; Cindy reminded me of my cousins in Wisconsin; Julie, the brunette from North Carolina, sat on the carpet. I had names for four of the ten wives. My own military couples concentration game—now I only had to match them with call-signed husbands.

They went back to talking about pregnancy and being only dilated to three but needing to push. After general agreement that the dislocated hips and the need to pee all the time and the pain was worth the end result, they moved on to the subject of potty training. Those with girls apparently had an easier time than the women with boys who could not be counted on to hit the target.

Good grief. I'd nothing to talk with them about and nothing I *wanted* to talk to them about.

I signaled panic to my new husband. You know—the wide-open, blue-eyed lemur look. He smiled, laughed at something Agile said, and turned back to watch an aerial hand dogfight, where a captain showed the lieutenants where they went wrong in some maneuvers. Maybe my prince didn't understand I needed rescuing.

My brother had moved to the faux-leather covered bar to talk to Toad while the lieutenant and his date listened in. Don didn't look my way. No rescue there.

"Excuse me. I'm—" I carried my wine across the room to stand next to Andy.

"Marcia, you remember Agile from the wedding reception?"

I murmured agreement. He did look familiar. Dark hair, a few inches taller than I was. Slender, but solid. Not that I remembered who his wife was.

"My wife's name's Cindy."

Cindy. The one who reminded me of my Wisconsin cousins. I smiled and nodded.

Agile smiled back. He had the nicest smile.

My Not-So-Charming kept talking to Agile. They spoke about some maintenance issue and complained something was in danger of becoming a hangar queen. Whatever a hangar queen was. Andy hugged me. Then there was more conversation about engine maintenance. A guy named Donut joined in the conversation, giving Andy grief about flying with leaking fuel tanks to North Island.

"What are you complaining about, RIO? I drained the internal tank for you."

"If it had been anybody else than you, Snatch, I wouldn't have flown in the backseat."

"We got there. It was fixed."

I was on Donut's side. Leaking fuel sounded like a bad idea.

The group of guys next to me, in their mid- to late-twenties, weren't all tall and handsome—for example,

Jaime's over-muscled, short body gave him more of the aspect of a blond bullfrog—but the radiating male confidence warmed and pulled me in.

Standing not quite in the circle of aviators and not quite out, I listened. I'd learned if I stayed quiet when my brothers and their friends were talking, sometimes they wouldn't chase me away.

"The way I heard it, they were flying intercepts out in W-291 and the radios weren't working."

"Fucking radios."

"They said they saw the other plane as they came out of the clouds and joined up." The lieutenant's two hands flew palm down, one trailing the other. The right hand swooped alongside the left. "Both canopies were gone and both seat guns extended. No one was in the plane."

The men around him shook their heads.

"The plane flew straight and level. Then it departed and arced down into the ocean."

Beers tilted up and drained down gullets.

"Where were they?" I asked.

The men shook their heads, looking at Andy, who hadn't heard my question and didn't notice the looks.

What? Why were they looking at him? I asked the question. "Why weren't they there? What happened?"

The lieutenant, who'd told the story, shook his head. "Ask Snatch. It's an active investigation."

Jaime mumbled, "No one knows, anyway."

More beer chugged.

17

I moved closer to my Andy. He smiled at me and continued the conversation about the utility hydraulic failure on number thirteen. Maintenance Officer stuff.

A captain at the back of the group lowered his voice. Must have been a joke. Chuckles. A few sheepish grins in my direction. Maybe an off-color joke.

Behind me, the women laughed and hooted. Potty training couldn't be that funny.

Andy had told me a pilot always needed to know what surrounded him, and the most vulnerable area was the rear. Aviators needed to know who was at the six-o-clock position to avoid getting a missile up the ass. I checked the group at my six. Still too many women over there.

The men's faces flashed the shining grins of joyful boys. They spoke of flying, of complex machines, and told dirty jokes. I'd journeyed to a foreign land with a foreign tongue telling the secrets of being one of the guys. I wanted to stay and learn their language.

Women spoke of babies, kids, and fashion—also a foreign language, but one I'd little interest in.

A hand on my shoulder. "Marcia, come help me with the food in the kitchen." Julie.

She'd come up on my six.

"Have you seen my other half?" she asked Andy and Agile.

Head shakes.

She looked at me, one eyebrow raised.

"No." I said. We walked toward the kitchen. I still didn't know which aviator was her husband.

"Julie?"

"Yes?"

"What investigation were the guys talking about? The lieutenant said someone joined up on a plane, and it was empty. No pilot or RIO."

A shadow trailed across her face. "The lieutenant talks too much. It wasn't our squadron. It was 323, the Snakes. They lost a plane Christmas Eve."

"Lost?" If another plane had been there, they should know where the plane went down. Then it wouldn't be lost, just crashed. Crashed in the ocean. Deep waters. Lost as in 'not recoverable'. "What about the pilot and RIO?"

She touched my arm. "Don't think about it. Don't worry about it."

I wasn't worried, just curious and unsettled. I wondered if I should worry. Julie seemed unsettled too. So I let it go.

"By the way," I said, "Andy said you're one of his favorite people."

She smiled.

"He said he could count on you to talk about literature and philosophy when he was a bachelor in Kingsville."

She nodded, smiling wider. "You married one of the good ones. I've always thought of your husband as a Renaissance man—he's interested in so many things." She nudged my arm. "It doesn't hurt that he's good-looking and doesn't know it."

He *was* one of the good guys.

I followed her into the kitchen and ran smack dab into her back and her gasp.

"Jake! What in the world are you doing?"

I tried to peek around her to see who she yelled at and why. She blocked me to the right. She blocked me to the left. I double-feinted and squeezed slightly into the gap between her shoulder and the door jam.

Bird, scrawny legs and all, stood naked next to the sink, his right hand clasped around his male member, a member wilting rapidly under our scrutiny. "Darling, I would think what I am doing is obvious."

I giggled and backed away.

Seems the guys had decided the party needed some enlivening, so some of them bribed, cajoled, convinced Bird to streak through in his altogether. With Bird's ego, it hadn't taken much.

The kitchen temperature left him shrinking, so Bird was caught, by his wife, in the act of trying to look good at the field.

"Darling," he said. "You want to be proud of me, don't you?"

"You are *so* dead." From the tone of Julie's voice, at the very least, he'd soon wish he were. Proud, she wasn't.

I moved away, laughing, to join back up with Andy.

Andy must have heard Julie yell. He arched an eyebrow in the direction of the kitchen.

"Oh," I said. "Bird surprised Julie." I'd already learned aviators low-keyed information.

Why did she marry and stay married to the walking-ego-incarnate Bird? His idea of a conversation involved big guns—unrelated to metal objects, he meant a sizable rack, double-deltas, bazooms—and making a score on deployment. What did she see in him?

20

Well, Bird was tall; he was a pilot; he had dimples. And he was—well—he had a big nose.

Still disconnected from most of the women; a tenuous thread pulled me toward Julie. We both loved our pilots. Bird might act funny, but Julie made me laugh. She faced up to her husband's less than best behavior without hysterics, with dignity. He'd lost his. She'd kept hers.

I dropped the worry about empty planes and lost aviators into my messy memory drawer and eased it shut.

Chapter 2
Officer's Wives Meeting

In the first months of my marriage, we had as our CO—Commanding Officer—a former POW. Andy told me Harley had been a prisoner of war in Vietnam for seven and a half years. Prisoners of war had the respect of all Marines. Our squadron was his twilight tour, a reward for enduring the unendurable. The general population might not have honored those who returned alive from Vietnam prisons, but every Marine bowed his head to them. Soldiers knew what it took to conquer pain and fear.

I'd met the CO, Harley, at Bird and Julie's squadron party where he sat to one side, quietly. Few bothered him. A man had the right to have space and peace after years of torture and abuse. I wondered as I watched him whether he'd ever free himself. A thirty-three year old Captain when taken prisoner, now he was a forty-one year old Lieutenant Colonel and CO of a squadron. He seemed old, so much older than the flyboys who amused themselves by streaking and drinking and bragging.

In a squadron, the CO was the boss. He made command decisions, ruled the roost, and if he thought it important—it was important. Number one mantra for a squadron aviator: Don't make your CO look bad.

The XO—the Executive Officer—was the paper-pushing, attention-to-details, pain-in-the-ass who made sure the big vision of the CO was turned into reality. He did a lot of the admin work and in any court-martial; he was in charge of the details.

The Marine Corps abhorred a vacuum in the command. In the mental and emotional absence of the CO, Hanley, the XO—supposedly second in the command structure—took on the job of running things. Harley and Hanley—sounded like a vaudeville comedy duo, but were anything but. So it fell to Margaret, the XO's wife, to host the first squadron wives' meeting since my marriage.

Andy and I had a running discussion in later years on who was the CO and who was the XO of our family. I maintained he was the XO since he paid the bills and did the worry-work over the administration details; and I was the CO, making command decisions on the big picture like how many children we would have, what the rules were for the children, and where we would live after retirement. He always snorted and shook his head after I reminded him of the qualifications, but he didn't really argue because he knew I was always right. Proof I was the CO. However, for my first official wives' function in the Marine Corps, I hadn't yet reached command of the family status. We had no kids and I barely commanded myself.

I rang the doorbell, checking to make sure no vestiges of breakfast or dog drool from my golden retriever puppy had dribbled on my shirt. I shifted on my platform shoes from my right foot to the left and back. Voices. Women's voices.

Shoot. Like I said before, I'd never been a part of a women's social group I enjoyed. Not confident in my wardrobe choices and uncomfortable in my own skin, I'd been a GDI—a God Damn Independent.

A GDI thoroughly convinced of my own inadequacies, I didn't know how I would find a place for myself, but I had to try. I had to try because I loved Andy and Andy's career could very well hinge on whether I meshed in the social life of the squadron.

Or so I'd been told by my mother.

Margaret opened the door and welcomed me. Her dark hair curled perfectly to her shoulders. Her tailored polyester pantsuit screamed I-know-how-to-dress-to-look-like-I'm-in-charge. I tried to remember if she'd been at the party when Bird had streaked through in his altogether, 'looking good at the field' except for his knobby, skinny legs. I couldn't remember. I couldn't picture her face in the crowd, much less if it registered surprise, laughter, or disapproval. No way to judge how serious she took this whole military business. She looked too put-together for me to feel comfortable with her.

"Can I get you something to drink?"

I laughed. "A margarita would taste good."

Her face froze.

Shit. I'd stepped in it right away. "Uh. Ice tea?" Okay. Different rules for behavior at squadron wives' meetings than at parties.

25

A Marine on parade would have been proud of Margaret's execution of an about face.

I grimaced, my cheeks blazing hot, before following her stiff back through the immaculate house, decorated in antiques, toward the sound of women's voices in the living room. Margaret must not be a California girl. I longed for my spider plants in macramé hangers and rust orange shag.

"You all remember Marcia? She's Captain Sargent's wife."

Twelve wives sat around the dark, polished wood coffee table, some on the sofa, some on spindly-legged chairs, two on silk floor cushions.

The first face I recognized, framed in straight dark hair, belonged to Julie, Bird's wife. I hadn't seen her since her party and my sight of too much of her husband. To her credit, she caught my eye and smiled, rolling her eyes and shaking her head. The smile welcomed me into the Ain't-The-Boys-Nuts? Club. I grinned back. I admired her ability to laugh with me at her husband's antics. Funny how one shared experience could connect me to a someone I'd hardly known before.

Fran, the CO's wife—his second wife, since his first abandoned him while he suffered in the Hanoi Hilton—sat in an antique wing chair, smoking a pipe. My eyes latched on the long and elegant curve down to a small bowl filled with glowing tobacco, then jerked away. I only knew one *man* who smoked a pipe, my grandfather. Plain, drab Fran reminded me of a West Virginia mountain woman. I darted sidelong glances at her. Just as her husband had earned space and quiet, the wife of a tortured man deserved her own space and quiet. Silence spaced with longer silences in between.

I doubted she'd be an ally. We existed on opposite sides of the wives' continuum. She was old. Compared to her almost forty years, I was impossibly young. She hid behind smoke and silence. I talked too much, too often, to the wrong people, saying the wrong things.

Margaret introduced me around. I remembered a few others from before. Cindy. She'd been at my wedding reception and the squadron party—not that we'd really had a chance to talk. Debby, closer to my age, the statuesque blonde. Kathleen, a large-framed woman I thought I knew from the party. I must have remembered her name wrong 'cause "Kathleen" wasn't it. I added one new name: Marilyn. Short. Dark. She had a pug nose and an impish smile. The rest of the women's names entered my ears but refused to take up residence in my head. Margaret pulled out another chair from her dining room, dark gleaming wood, curved legs to small lion paws. Old furniture. Hmmph. I loved my Danish modern.

I sat between Debby, the blond, and another dark-haired woman whose name escaped me. I smiled at the unnamed one. At least I could be friendly.

Cindy and Kathleen sat across the coffee table from me on the red tufted sofa. Margaret set the ice tea in front of me on a crystal and silver coaster. My face had almost cooled down.

Margaret sat in a delicate, mahogany chair with petit-point armrests, settling a black notebook on her lap. "Now, ladies. To business."

Business? Andy said I'd be getting to know the wives. What business?

"Marcia's new, so she needs a squadron roster and a copy of the calling tree." A pause. Direct stare at me. "You *do* know not to call me or Fran to start the calling tree unless it is a bona-fide emergency? We can't be bothered with every little thing that you might worry about." Her condescension condensed into a fog, obscuring the faces around me.

My nose prickled. Eyes welled. I picked off a piece of lint from my pan"I'll give her the debrief." Kathleen reached out to take the papers Margaret thrust in my direction. Kathleen's voice graveled with cigarettes and the broad vowels of New England. She caught my eye and winked. "New wives have better things to do than worry about protocol or paperwork."

Snickers.

The conversation, led by the XO's wife, veered to discussion of the Easter picnic and egg hunt. They spent considerable time on who would boil and decorate the eggs—should dyeing them be something the kids of the troops helped with? General consensus—no. Then, volunteers to get baskets and plastic grass put together. Food would be potluck for everything except the hamburgers and hotdogs. The guys would get those at the commissary, the military base grocery store. And they'd get the beer at the package store, the base liquor store. Location? The base picnic grounds, as usual.

I sat quietly, worrying about whether I should sit with my ankles crossed or ankles together and tucked under my chair. I fidgeted between both. I took a sip of the ice tea. Unsweetened. Blech.

Julie broke in, her voice low, "And have we heard anything more from 323 about assistance for the families?"

VMFA 323, the Snakes—another squadron at El Toro.

Margaret closed her notebook. "The XO's family's down in Miramar since he was in the Tomcat program there. But the squadron here has circled the wagons."

Why did they circle the wagons? What had happened?

"I heard she was going to move back to Georgia, where her family's from." One of the wives on the floor cushion. A brunette.

"She has to move. The two months are almost up. They're kicking her out of housing." Kathleen sucked smoke deep and blew it out. The cloud thinned and spiraled up to join the blue haze near the ceiling from Fran's pipe.

"Kicking her out? Her husband just died!" Blonde Debby next to me. She sounded as if they were kicking *her* out.

In some ways, they were. All of the women risked losing their husbands and then their spot in military housing. It didn't seem right or fair. I lived in a house off base, so did Marilyn and Cindy, but most lived in government housing. The cost was low, the location close to the squadron. Convenient—until it wasn't.

Cindy leaned forward. "At least it's better now. Five years ago, the widows had ten days."

The babel of voices escalated. My eyes tracked from one face to another to another.

"They're presumed dead. Remember—SAR, Search and Rescue, never found anything." A woman dressed in a suit my mother would have worn, though she couldn't be older than thirty.

"After disappearing on Christmas Eve. Those poor kids."

Oh. The aviators the lieutenant talked about at the squadron party. The accident Julie told me not to worry about.

"Yes. The XO had three and the pilot had a couple, I think."

"Disappearing on Christmas Eve. Doesn't it seem, well, eerie to anyone else?" Debby asked.

"Tom says they think it was an inadvertent ejection." A petite brunette.

The other wives seemed worried.

"Inadvertent? I thought they had to pull the face curtain down. How do you do that not on purpose?" Cindy's voice rose in exasperation.

"Tom says there's a pull handle on the floor. Maybe one of them caught something on it." The petite brunette again.

"Duff says another guy once caught his flight suit on the ejection handle climbing out of his airplane in Yuma." Kathleen stubbed out her cigarette.

"Was he okay?" A woman with long brown hair. Bet she ironed it.

"No."

"Oh." Blonde Debby.

Oh. 'Not okay' meant dead. Perhaps Julie hadn't meant what I thought when she told me not to worry. I thought she meant there was nothing to worry about. She must have meant that worrying wouldn't help.

In the ensuing silence, Margaret opened her black notebook with an audible snap. "Ladies. Enough. Any *helpful* suggestions?"

Cindy suggested designating a contact person to call the Casualty Assistance Officer at 323. Julie volunteered.

The dark-haired young woman next to me whispered under the hum of agreement, "She'll know what to do. Julie's first husband was shot down in Vietnam."

I looked at her. She nodded to confirm her words.

I studied Julie's face. Bird was her second husband? Nothing showed. Doesn't death and loss change everything? I expected it to show in her eyes or the twist of her lips. I didn't expect she'd have married a guy who ran through parties in his original packaging.

The rest of us sat up straight, listened to the final bits of business Margaret presented, and kept our mouths shut.

Kathleen walked me out to my car at the end of the meeting. "I know you don't need instructions on when to use the calling tree. Margaret has a poker up her patoot. Always has, probably always will." She laughed, an Irish washer-woman's booming laugh. "Some women wear their husband's oak leaves on their own shoulders. Too heavy a burden for me." She patted me on my shoulder. "Don't worry about it. New young wives are forgiven a multitude of sins."

"Thanks, Kathleen. Uh. Who *is* your husband? I can't seem to match up the spouses with the call signs."

"Kate. Call me, Kate. Margaret tries to make silk purses out of sow's ear. Her problem, not mine. I've never aspired to pursehood."

Kate—that was the name I remembered.

"My husband's Duff. He's not a pilot. He's a Warrant Officer."

I looked blank, I guess.

"He's a non-commissioned officer promoted from the enlisted ranks. You'd remember him better if you had any boobs to mention."

The wave of heat washing from my head down to my barely-existent chest felt like a neon light shining in the middle of the afternoon.

The booming laugh again. "You're lucky. They're a pain in the neck—literally." She straightened her shoulders, only emphasizing her impressive shelf. "You'd remember Duff better if you were stacked, because he'd have pissed you off. He'd never know what color your eyes are because he'd never look above your chest. He's a little redheaded worm who stares at women's breasts like he was plucked off the nip too young—and he's short enough to have had it stunt his growth. First time we met, I coldcocked him with a beer. Then I married him. Guess I shoulda known what I was getting into."

Who was this woman? Why was she sharing so much as we stood in the middle of the street in base housing? The crabgrass lawns encircled Mediterranean-style suburban homes. Yet the street we stood on curved

32

up toward the foothills and down toward the El Toro runway.

A roar built and built—a jet taking off. The vibration filled the air and my ears and my bones. As it veered off to the south, I saw white lettering 'VW' on the black tail. One of ours! Maybe Andy. Awe at his being one of the few who flew something so fast, so loud, so—I didn't have words—I wanted to fly one. Kate's lips moved. "Did you say something?!" I yelled.

"I said, 'There goes the sound of freedom.' That's all. You've got it bad, don't cha?"

"What?" I watch the last flicker of the plane disappear into the smog.

"P-envy, short for pilot-envy, a form of penis envy." She laughed. "We wives have to stick together, since they won't let us play with their toys. Come over anytime. We'll drink some wine and bitch about our husbands. Oh. Oops! You're a newlywed. You won't start bitchin' and moanin' until the honeymoon wears off. Say—during the first deployment."

She waved as she drove off in her Volkswagen bug. I liked her. I didn't believe her. The honeymoon would never wear off.

Chapter 3
The First Deployment

The dark woven wood shades had been pulled up to reveal the bright morning light. I stood in my quiet kitchen, way too far away from my guy, holding the phone receiver to my ear. I could barely hear him over the roar of jet engines and men laughing in the background.

"Can't talk long. Got another hop in an hour. Come down here."

"To Yuma?"

"Yeah. I miss you."

"I miss you, too, but—"

"Drive the Volvo."

"What?" I couldn't have heard him right.

"Drive the Volvo." The words grated past his reluctance.

That's when I knew he really did miss me. His beautiful British Racing Green Volvo that he'd had when we'd married a month and a half ago. His stick-shift-almost-new Volvo I'd never been allowed to drive, with good reason. I didn't know how to drive a stick.

Actually, technically, I did. Unfortunately, practically, I never had.

"I love you." My whole heart went into those three words.

"Yeah. Same."

I didn't love the 'Yeah. Same.'—but he'd told me before that mushy talk over the phone in the ready room looked bad at the field.

It didn't matter. He wanted me with him as much as I wanted to be with him. I could get by when he was gone—after all he'd been gone last night and I hadn't died of loneliness—but I didn't want to spend nights away from him. Somehow with him I was smarter, stronger, better.

First I had to get to him.

Stick-shifted cars crow hop when the gears aren't done right. Going over the mountains from San Diego to Yuma, Andy's green Volvo might as well have been a frog. I gritted my teeth and pressed on. The gears gritted their teeth, too, making grinding sounds that threatened the imminent departure of the engine or the transmission onto the road.

Quitting wasn't an option. I was on a mission.

When the car and I finally lurched into Yuma, my head hurt from squinting against the light glaring through my windshield. I checked into a motel on Fourth Avenue, drew the dusty drapes almost closed, and flopped on the bed to wait for my honey to call.

The plan was to join up outside the BOQ—Batchelor Officer's Quarters—when the flying day was done and he'd drive us to dinner.

Heaven forbid I called the squadron to let him know I'd arrived. That was always a bad thing to do—but a worse choice when the squadron had deployed. The classic line stated, "If the Marine Corps had wanted you to have a wife/family, they would have issued you one." So pilots expected the wife and family to stay off the airwaves to the squadron, letting them pretend they were footloose in Neverland.

The squadron was on deployment.

The number one job of an aviator was to log as many hours as possible flying the airplane. A cross-country was generally a weekend spent in the plane going somewhere and then coming back. If the pilot could get out Friday, he could land somewhere and spend the night; then fly somewhere else on Saturday and spend the night; then return on Sunday—three legs, more flying.

A TAD—Temporary Attached Duty—involved a longer period of time, sometimes with one aircrew—pilot and RIO, sometimes with more. Getting selected for the Navy's Top Gun school was TAD, so was Red Flag at Nellis Air Force Base where pilots flew against 'enemy' combatants to practice ACMs—Air Combat Maneuvers. There was another black—super-secret etc.—program near Nellis where American fighters flew against so-secret-I'm-gonna-have-to-kill-you-if-you-find-out-about-it something or somethings. Rumors were they had Soviet MIG fighters. How did wives know about any of this? We listened when the guys stopped talking, and usually we were listening before—when the guys had forgotten wives were present.

A deployment involved all or most of the squadron, officers and planes, often with troops to take care of the planes.

On deployment, Andy had explained, it became even more imperative for the wife to be neither seen nor heard.

So Peter Pan—all he had to do was fly and save the world from the bad guys. A call from the wife reminded them that they should be grownups—with wives, kids, and responsibilities.

Andy told me the other problem with my presence on deployment—the players in the squadron. Players were guys who, when away from the cat, played with any mice they could find. Some aviators went cross-country for the hours. Some went for the action—in the Officer's Clubs on far-flung bases, or in the bars well known for female players. Sometimes a female player would be single, but sometimes she'd be married and unhappy, or married and lonely—which qualified as unhappy. Aviators who were players flew planes by day and flew into any willing arms at night. They thought they contributed to the general wellbeing of the world—as long as their wives at home didn't find out.

The advantage to playing around on cross-countries, TADs, or deployments involved the deniability factor to the wives waiting at home. Ideally, nothing had to be denied because wives discovered nothing. The presence of other wives interfered with safe play because of the unofficial wives' calling tree.

I hated that the aviators sanctioned infidelity with their silence. When I said to Andy that none of that seemed right, he shook his head and said it was the way it was.

I wanted it to be different.

Finally, fifty pages into my romance novel, *The Wolf and the Dove*, Andy called. "Come get us." None of guys joining us for dinner were players. The players had been told where I'd be, so they could be elsewhere.

The Marine guard at the gate had to be my age, but he saluted and called me "Ma'am".

I loved being saluted. Andy said they saluted the rank on the car, but the truth was they might have to salute the officer's sticker—but they smiled at me. I smiled back and took the grin and the salute as my own. Polite and helpful when I asked for directions, the guard didn't even laugh when I jackrabbited away.

I jerked to a stop in front of the long, low BOQ building, the Volvo shuddering with relief. Standing with Andy were four men dressed in civvies. Three RIOs: Jaime—the muscular blond bullfrog, Trigger—a Texas calf roper in college, Pops—an old man at twenty-seven. The fourth, Cindy's husband, Agile, a pilot, kissed me on the cheek when I got out of the car. Agile was one of my favorite men. I had lots of reasons. He liked me and always made an effort to include me in the conversation. He loved his wife—a very attractive trait. And he had a great grin.

They crowbarred themselves into the backseat, Andy took command of the gearshift, and we were off to Chretins.

Famous, infamous Chretins. I'd heard about it since the first time my brother flew to Yuma on a cross-country. I'd been raised on tacos, enchiladas, and tostadas. With six kids to feed, my mom had discovered beans, cheese, tortillas, and salsa went a long way. I loved

Mexican food. Blue-eyed, with ancestors going back to the Mayflower and to Cherokees who traveled the Trail of Tears, still I considered tacos soul food. Now was my chance to savor all things tortilla at a restaurant of renown.

Pops rumbled in my ear, "I can taste those *jalapeños* now. The hotter, the better."

Trigger's Texan drawl curled around his words, "I'm sauntering over to that Pizza Hut next door. Save some beer. That Mexican food doesn't agree with me."

I wondered if they named Trigger after Roy Rogers's horse or after the trigger that had to be pulled to fire shots? Andy would tell me—if he knew. Maybe they teased him about being quick on the trigger on bombing runs. I blushed. Or in the bedroom.

Before I married a Marine I would never have thought of that.

"Beans don't agree with Pops neither." Jaime piped up. "Whee-ooo. And we're sharing a room at the Q."

"Hey!" Pops protested. "Not in front of Snatch's wife."

I smiled. "It's okay. I have brothers."

Trigger said, "That's right. In fact—"

"In fact, her brother is a Marine aviator, too. Bullet." Agile patted me on the shoulder. In sympathy?

"Bullet's her brother?" Jaime whistled. "Well, shee-it. Now I've really got to behave. He wouldn't like anyone messing with his sister."

"And he's twice as tall as you are," Agile pointed out helpfully.

We parked in the heat-shimmered parking lot.

Trigger held Chretin's door for me.

Honestly, the place didn't look like much. In fact, I couldn't see much. Amber glass lamps with 10-watt bulbs barely cast shadows in the shadows.

"I think this is called 'ambience'," Agile said.

"I think it's called, I-can't-see-what-I'm-eating. I'll be back with my pizza." Trigger exited out the back door.

Andy guided me by the elbow to a long table. "At least today Joe Chretin hadn't gone out of his way to pick us up at the flight line and bring us here. The first time that happened with Trigger and he walked out the back door for pizza, I didn't know what to say."

"Yes, you did. You thanked Joe and ordered a beer and nachos. You thought it was a great story," Pops reminded him.

Andy laughed. "A story to show what we have to put up with from you RIOs."

The guys ordered. I ordered a margarita, having never acquired a taste for beer. They ordered three pitchers of *cerveza* and three trays of nachos—two with *chorizo*. No one looked at a menu. I guessed dinner would come after the appetizers.

The nachos arrived with the beer. Golden circles of tortilla chips with greasy cheese baked on, and a huge green slice of *jalapeño* sitting on top of each one.

Eww. *Jalapeños* blistered my mouth. Maybe I could pick them off.

Jaime and Pops had no problem with the spicy peppers. They'd finished a tray each by the time Trigger returned, carrying his pizza. Sweat beaded Pops's bald head, rolled down his forehead and into his shirt, soaking the front.

Double eww.

"Hey, you guys hear about the VMFA 101 instructor who filed a supersonic flight plan from Yuma to Miramar?" Jaime wiped his fingers neatly in between bites of nachos.

"Not a student—an instructor?" Andy shook his head.

"He filed a flight plan to go to San Diego with afterburners lit?" Agile smiled.

They all grinned—the grin boys get on their faces when someone else does something fun.

"Yep. And they approved it. I hear the good people of El Centro and San Diego got an earful." Jaime ate a nacho. "The CAG had to have gotten complaints."

"CAG?" I asked.

"Commander of the Air Group." Agile said.

"Wait, why are lit afterburners a problem?" I knew afterburners did just that, burn jet fuel visibly at the rear part of the engine. Very pretty at night.

Andy hugged me to him. "Afterburners make F-4's go very fast, kind of like being rocket-propelled."

Agile grinned. "And when F-4's go very fast, they are very loud."

Andy nodded. "Breaking the sound barrier the whole way to Miramar added to the loud factor."

Pops swallowed and wiped chorizo off his mouth with the back of his hand. "I heard it rattled some windows."

"Broke some windows, more like," Jaime corrected.

"Well, idiots aren't supposed to be flying multi-million dollar military jets." Agile frowned. "Approval or not, he's going to be in deep kimchi."

"Deep kimchi?" I asked.

Agile answered. "Kimchi is fermented, spicy, stinky cabbage from Korea. Being buried in it would be worse than being in deep shit."

"Should've known better." Andy growled his disapproval of the unnamed instructor. "The war's not going on anymore. Can't piss off the civilians."

Jaime waved his beer in the air. "That's a depressing story. Have you heard the one about that lieutenant who discovered a third way to eject from a fighter?"

"Wait," I said. "What are the first two ways?"

Agile leaned toward me so I could hear over the Mexican mariachi music blaring from the speakers above our table. "The first way, the pilot or RIO reaches up above his helmet with both hands, and grasps the face curtain—a striped double loop—then pulls down. The second way, the aviator reaches between his legs and pulls up on the ejection handle, another striped loop."

"So what was the third way to eject?" I said.

"I thought you'd never ask." Jaime smiled.

Andy said, "I can tell this is going to be a good one."

Pops was laughing. I think he'd already heard it.

"The third method is not to eject. This has only been successful once I know of. The pilot was making a Red Eye tracking run at the Yuma Proving Grounds and made a very low pass. Too low a pass."

Trigger closed his teeth, opened his lips, and breathed in. A short wet whistling sound—a double tooth suck—a warning of incipient danger or stupidity.

"He ran out of sky and bottomed out on the desert floor." Jaime gulped a mouthful of beer. "Next thing he knew, he sat amid the sage and scrub in his ejection seat, but without a plane surrounding him. It had disintegrated into pieces in the crash. He had not."

"Unbelievable."

Jaime paused. Waited for our complete attention. "It's known as the immaculate ejection."

Laughter. More laughter.

No pilot claimed fallibility or stupidity—except after he escaped by the skin of his plane from the teeth of death. Then he had joined the "goddam lucky bastards" club and he was golden.

Grins all around.

Nachos were chewed and swallowed. More elbows bent to pour beer into mouths.

I used a napkin to wipe *jalapeño* juice off another nacho. Pops took my pile of discarded peppers and piled them on his nachos.

Agile turned to Pops. "I heard a rumor you got the best of the disbursing chick."

"You mean the gray-haired lady with a stick up her ass?"

"Are you talking about Mrs. Boston?" Trigger leaned in.

"I knew they were holding your pay." Andy turned to me. "To give you some background, Pops drives a red MG ragtop—"

"—With the ragtop cut off," Jaime pointed out.

Pops chewed a nacho and swallowed. "There were a couple of holes in it. It looked ratty. Now it has a nice clean line."

Jaime rolled his eyes.

"One day last year—long before you had your run-in with Mrs. Boston," Andy said to Pops. "We were cruising around the base before a cross-country, and Pops decided he needed some cash. He asked me to reach under the passenger's seat and pull out a paycheck. Mind you, the MG had been exposed to the elements, so everything under the seat was a bit damp. I reached under and pulled out a handful of papers. They were all U. S. Government paychecks made out to Pops. He had to have had fifteen thousand dollars in checks moldering under the seat. He'd never bothered to cash them."

Trigger shook his head. "Rich, young bachelors."

Pops took up his own story. "I had a travel claim from a deployment I was supposed to liquidate. I told her to take it out of my paycheck or add it in—whichever. I have better things to do than run down to disbursing to keep Sarah Boston happy. So she couldn't clear out her books. She called me up and told me I wouldn't get my pay until I settled my claim. It pissed me off. I told her, 'I'm not a rich man, but I can hold out longer than you.'"

The guys all laughed.

"Bet the bank loved cashing those wet checks from under the seat." Agile tilted back his beer.

"When the next scheduled financial audit came about, Mrs. Boston's books still hadn't been cleared.

45

The head honcho apparently asked, 'Who is this Captain you owe six months pay to?' I'm sure the lady tried to explain. No joy. Her orders were to 'Get him down here and pay him.' I accepted the check and no one asked me about my TAD discrepancy."

Laughter rolled through the room, a laughter filling the restaurant until everyone wanted to be where I was, sitting with the guys, these aviators, and swapping stories.

I wished I had stories to share, but I wasn't a flyer, wasn't a Marine, just Snatch's wife. All I could do was listen. And remember.

I don't remember ever actually eating anything except nachos carefully cleared of *jalapeños*. I drank in the camaraderie and hungered for more.

Chapter 4
Change of Command

The sun crisped the top of my curly brown hair, and the aluminum bleacher blistered the backs of my thighs whenever I didn't pay close attention to perching forward in my mini-skirted dress. July in Southern California seemed a poor choice for a Change of Command ceremony. Actually, July in Southern California was a bad choice for any ceremony on a black tarmac surface. The sun radiated on to the black and the metal, reflecting upward in distortions of heated air. A trickle of sweat snaked down my spine. If I had my druthers, I'd be elsewhere. My druthers were not important. Being here was.

Andy told me so that morning.

"Do I have to go to this thing?"

He nodded. "'This thing' is the Change of Command Ceremony, and it's a tradition. In the Marine Corps, traditions are important."

"But I'm not a Marine."

"You're my wife, and so you're part of the Marine Corps."

Morality had held no conflicts for me before I met Andy. Peace was good. War was bad. War killed people. People killed people in war. Somehow, I hadn't realized that in marrying a pilot, I'd married a Marine Corps officer who practiced war. I hadn't even wanted him in uniform at the wedding—or to use a sword to cut the cake.

He'd wanted the uniform and the sword—he said he'd gone through a lot to earn the right to wear them, they'd cost him a pretty penny, and he wasn't going to rent a monkeysuit.

He had worn the uniform and we cut the cake with his sword—and with my engraved sterling silver cake knife. Marriage is all about the art of compromise.

"Everyone in the command, enlisted and officers, and their wives will be there. For us, it's mandatory. For the wives, it's expected. It will be noticed if you're not there."

His tone made it an order.

Yes, sir! End of discussion. Tears, ever close to the surface, threatened. I wasn't a Marine, but I had to be a Marine officer's wife.

And I feared I'd fail.

Short dresses and bleachers were a bad combination when dignity and decorum were expected. Why did I wear this dress? What did it matter? All my dresses were this short. I crossed my legs at my ankles. Hand strategically placed, in front of hemline, between knees close together. Heaven forbid anyone got an inappropriate view. Heaven forbid anyone thought there was an inappropriate view to get.

Proper and decorous came with the position of officer's wife. A proper and decorous officer's wife should never perspire or sweat. To paraphrase etiquette class: horses sweat, officer's wives glow. The rivulets down my spine exposed my failings, if only to me.

Margaret, the XO's wife looked put together and calm. No dress squirming for her. She caught me looking. I waved, smiling. I didn't mean it, but she made me nervous.

She wore clothes I wouldn't be caught dead in—a dress to the knee probably with stockings attached to garter belts. Why dress like an old lady when just a bit over thirty? I didn't get it. Unfortunately, my miniskirt required pantyhose. Pantyhose trapped heat.

Looking on the other side of the bleachers, I recognized gravel-voiced Kate from the wives' meeting. She didn't look up, busy in her big bag of a purse. Cindy, Agile's wife, sat with Julie, Bird's wife, three rows down. Cindy arched around, scanning the bleachers. She saw me, smiled and waved.

A brash, young voice, "Excuse me. Excuse me."

Marilyn, Donut's wife, sidled across to sit next to me with a deep sigh. "Hoo-ee! It's burning up today. What are they thinking having this in July? Should we stop them right now and tell everybody to come back in November?" Her laugh, an infectious chuckle, welcomed all around us into the joke. She fluffed dark curls tightened from heat and perspiration.

Only a few years older than me, nothing seemed to intimidate her. Since she had nothing to prove, I wasn't intimidated. Sitting with her would be fun.

Out toward the runways, the Phantom F-4 jets of VMFA 314 framed the parade ground, their tails with VW written large slanted away from where I sat, the radomes and cockpits pointing inward. The troops for the squadron lined up in the open space between them, their feet a shoulder's width apart, their arms behind their backs—the 'parade rest' position. The Marines might all be sweating, but no sign of it showed. The officers also stood at parade rest. Somewhere in those crisp, disciplined lines of men, my Andy stood.

I tried to spot him in the officer's formation. No luck.

An officer stepped to the podium, Bill Jackson. I never knew his official call sign. Andy called him Unsafe at Any Speed. "Ladies and Gentlemen, please take your seats. The ceremony will begin in five minutes."

Another officer marched to the center of the stands, faced us, and barked the command, "Staff—fall in!" I recognized the XO's florid, squashed tomato of a face.

Other officers in formation stepped up to join him. "There's Andy!" He looked serious.

"We can always spot our own 'cause they look so cute, don't they?" Marilyn grinned. "I like them best in their flight suits, showing their tight ass-ets."

I covered my mouth to keep from bursting out laughing, but snickers slipped through my fingers. Marilyn's giggle didn't help me keep quiet. I snortled.

The XO's wife glared at us.

Unsafe read into the microphone, "Good afternoon, Ladies and Gentlemen. On behalf of the Commanding Officer, Lt. Col. Harley Chapman, welcome to VMFA 314's Change of Command Ceremony. Lt Col. Chapman will relinquish command to Lt. Col. Michael Wadsworth. The Commander of Troops for today's ceremony is Major Hanley. The adjutant is Capt. Duncan."

I nudged Marilyn with my elbow. Capt. Duncan was her husband, Donut.

She nodded, eyes on the parade ground, searching.

"Please rise for the invocation by Commander Johnson, 3rd MAW Chaplain, United States Navy."

The chaplain looked like any other Navy officer, a little pudgier than most of the Marines I knew, dressed in blazing whites, with tiny crosses instead of rank insignia on his collar.

"Let us pray."

I teetered on the riser in my platforms, and bent my head.

"Heavenly Father, bless all here assembled to bring grace on Harley Chapman and wisdom to Michael Wadsworth as they venture into their new lives and responsibilities. In Your name we pray, Lord. Amen."

"Ladies and Gentlemen, please be seated."

We sat.

Ouch. Sun-barbecued metal. I scooted farther forward and tucked my skirt under me.

"Take your post—Sir!"

Capt. Duncan, better known as Donut, marched to the right side of the first group of troops.

Marilyn bounced on the seat. "That's my Willie!"

My turn to grin at her.

Unsafe read, "Present day ceremonies in the Marine Corps have their basis in both history and tradition. The line formation made possible the massing of firepower from the muzzle-loaded muskets of yesterday. In earlier days, the line of battle was just that, a line of two or three ranks and much like the parade formation you will see today as the adjutant forms the line for battle."

He might be Unsafe-At-Any-Speed in a plane, but he spoke well in public. Too bad that would never be enough to change his call sign. Actions trumped words for a pilot.

"Sound—attention!"

The band sounded something. It must have been 'attention'. Four notes on a bugle: Ta dah, ta dah!

It called me to attention. I straightened my shoulders.

Officers in front of each group of men on parade called out, "Company—attention!" The troops straightened up so much they almost curved like a tight bow, arms at sides, feet together.

"Right—shoulder—arms!" The troops lifted their rifles, put them at an angle across their chests, straightened them to the vertical, and then shouldered them.

The snap of rifles met hands in unison across the parade field.

I admired the precision. If I'd been in the formation, I'm sure all would have heard the clunk of rifle barrel knocking an unwary Marine to the tarmac.

"Sound—Adjutant's Call."

The bugler played, *Da ta da* dah! *Da ta da* dah! *Da ta da, da ta da, da ta da* dah!

My pulse quickened. I decided I liked bugles.

A heavy drum beat.

"Forward—march!"

As one, the troops stepped off, the thud of heel to toe magnified by two hundred.

"Staff—forward—march!"

The box of officers, including Andy, marched forward until they were midway between the line of troops and us, their audience. The color guard stepped forward with the American flag, the Marine Corps flag and another flag almost completely hidden by red, white, and gold ribbons.

"Guide—online!" The troops at the corners switched the rifles to their left shoulders and did a kind of fast marching, before facing Donut and halting.

"Mark time—march!" The companies marched in place—four to eight seconds of going nowhere.

"Company—halt!"

"Order—arms!" and "Left—face!"

"Dress—right!"

With barely seen adjustments, the troops straightened like billiard balls racked up for the break—only the wooden rack framing them had to be hours and hours of practice, discipline and following orders.

Two hundred or so troops perfectly aligned with no lines on the tarmac.

Marilyn whispered, "And I can't get him to put his shoes neatly in the closet."

I glanced at her, startled. "Isn't that a wife's job?"

She put her hand on mine and squeezed. "Oh, honey. We've got to talk."

"Ladies and gentlemen, please rise for the Marching on of the Colors and remain standing for the playing of the National Anthem."

53

MARCIA SARGENT

We stood.

"March—on the colors!"

The band played as the color guard marched in front of us. They carried the three poles of flags: two dipped low, the American flag standing tall.

The music sounded notes of bright patriotism. The program called it The National Emblem March. I wiped tears from the corners of my eyes. In spite of the heat, maybe because of it, the pageantry touched a primal place in my subconscious.

I blamed it on my Fourth of July birthday. Until I was five, I thought the parade and fireworks were for me. Afterwards, I shared a birthday with America and took on pride in my country as my birthright.

Marilyn dug in her purse for tissues, handed me one, and dabbed at her own eyes with another. "It always gets to me, too," she whispered. And she hadn't been born on Independence Day.

The officers saluted the colors as they passed. The color guard turned and halted.

"Present—arms!"

"Staff—present—arms!"

The last note of music.

"Staff—order—arms!"

Unsafe asked us to all be seated.

Have I mentioned that I married a Catholic as well as a Marine? This began to feel like Mass, a formal Mass—a lot of stuff that I didn't understand that everyone else seemed to know, and a lot of standing and sitting. While so far no one had ordered me to kneel, the endless marching about and calling of orders and

54

the sun blazing into my eyes wore on my attention and enthusiasm.

Of course, it wasn't over.

"Post the colors!"

The color guard marched in place, but moving, turning around an invisible center point until they faced the front and halted.

"Parade—rest!"

All the troops went to parade rest.

"Sound off!"

The band played a song that made me straighten up like the little hairs at the back of my neck. Even with all the turning and marching and the serious focus of the men in uniform, the music brought it back to emotion.

The band paraded in front of the assembled Marines.

"Squadron—attention!" The troops snapped straight.

"Present—arms!" All saluted or held their rifles in front of them.

"Present—colors!"

Donut faced about, saluted the commander of troops, and reported, "Sir, the parade is formed."

The XO returned the salute. "Take your post!"

Donut marched to a position on the right of the XO.

"Order—arms! Port—arms! Right shoulder—arms! Port—arms! Left shoulder—arms! Port—arms! Order—arms!"

The entire formation of men snapped their rifles from out front to right to front to left, then out in front.

Rifles again. I cringed. What was I doing here? I liked puppies and flowers and reading. I hated war and killing and expectations of decorum.

"Receive the report—sir!"

"Report!"

One by one, the officers in front of the troops reported, "Sir—all present and accounted for!"

Donut saluted, then faced about, and saluted the XO. "Sir—all present and accounted for!"

My brain was only partly present and accounted for.

Andy stood at attention in the group of officers from the squadron. I knew my Andy wasn't a killer. He flew planes and loved me. I wanted to wave at him, but his eyes were locked forward.

"Publish the orders!"

"Attention to orders! Headquarters, VMFA 314, Third Marine Air Wing, the Officer of the Day today is Captain Samuels, the Officer of the Day tomorrow is Captain Jackson, by order of Harley Chapman, Lieutenant Colonel United States Marine Corps Commanding."

Officers and soldiers marched and saluted and moved their rifles to different positions. The color guard moved the flags around to different places. The band played more military music.

Something about the fluid structure, the rhythm of men moving to ordered commands I barely understood, moved me to an awareness of the cadence of time and tradition in the Marine Corps.

I started to understand why Andy had wanted his uniform and his sword as part of our wedding.

My nose prickled again with incipient tears.

Would I ever truly belong to this?

I knew, sometimes, I'd have to walk in step with others and pay attention to commands. Following commands provided precision in difficult tasks, like practicing first aid until CPR became second nature. I might even get to call out the orders. But watching the men marching under the looming Phantom F-4s on either side of the parade ground, a piece of me stepped back out of line and said, 'This is not who I am."

Perhaps Marilyn saw the panic in my eyes. She patted my hand. "Don't let this kick ya in the ass. The guys do this, but it isn't what they are. We're here, but it sure as hell ain't what we are, either."

The XO's wife shushed her.

Marilyn shook her head and whispered only for my ears, "Bitch."

I smiled. I wouldn't say that out loud, but I truly appreciated that she had.

Chapter 5
Commanding Change

Still sitting on metal bleachers in the hot July sun watching my first Change of Command. Still dripping sweat rivulets down my back.

"Ladies and gentlemen, please rise for honors to VMFA 314 Commanding Officer, Lieutenant Colonel Harley Chapman."

We stood. I sighed.

Unsafe read commendations and awards for the CO. There seemed to be a lot of them.

We sat.

Was this ever going to be over?

Then Colonel Chapman spoke, briefly. I appreciated the brevity of his words, the sparse way he recognized all who had served with him and the honor it had been for him to be a part of the Marine Corps family. He cut to the chase eloquently. More words in summer heat do not a better speech make.

The troops snapped their rifles. The CO and Major Hanley, Donut, and another Lieutenant Colonel I didn't recognize started moving around. There were salutes and the audible click of shoes on tarmac.

"Sergeant Major, deliver the colors to the commanding officer!"

At this point, the guy holding the flag with all the ribbons and tassels stepped with smart turns and heel clicks and finally to the CO, Harley Chapman.

"Ladies and gentlemen, we now come to the ceremony's most solemn moment, the actual passing of command. The battle colors of a Marine Corps unit symbolize the authority and accountability of command. Transferring the colors during the ceremony symbolizes the relinquishing of command by Lieutenant Colonel Chapman. By accepting the colors, Lieutenant Colonel Wadsworth accepts command and confirms his total commitment to the Marines and sailors he will command. Sergeant Major Martin is delivering the colors to the commanding officer."

I wondered what the new CO's 'total commitment' would mean to Andy. I hoped he'd make life good for my guy.

The Sergeant Major carried the flags to Harley Chapman.

We were ordered with a 'please' to stand again.

A breeze kicked up, streaming the flags, which flapped audibly like a brisk clapping of hands.

"From: Commanding General, First Marine Aircraft Wing. To: Lieutenant Colonel Chapman. Subject: Wing Special Order 4335. Effective 0900 1 February 1975. You stand detached as the commanding officer, VMFA 314, and are directed to detach from the Marine Corps. Signed, John K. Davis, Brigadier General, U. S. Marine Corps."

Truth was: Harley Chapman had been detached from life since he'd been a POW. Solitary confinement and torture required a man to play mental games to survive. He disconnected from the outside world to strengthen his inward defenses, and as far as I could tell, never attached back again.

The Sergeant Major handed the colors to Colonel Chapman and then saluted.

Harley and the other Lieutenant Colonel faced each other.

This must be Colonel Wadsworth, who was taking command of the squadron.

"Lieutenant Colonel Wadsworth: From the Commanding General, Third Marine Aircraft Wing. To: Lieutenant Colonel Wadsworth. Subject: Wing Special Order 4336 effective 0900, 1 July 1975, You stand detached as the Executive Officer of HMMS and are directed to report for duty as VMFA 314 Commanding Officer. Signed John K. Davis, Brigadier General U. S. Marine Corps."

Chapman handed the colors to Wadsworth. I imagined Harley Chapman sighed in relief after relinquishing the flag. I hoped his life after retirement brought him a chance to breathe in peace.

They exchanged salutes, shook hands, then traded places.

I hoped the pageantry was almost over.

I wasn't the only one wanting the ceremony over. A blond boy, thin and wiry, drummed on the bleachers with his feet and pulled the hair of the younger girl next to him. I shifted my weight on my shoes. The boy started making some odd animal noises. I heard a clap, just one clap. The boy looked up at the clapper, gravel-voiced Kate, Duff's wife, whom I'd spoken with after the squadron wives' coffee.

Kate raised one eyebrow in his direction, lifted her right hand in front of her, pointed at the boy, and brought together her thumb, index finger, and middle finger with such quick emphasis, I expected a sound.

Instead, the boy stopped making the animal grunts.

She put her right index and middle fingers on the index and middles of her left, forcefully and silently.

The boy sat on the bleacher, feet still.

I lost focus on what was happening on the parade ground. I wanted to be able to get my husband to do what I wanted without a word spoken.

Okay, that was unlikely.

But someday, I might have kids. I considered the possibility more probable each day I decided to stay married. Disciplining children with a gesture verged on a miracle. I needed to talk to that miraculous mother.

Everyone sat down around me, so I guess they ordered us, again, to sit. I sat, too.

Then, the new CO spoke. By this time, my head hurt with the heat, and I felt like a saran-wrapped hotdog in the microwave. The new CO liked to talk. The wind had died again. I used the Change of Command program to more vigorously fan my face, wondering if the movement raised my body heat and the moving air only fooled me into believing it helped.

The CO stopped talking.

Amen.

They presented flowers to the CO's wives, outgoing and incoming.

The staff and troops came to attention, and the new CO commanded, "March the command in review!" His voice was deep, but alive.

I felt a change—a change in attitude, a change in command.

The new CO saluted Major Hanley who also saluted. "Aye, aye, sir."

Again Donut and the XO took turns calling out orders, officers and soldiers marched and saluted and moved their rifles to different positions. The color guard shifted the flags around to new places on the parade ground.

The band turned in formation to march in front of us, and the notes of 'The Marine Corps Hymn' clarion-called to my heart. The last words of the first verse played in my head. '...*First to fight for right and freedom and to keep our honor clean. We are proud to claim the title of United States Marines.*'

Marilyn and I both sniffled.

Major Hanley saluted the new CO, who returned the salute. "Sir," he said. "This concludes today's ceremony." Then he turned, faced the officers, and said, "Staff—dismissed!" The officers saluted and marched off the parade grounds.

"Ladies and gentlemen, this concludes today's ceremony...."

Yes.

I didn't hear the rest until he said, "...would like to extend an invitation to join them in the hangar for a reception."

Marilyn and I, united by our previous laughter and now subdued attitudes, wobbled off the bleachers, down to the parade deck, and into the hangar.

It took a few moments for my eyes to adjust to the shade in the hangar.

"Red punch and white cake?" The reception, quiet and reserved, resembled the beginning of a wedding reception before the drinking starts. I'd expected a wild and crazy celebration. This resembled Margaret Hanley's wives' meeting—but with husbands in uniforms.

Marilyn patted my arm. "The real party will be at the Officer's Club later." She looked around. "I need to find Duncan".

More than half the time she called her husband by his last name.

She slipped into the crowd of troops, officers, and the families.

Maybe that was the reason for the formal tone. The troops were here: the enlisted and their families. I thought about the public face of an officer. Command would suffer if the officers ran around naked and drank to stupidity. Cake and punch and decorum made sense.

I walked up to Kate, who stood next to her short, redheaded, freckled husband Duff. The blond boy danced around on her right, arms and legs moving at odd angles and rhythms.

"Hi, Kate! Who's this little guy?"

"Hi, Marcia. This young man is my son, Michael."

He stared at me—all skin, bones, and curly white-blond hair.

I smiled. "Hi, Michael. Did you like the ceremony? Are you into airplanes like all the other men around here?"

"He can't hear you. He's deaf."

"Oh, I—didn't—"

"It's all right." Kate turned and started talking almost silently to him while moving her hands and lips in a ballet. She seemed to be translating what I'd just said.

He grunted some sounds and, grinning, moved his fingers and hands.

Duff reddened. "Teach him to speak properly. If he could read lips—" He looked at me, flushed darker, turned and stalked to the other side of the hangar.

"—If he could read lips, you could talk to your son yourself." Kate spoke to his back, but softly. "Sorry you had to be here for that. Duff won't learn sign language."

"He can't talk to his own son?"

She grimaced at me. "He knows how to be a Marine. I don't think he knows what to do with a child he can't fix like he can the airplanes."

My heart hurt for her and for Michael—but not much for Duff. He could have chosen to be the grown-up, instead of the sulky boy.

By this time in our marriage, I'd already started calling my husband, 'Handy Andy.' He could fix anything around the house and, from what I heard, as the squadron Maintenance Officer, anything in the hangar. What if our marriage broke, or our as-of-now-nonexistent kids were irreparably damaged? Would he give up on what he couldn't fix?

My nose knew Andy's spicy aftershave, even before his warm arm embraced my shoulders. "Hi, Kate. Hello, Michael." He raised a pilot's thumb's up. Michael returned the gesture. They grinned at each other.

And at that point, I realized my husband might be one of the boys, but he knew how to be a man. I trusted him to learn to talk to our children. I trusted him and knew trust was not easy to come by.

I wrapped my fingers over his, looked up to his beloved face, and wondered: if I accepted the colors of a Marine wife, must I also be willing to follow the military's commands?

Chapter 6
The Officer's Club

Any aviator worth his wings knew when to lock his pipper on the O Club, or Officer's Club, the predicted impact point of wild and crazy pilot life: Friday afternoon, squadron day done? Tuesday evening, date life slow? On a cross-country to someplace your mother had never heard of? Go to the O-Club and find fellow aviators with whom to drink beer, roll dice, and swap stories.

With the new CO, Col. Wadsworth, Happy Hours at the O-Club again became mandatory any Friday the guys didn't take a cross-country.

Drinking was an expected activity for all squadron aviators. The bonding benefits of alcohol were well-documented in male social organizations. Pilots needed time away from the airplanes to debrief and detour from the stress of flying high-performance aircraft. Happy Hour started on Fridays after the squadron shut down for the weekend, sometime between 1600 and 1630—4 to 4:30 pm. Wives and girlfriends joined their drunken other halves at the club as soon as the babysitters came, typically 1800 to 1900. Single women, looking to play, filled up the barstools and walls by 2100. In the days before a DUI would end their career, aviators without semi-sober wives at the O-Club just drove slowly on the way home and watched out for MPs, the Military Police. Or drove not so slowly. Donut discovered orange trees in 1976 cost $3000 to replace when he crashed into and knocked over a prime specimen on his way home from a raucous Happy Hour at the MCAS El Toro Club.

The week after the change of command, Andy briefed me at O-dark-thirty in the morning that he'd put the Officer's Club at MCAS—Marine Corps Air Station—El Toro on our flight schedule.

I remained burrowed under the covers on my bed, my sleep-fogged brain barely registering the details.

His projected take-off time: sixteen-thirty in the afternoon. I should man-up by eighteen hundred, or six pm civilian time.

Man-up. In a ready room brief the term referred to the time to be in the plane ready to strap in. Andy meant he'd go to the O-Club earlier, direct from the squadron, and I should drive over and join him an hour and a half later.

Taking orders in pilot-speak took some getting used to. Taking orders took some getting used to. Andy had already learned that putting anything on a mandatory get done list guaranteed I would *not* get it done. Six months into married life, I still had random urges to go AWOL, leaving his military expectations behind and returning to my true civilian self.

But I liked the O-Club.

"Mmm-hmh. I'll—" I yawned a jaw-cracking yawn. "I'll be there."

"We'll knock off to head home from the O-Club at twenty-two hundred hours."

Was it his military briefing experience that required him to clarify exactly what time we would return to home base? The sun hadn't risen, we hadn't gone yet, and he had command-ejected both of us from the Club.

Curfew was a major sticking point in our marital happiness. I loved a party. Energy flowed into my grin the longer and wilder the festivities. I'd rather wait and stay as long as anything interesting went on—generally until they turned the lights off. Not my Andy. He hardly drank—just enough to hang out with the boys—and he recharged in his alone time.

My O-Club flight schedule involved lots of time with pilots and RIOs who liked me, being slightly suggestive when they paid attention to me, and listening to aviator stories when they didn't. Oh yeah—and getting a bit of a buzz on so I didn't worry nearly as much about whether I made a fool of myself. Six months into our marriage I knew the O-Club was the designated area for foolish behavior without repercussions.

Andy's planned hop involved talking quietly with guys he liked and listening intelligently to wives he liked—wives like Bird's Julie—while sipping a beer, maybe two and keeping an eye on me.

Officers had achieved alcoholic camaraderie well before I walked in the door. Men's voices and drunken laughter boomed across the room. The ratio of men to women? Almost ten to one, even counting the waitresses.

My heart rate increased—so did my desire to smile.

Keeping my radar active for Andy's voice or laugh, I employed VFR—visual flight rules—to sort him out from the chaff of other uniforms and flight suits.

Officer's Clubs had certain characteristics in common, and the Club at MCAS El Toro deviated little from the norm. First, the lighting was low, but not too low. Aviators wanted to find attractive women, avoid the brass wanting to chew their ass, find their wingmen, and see the dice.

I acquired a visual on my Andy halfway between my position near the door and the bar. Blood thrummed under my skin. There was something wonderful about taking off into an Officer's Club as the youngest wife, afterburner lit, sure my guy would protect me from the bogeys—the bad guys—and indulge me when I went on the offensive. He knew I'd flirt. I knew I'd flirt. And I also knew I'd be landing at my home airfield with the one I loved, no worse for wear.

This O-Club, like all O-Clubs, had a bar at the back of the room large enough for plenty of elbows and naugahyde-covered barstools. The size of the bar and the number of thirsty clientele required two or three bartenders and several sections of cocktail waitresses. Men in flight suits bellied up to the bar, presenting very fine rears to the rest of the room.

Tables and chairs scattered about the perimeter of the room, the walls covered with duty-issue dark wood paneling. A bar lounge in a Holiday Inn had a better quality of atmosphere, except for one thing—Marine Corps O-Clubs were filled with officers, some in uniform, some in flight suits, and all with an indefinable attitude that said, "Damn, I'm shit-hot."

Weeks ago, before my first flight through the Club, Andy had given me a preflight brief on the Rules Of

Engagement in the Officers' Club. The aviator's ready room brief covered ROEs. Pilots needed the rules and expectations for any hop to take away unpredictability—so they could come back in their plane and without looking bad at the field. The rules were like a good wingman, the pilot knew ahead of time what the other aviator would do in any given situation.

One of the rules for pilots was 'right to right'—in any potential nose to nose collision, each plane was to turn right, veering away from disaster. Jet fighters went very fast. How fast? Well, if an aviator told you the maximum speed, he'd have to kill you. Fighters routinely flew toward each other at one thousand knots—1150 mph—of closure. Without prior discussion, a pilot had a fifty-fifty chance of turning the wrong way in a head-on confrontation. Bad odds for planes. Worse for aviators.

So when I spotted Margaret, our XO's wife, I applied the 'right to right' rule, and veered right around a group of lieutenants with beer and bravado sloshing. Margaret must have had the same brief—she angled to their other side. Why stay on a collision course if able to turn away?

Andy had also cautioned me to steer clear of aviators out of control. ROEs mandated disengaging from and steering clear of planes out of control. Just as a weaving car on a road indicated the driver was non compos mentis—drunk out of his mind—and should be avoided at all cost, so aviators avoided the pilot who lost control of his plane for any reason. The out of control drunk wouldn't be looking out for other drivers; an out of control pilot didn't have the time or the ability to steer clear.

I altered course to avoid the lieutenant who had stripped his flightsuit down to his waist and had started to bend over, thumbs hooked in his tidy whities. I'd missed the moon at my wedding and didn't have any problem missing this one.

Someone yelled from across the room, "Fer God's sake, buy Jimbo a beer before we have to see any more of him!"

I'd almost navigated the tables and the drunks to reach Andy's side.

"Snatch!" Donut called from across the room. Marilyn waved welcome next to him.

The four of us planned our intercept with hand signals.

Within a minute of maneuvering, we joined up.

Marilyn hugged me. "The Change of Command last week doesn't seem to have caused any permanent damage. Congratulations."

"Thanks for keeping me company," I yelled, leaning in. The din of male voices and laughter drowned out any coherent speech more than a couple of feet away. "You had a lot to do with my survival." I patted her husband on the arm. "Donut, you looked good as adjutant."

"Duncan always looks good." Marilyn nudged him with an elbow and a smile.

"He does." I agreed, then blushed. Would Marilyn be okay with me admiring her husband?

Donut flushed.

Marilyn smiled.

Okay. Not a problem.

"Hey, we never briefed two vee one." Donut looked to Andy, maybe for help to protect him from the women. Marilyn and I weren't fighter planes, but we definitely had an advantage at the start in this dogfight against shy Donut.

"I'm not flying on this hop." Andy held up both hands in surrender.

"Whoa! Empty hands. What can I get you?" Donut seemed pleased to have a task away from our live fire.

Andy ordered a beer. I ordered a rum and coke with lime. Donut snagged a waitress on his way to the bar.

I liked Donut even though he never flirted with me—maybe *because* he never flirted with me. Easy to appreciate a true-blue man.

And then the bar phone rang.

Everyone froze. Voices hushed. Laughter cut off in mid-guffaw.

I heard the ice clinking in the glasses carried by the waitress four feet away from me.

The phone rang again.

One of the bartenders picked it up. "Hello?"

Andy and Donut smiled at each other.

The bartender, his burly arm holding up the phone receiver, called out, "Is there a Bob Jacobs here?"

Arms pushed someone forward.

"It's your wife."

Voices and laughter roared through the O-Club.

"The drinks are on Bob!"

"Thanks, Bob!"

"Thanks, Bob's wife!"

A surge of uniforms toward the bar.

"What?" I asked.

Andy said, "Don't ever, ever call me at the O-Club. If it's a real emergency, call the duty officer at the squadron and he'll call me."

"Why—?"

"If any woman calls someone at the O-Club, the poor bastard buys drinks for everyone there." Donut's breath sucked in through his teeth. "Bob will be out about three-hundred bucks on this one call."

The infusion of free alcohol had raised the noise level to a happy afterburner roar.

Our drinks were delivered.

Bob sat in a corner, his head in his hands. The guys raised their beers in mock salutes in his direction and tilted bottles to their mouths.

"Couldn't happen to a nicer sap." Andy's tone said the opposite.

"Idiot." Donut mumbled. "He actively works on getting himself and his RIOs killed."

Killed? I laughed, thinking he was kidding.

No one else laughed. Marilyn stopped smiling.

"And he has the worst job in the squadron."

"What's that?"

"He's the Voting Officer."

"Why is that the worst job?"

"He has to make sure everyone has absentee ballots if needed."

Later, when drug tests came into vogue, the VO made sure guys peed in the bottle. Part of an aviator's

74

mystique and power was tied to the importance of the job he had in the squadron and the excellence in which he performed it. Absentee ballots and drug tests were completely non-essential to flying, with no opportunity for excellence. In fact, being excellent at getting your fellow pilots to pee in the bottle pissed them off in more ways than one.

I added Bob to Andy's list of aviators to avoid centering the dot on. A pilot in South Korea on an ACM— air combat maneuver—centered the radar dot—pointed his plane at the same piece of sky as the bogey and maintained the collision bearing—within a mile of the intercept. A mile at a thousand to twelve hundred knots of closure left little time to avoid a midair collision. The pilot found the bogey all right—very quickly and close enough to touch. Oops! Imperative in ACM and formation flying: 'no touch touch—however slight'. It takes very little contact to make parts of planes fall off—often with catastrophic results. The F-16 lost most of a wing, the pilot ejected safely. The F-4 ended up damaged, but flyable. The result? An ROE that forbade centering the dot within a mile of the opponent.

If I didn't see Bob, or move toward him, my honey wouldn't have to worry about being in the same piece of sky.

But Donut was a RIO. He had to fly with pilots like Bob and Unsafe-At-Any-Speed, and without a control stick to guide the plane away from disaster. A cool breeze brushed the nape of my neck. I shivered.

RIOs lacked control in the air—except through the radio yelling at their front-seater to land before they ran out of fuel and through a RIO's ability to command eject. They could decide to eject both seats if the pilot was incapacitated—or too stupid to realize he had reached the point of no return to controlled flight. Since some pilots would rather be dead than look bad at the field, the decision to abandon a multi-million dollar airplane often rested on a RIO's realization that staying alive allowed for redemption, while a smoking hole in the ground did not.

The main job of an officer in the squadron was to be a pilot or RIO. Pilots were judged on their competency in the air, whether they were 'a good stick'. The ranking went on a scale from "a damn fine stick' to 'unsafe at any speed'. Pity the pilot in VMFA 314 known by the call sign Unsafe-At-Any-Speed. Pity him, but don't respect him—and if you're a RIO, try not to fly in his backseat.

As a wife, I just wanted to know my guy's skills kept him safe in the air. On the ground, his skills kept me happy and I participated enthusiastically in keeping him happy: well-fed, well cared for, and lots of between-the-sheets time.

An arm snaked around my waist. "Hey, good looking."

Jaime, my favorite blond bullfrog. I looked level into his twinkling blue eyes.

Where Jaime was, Pops wasn't far behind. "Hey, Jaime. Hey, Pops."

"You guys know Gazelle?" Jaime asked.

"Haven't had the pleasure," Donut said.

"He flies out of Beaufort. He's here tonight. Make a point of meeting him."

76

All eyebrows raised and we looked at Jaime.

"He's known for having kissed every Marine general—"

We waited.

"—On the lips!"

"Oh come on." Andy shook his head, disbelieving.

"Really. They see him coming in reception lines and put one hand out to shake and the other one across their mouths."

"How does he get away with it?" Marilyn loved those who pushed the envelope.

"He's Gazelle." Jaime said it like it explained everything.

Pops nodded. "Some guys can get away with anything."

"Others step on their cranks one time," Andy said, "and find themselves flying trashhaulers and getting out before retirement age."

"Speaking of stepping on one's crank," Agile said. "There's a new CO in the other squadron. Did you hear about his first AOM?"

"No."

"What's an AOM?" I asked.

"All Officers' Meeting," Andy explained.

"The meeting was so memorable, the squadron officers christened him with a new call sign afterward."

"What'd he do?"

Agile gestured with his beer. "Okay—so picture the pilots and RIOs sitting in the ready room for the first AOM, eager to hear the words from their new CO. The guys sat there wondering if he'd be a good stick, or a stick-in-the-mud, or both. Would he operate a flying club—where his favorite guys got the majority of the hops—or would he be interested in keeping everybody up to speed, newbies and buddies alike?"

The guys nodded. Familiar territory to them.

"They wondered if he'd be a micro-manager or a laissez faire, hands-off kind of leader? Would he be a screamer or silent and deadly when crossed? So they lounged in the ready room chairs ratcheted to a reclining position; or sat in decommissioned ejection seats or perched on window ledges with their morning cups of joe, or a cigarette, or both—and the new CO stalked in."

"A stalker? Bad sign. I like saunterers myself."

Agile told a good story. "What did he do?"

"It wasn't what he did, but what he said," Agile clarified. "His speech went something like this: "Good morning, a—holes. Welcome to my f—ing squadron. You may not know much about me, but if you're f—ing pussies about my f—ing language, you can shove it up your a—-, and walk right out the g—damn door right now. I don't give a flying sh—t about your f—ing sensibilities and I won't be watching how I f—ing talk around you."

I didn't know if I should laugh. Would someone like that be a good CO or a bad one?

"He filled in all the blanks—which I won't do with ladies present. He went on for much longer, and the faces in the room were red from laughing or were transfixed by the level of skill required to incorporate that many body parts, bodily functions and irreverent verbs into one speech."

78

Donut nodded. "Generally, a CO is expected to demonstrate a higher standard of behavior than a lowly lieutenant. In this case, the colonel performed past all expectations."

Andy agreed. "A lot can be forgiven a good stick or a great RIO. Excellence in any area looks good at the field."

Excellence in cursing?

"Did anyone walk out?" Marilyn asked.

"If they did, their call sign would also be changed to 'Pussy'," said a lieutenant who'd been listening in. "Uh, excuse me, ma'am."

"Yeah, watch your mouth, Slack." Pops punched him in the arm.

"What is their CO's new call sign?" I asked.

"Col. Profane," Agile said.

We all laughed. Others, who had been listening to the story from the edges of our group, joined in.

I craned my neck. "Is Col. Profane here tonight?"

"Nope. Just the legendary Gazelle," Jaime said.

"What does Gazelle look like?"

Jaime pulled at the collar of his shirt. "Uh. He's not in here right now."

"Where is he?" I asked.

Pops grimaced at Jaime, looking like a short Oliver Hardy. "Now you've done it."

"He's probably in the back room with the strippers." Cindy stood at my elbow.

"Oh hi, Cindy. Strippers?" That sounded interesting. "There are strippers? Here?"

MARCIA SARGENT

Pops conked Jaime on the head with his empty beer bottle, gently so it didn't break, hard enough to make Jaime wince. "Snatch is going to have your balls for this one."

I turned to my sweetie. "Let's go see."

"No."

"But I want—"

"Doesn't matter what you want. No women allowed."

"That's not fair."

His eyebrow raised.

Cindy patted me on the arm. "He's right, you know. Women aren't allowed."

Was she chastising me? This wasn't the fifties. The women's liberation movement maintained women could go anywhere, do anything. The sexual revolution had taught me to be open-minded about nudity and voyeurism. At least, I wanted to be open-minded.

As a matter of fact, I didn't know if I wanted to go see a strip show. Naked women didn't sound all that much fun. I didn't like being told I couldn't. I hated being reminded I wasn't really a member of the fraternity.

"Did you go see them already?" I asked Andy.

"No."

"Are you going to?"

"No."

"Do you want to?"

"No."

Darn. Now I couldn't use the argument that if he could, I could.

Jaime, Pops, and Donut pretended we weren't having this discussion in the middle of our little group in the middle of the MCAS O-Club. Cindy and Marilyn were happy to listen in.

Marilyn put her hand on her hip and confronted Donut. "I want to go see the stripper."

"No."

She looked ready to break away from the allowed flight path.

Marine aviators loved to push the envelope—especially if it would win them glory. In aeronautics, the envelope was the known limits for the safe performance of an aircraft. Test pilots had to test (or push) these limits to establish the exact capabilities of the plane, and where failure was likely to occur—to compare calculated performance limits with ones derived from experience.

ROEs for Marine aviators established the ground rules, but the main requirement for being a good stick involved knowing when to push to the edge of the rules and when the rules didn't apply. Marines were told what they couldn't do; Air Force pilots were told what they could. Air Force pilots flew by the book and had itemized checklists for all contingencies. True, they lost fewer planes on the average, but in a 1v.1 with a good Marine pilot, they were beat like a rug.

Obviously, the parameters for the wives were more like the Air Force's.

"There's Gazelle." Jaime's sigh of relief whooshed across my cheek.

"Who?" I asked.

"Gazelle. There he is. I'm, uh, going to talk to him."

Pops went with him. Andy and Donut thought about it, I could tell. But sense and valor won out. I think they both feared if they left Marilyn and me alone, we'd walk through the door into the back room of the O-Club.

Maybe they were right. If Marilyn went, I'd follow. Although sure of my entitlement as a young woman, I needed a wingwoman to push the edge of the envelope.

Cindy shook her head. "I have no interest in watching strippers."

I admired her I'm-old-enough-to-know-what-I-like-and-what-I-don't-like attitude. I also felt sorry for her. She seemed so old. I hoped I'd be able to stay young even when I got to be over thirty.

Marilyn laughed. "I'd be a lot more interested to see one of the guys strip out of a flight suit."

Safety Question of the Day: How many rules should a wife be willing to break to see something she didn't really want to see? Answer? None. So Marilyn and I stood down, but—at least on my part—it was only a temporary cessation of offensive action.

Why did the guys watch strippers? Psychologists might know a bunch of reasons, but I figured the guys liked being bad boys—bad little boys whooping it up in the back room, and then walking through a door into the O-Club bar, to the ladies and rules of decorum. After all, even Peter Pan wanted Wendy to mother him.

Decorum. Not exactly—more like *relative* decorum. I watched the drunken hand movements of simulated air-to-air combat maneuvers, listened to guffaws of laughter, and observed lieutenants flirting with the waitresses. Jimbo had never finished his moon. A free beer had brought him down from his perch and zipped up his flight suit.

A high-pitched giggle from the corner.

My head whipped toward the sound. That sounded like *a guy* giggling like a maniac.

Andy took my elbow. "Let's go meet Gazelle. I think that may be him."

Chapter 7
The Boys' Club

Andy led, holding my hand as we wound our way through the murky maze of tables, drunks, chairs, and sloshing drinks to our objective.

Gazelle-who-had-kissed-every-Marine-general-on-the-lips didn't look like much. Shortish, a little bit pudgy, he looked more like a garden gnome without the beard and the red hat, but dressed in a green flight suit.

Jaime introduced us.

Gazelle's hand was as warm as his eyes. "Hello, darling."

After Gazelle and the other boys acknowledged Marilyn and me, they turned their attention to aviators and places they had in common—the Marine aviator not-so-secret handshake. *You flew out of Cherry Point in '73. Did you know Capt. Umptifrish? Yeah. I flew with 232 in Iwakuni in '68. Oh that guy Macgillicudyfratz was a wild one. Do you remember the benjo ditch races?*

Not knowing any of the cast of characters or the settings, Marilyn and I stood slightly out of the circle of testosterone and commiserated about the not-so-nice elements of being married to a jet jockey. We agreed we hated the smoke permeating their clothing from the ready room and our clothing after being at the O-Club. By this time in the evening, the smoke layered a second hazy bluish ceiling just above my reach.

"Speaking of smelly." I shared about a recent evening when Andy had returned home after three hops, "—and I made him take a shower. No way would we be going out to dinner with his helmet head."

"Helmet head, darling?" Gazelle giggled, a high cackling giggle of a laugh. "He had helmet head?"

I didn't think anyone else had been listening. My face warmed. "Uh huh. You know—when you guys take off your helmet after flying all day? Helmet head. And it stinks!"

"Oh I bet it does, darling. I bet it does."

About that time I figured out Gazelle had put a completely different meaning on 'helmet head'. As far as he was concerned, he'd gotten a completely clueless sweet young thing to talk about a stinky dick head in public.

He giggled again and started in on Andy. "Snatch, you've got to stop coming home with helmet head. Beverly made me promise to, years ago. Saved our marriage." His little boy grin illuminated his face.

Even though the joke was on me, I laughed, and blushed, and punched him on the arm. "You are a bad, bad boy."

"I know, darling. And you love me for it."

I did.

Gazelle's attention was grabbed by a couple behind him. "Talk with you later, darling."

"Snatch," Donut said. "Did you hear three more P-3 birds came back without their drag chutes this week?"

"Way to look bad at the field."

I shrugged, asking Marilyn wordlessly if she knew what chutes had to do with anything.

Marilyn tugged on her husband's sleeve.

He said, "P-3's notorious for coming back without their chutes."

I still didn't understand.

Andy said, "It's bad because it means they departed the airplane—" Translation—they lost control of their flying machine. "—And had to deploy the drag chute to bring it back under pilot control."

"The drag chute is that little parachute that twirls at the back of a fighter having a troublesome landing— it helps slow it down." I suspected Donut simplified it more than he had to. "Little" and "twirls" were the key words indicating mild sarcasm.

I could handle sarcasm. I hadn't tired of asking questions.

"And P-3?" I asked.

"VMFP-3" Andy took a drink of his beer. "They're an aerial photo-reconnaissance squadron. They fly special F-4s with cameras."

"And most of them fly like hamburgers." Agile moved a chair to stand next to me.

Flying like hamburgers—respect's kiss of death. Aviators only admired those who were good at what they did—and aviators flew planes—or, if a RIO, helped pilots fly planes.

"Case in point, the missing drag chutes," Donut said.

"P-3's where bad pilots go to stay alive. They fly straight and level taking pictures. Hard to fuck that up."

87

The lieutenant, Jimbo, staggered past on his way to the bar. "My beer's gone. Need more beer." He reached into his pocket, pulled it inside out. "Money's gone. Need beer."

He stopped and swayed gently back and forth.

Then he threw himself to the ground, laid on his back, put his hands and feet into the air, and yelled, "Dead bug!"

Andy grabbed my arm. "Down! Down!"

I crouched on the floor.

"No! On your back!"

I assumed the position, laughing hysterically. "What—?"

Marilyn had thrown herself almost on top of Donut, who had already crashed down and flopped on his back quicker than a dying cockroach. She flipped onto her back and wiggled her platform shoes in the air.

Donut held his beer aloft. "Didn't spill a drop."

Others had, the yeasty sour smell wafted over me. I lifted my hair off the carpet—just in case.

I looked around through the legs of tables, the legs of chairs, the legs of barstools and saw lots of arms and legs in the air. Some covered in flight suit green, some in Charlie uniform green, some bare—oh the poor women in skirts—and mine in bell-bottomed pants. I had to bend my knees so the pant legs wouldn't slide up to my thighs.

Were the chaplain and his wife on their backs on the floor?

Yes.

She waved at me. I waved back.

By now I laughed so hard I could hardly breathe. I loved the games boys played.

"And we have a winner!"

Guffaws rolled from the far corner of the room.

"Who is it?"

"Who cares?"

"I don't care."

"Some FNG who didn't want to put his beer down."

"Or look foolish in front of his date."

A captain next to the bar raised a Michelob high. "Here's to all FNGs. May they buy my drinks forever!"

The lowest rung on the O' Club ladder was the FNG, the Fucking New Guy. An FNG could be a new 1st lieutenant, but usually an FNG was an Air Force puke, or a Navy pilot, or a ground Marine who hadn't spent time with aviators. It almost didn't even count to mess with their heads because they wanted to be one of the boys so badly they'd do anything to be accepted. Also, most of their brains were newly minted and/or not used to playing the game. What game? Any game.

The best games to play with FNGs were games that allowed the FNG to buy all the drinks and all the meals—for everyone. FNGs were never told all the rules.

Andy stood up and pulled me to stand next to him.

"Where's my drink?" I looked around on the tables near us.

"Don't worry about it. You get another courtesy of the last guy to hit the deck."

The rush already had hit the bar. Waitresses circulated taking orders. The noise level rocketed.

Dead bug—another game to get free drinks—and to get women on their backs with their legs up in the air.

Not only did aviators have their own code words and call signs, they also had their own games to play. I found the guys and the words and the games entertaining. Nothing I said or did seemed nearly as exciting.

Agile, Cindy, Andy and I found a quiet corner to watch the escalation of the festivities, powderkegged by alcohol.

I spoke earnestly about the Change of Command ceremony and how I felt about my guy having to follow orders and call colonels and lieutenant colonels, 'Sir'. I'd met a lot of lieutenant colonels and colonels, even a general or two. No way were some of them 'superior' officers. So I didn't get it.

"You're married to a military officer," Cindy said. "What did you expect?"

I didn't get her, either. It wasn't just her perfect brown pageboy making me nervous. "I expected my guy to be treated with respect. 'Yes, sir.' 'No, sir.' 'Of course, sir.' 'I will, sir.' is ridiculous. My Andy shouldn't have to talk to anyone that way."

Agile patted me on the head and grinned.

"What? What did I say?"

Andy smiled. "She's talking about when I called the group CO at El Toro to find out whether I would be going to a squadron or not."

Agile joined Andy, laughing.

Cindy shook her sleekly coifed head at me. "You are so young."

That was a crime?

Agile explained, "The group CO was the full colonel who had all the power to decide if your husband, our beloved Snatch, flew airplanes in a squadron or flew a desk doing picayune shit for other shits who outranked him. Of course, he was extremely respectful. If there was ever a time we'd all kiss ass, that would be it."

"Oh."

Gazelle's distinctive giggle worked the room. Sometimes it sounded from a far corner, sometimes from the door, usually it remained in close proximity to the bar.

I went to the ladies' room with Cindy. On our way back to the guys, we passed right behind Gazelle. Laughter exploded.

He turned around, arms wide. "What? What's the problem?"

Spotting Cindy and me, his eyes ignited with glee. "Darlings! Hello, darlings!" He swayed, arms all the way out from his shoulders. "You'll talk to me, darlings, won'cha?"

Something wasn't right. I knew it, but couldn't put my finger on it. Good thing I didn't.

"Gazelle!" Cindy's gasp echoed.

I followed her line of sight to the crotch of Gazelle's flight suit. And there, sticking out, looking incredibly alien—were two hairy, wrinkled purplish balls. Gazelle's hairy, wrinkled purplish balls.

Flight suits zip from the bottom as well as the top to facilitate leak taking in flight. Gazelle had unzipped his suit, pulled out his scrotum, and re-zipped it. Now he spread his arms, delighted we had spotted his display, and pretended he had no idea his privates were not-so-private.

Not decorous. Not at all. But Gazelle could show his bad little boy side—and his hairy balls—in public and I loved him anyway. He lived in Never Neverland, flew with the Lost Boys, and defeated the forces of destruction who wore sharp hooks to cover up their deficiencies. He had fun and I had fun with him.

"Gazelle, quit your ball-walking ways near my wife." Andy wrapped an arm around my shoulder and turned me away.

I checked my six. Gazelle wandered off to find another unsuspecting female.

"Marcia." Andy sliced the tips of his fingers across his neck: the universal pilot signal for 'Cut the engines'.

Hand sign for the end of a flight.

I knew my guy figured I'd flown enough around the O-Club. Much longer in the air and I might be bingo fuel, out of gas, once we reached home and bed. A tits-up wife—in the horizontal position and on her back—was good. A sleeping tits-up wife?—not so good.

I reached up to pat his slightly scratchy jaw. "Okay, honey. Let's go home." I knew he'd make it worth the landing. He didn't need games to get my legs in the air.

Chapter 8
Fallon and Live Fire

I looked up from my still flat stomach.

Pregnant.

My face distorted to twice its width in the mirrored tile on the wall—terror and elation deformed. I crossed my eyes and stuck out my tongue, hoping comic relief would help, but I couldn't see what I looked like with my eyes centered on my nose. I uncrossed my eyes and assessed my reflection. Fat, fat and fatter—except for my chest, worse luck. Even in warped mirror tiles my chest remained unremarkable. Each tile stretched out a different piece of my anatomy: my stomach, my hips, my face. The mirror tiles were slightly convex—I should have checked them before taking them from the hardware store.

My body tended toward long and lean until the past month when I'd gained twenty pounds. Twenty pounds! Was I already acquiring a moon face to go with the soon-to-be Buddha belly? Puffing out my cheeks, and then sucking in like a fish, I was dismayed to see little difference. Andy thought I even looked good when I woke up in the morning. I remained unconvinced. C'mon. Drool trail from my lips down my chin, eyes half-glued shut with sleep, my hair fuzzed out and sticking every-which-way? So I wasn't really worried about losing his admiration by gaining weight and looking pregnant.

The true problem? The idea of having a baby scared me to bone-deep trembling. Babies scared me. They were so darn helpless. Helpless baby, clueless me—a bad combination.

Five weeks ago, I'd been excited for my sweetie to return from the Fallon deployment and see how much bigger our bathroom looked. Nothing like redwood and mirrors to transform a place. I'd hung spider plants in the hangers I'd macraméd—our own lush, mini oasis. A surprise.

He'd hardly noticed it—we'd better things to do than admire the hanging plants.

Getting pregnant after that was a surprise, too. It shouldn't have been. After the Change of Command, I knew I believed in Andy and I believed in our marriage. Maybe some of Kathy's magic dust had sprinkled on me. I'd agreed to start the baby thing. We'd been practicing almost every day, morning and night. I loved Andy's smile when he'd said, "Making babies takes practice. Practice, practice, practice." We practiced for weeks, and nothing—until he returned from that two-week deployment of target training at Fallon AFB, Nevada.

The surprise was—I spent my early twenties trying not to get pregnant by boyfriends, or by Andy before we were married and in the first months of our marriage. I'd always figured it only took one time, one slip. Heck no. When I went off the pill, it took weeks of practice and fourteen days of abstinence to get a positive result. No 'Oops!' just, 'Come *on*, already.'

Today, finally, the Ob-Gyn had confirmed my diagnosis.

Time to tell him. Andy would be excited enough for the both of us.

"Honey?" he called from the bedroom.

"Be right there." I washed my shaking hands, and walked into the unknown.

———

"Wait right there." Andy ran around the car to open my door.

I almost laughed. Until I'd announced I carried his heir, I'd opened my own car door. As if being a few weeks pregnant completely incapacitated me. I didn't even have morning sickness.

Not wanting to anger the gods of pregnant women, I knocked on the faux wood inside panel of the Volvo. Didn't want morning sickness. Not wanting to discourage Andy's solicitude, I waited for him to open my door.

He put his hand under my elbow to help me up out of my seat and on to the sidewalk.

Marilyn and Donut's home near Culver Road and the 5 Freeway in Tustin was a bit older than our Mission Viejo house—built in the early- rather than late-sixties—so it hadn't completely abandoned the post-war-building-boom-tract-homes-of-southern-California look for the Spanish mission style. Dark rough-cut wood framed its gray-blue stucco. Clumps of knee-high, shiny green Peter Pan agapanthus marked the walk, their long stems topped with clusters of light blue flowers.

A burst of male laughter roared through the door. A high pitched woman's laugh followed. The squadron sounded all present and accounted for.

MARCIA SARGENT

Andy knocked and opened the front door without waiting for anyone to answer.

Young lieutenants and captains wearing Hang Ten t-shirts or madras button-downs over jeans packed the living room to capacity. Apparently, no one wanted to miss Donut's party to introduce his baby girl to the world of aviators. The word had already been passed—there'd be lots of alcohol, lots of food—but all smoking went outside. No messing up Randi's newly-minted lungs.

I knew Marilyn had turned baby-crazed. And I was happy for her—really I was. But I thought all newborns looked like W.C. Fields or Winston Churchill—even the girl babies. Babies also smelled—at best like sweet powdery yuck, at worst like sour milk, pee, and poop. And. I. Was. Pregnant. So far, all anyone wanted to do when they heard my news was talk about 'the sweet widdle hands and the sweet chubby widdle toes' and 'ooh, the precious widdle darlings' until I wanted to puke, even without morning sickness.

So I prepared for the onslaught of wives, including Marilyn, my former partner in I've-not-bought-into-the-whole-officers'-wives-hoorah. Traitor. Good thing I loved her and was happy for her and Donut. She was older—almost thirty. He was older—over thirty. They *should* have a kid.

And I figured their party was the most perfect and the worst place to brief the squadron that Snatch and I were also going to have a baby—in eight months or so—which seemed like the far-far-distant future. I knew I'd be leading the brief. Andy would take the congrats, but he preferred not to chatter about personal details.

It was the perfect place for an announcement, because most of the wives and husbands would be there—so I would get it out of the way quickly—in one 'Aaahh-hh'.

But the reactions would be magnified and I wasn't even sure I could handle one baby-nutty comment, much less a whole squadron worth from guys and wives. Hopefully, everyone would transfer most of the weirdness to Donut and Marilyn since that was the reason they had invited everyone to their house.

My nerves got the worst of me, and the lid rattled on the Corningware dish full of Cathy's Chicken: a casserole of chicken, broccoli, cheddar cheese, rice, and cream of chicken soup.

Andy took it from my hands.

"I can carry it."

"You're carrying enough." His smile looked a bit too much like gloating. He loved babies and had been lobbying to start our family since the wedding.

I wanted to kick him.

Andy and I passed the guys on our way through the living room.

He carried the dish through the mostly female crowd in the family room to the kitchen.

"Marcia!" Marilyn hugged me with enthusiasm. She looked good. As good as deep dark circles and twenty extra pounds could look. Shouldn't all the weight have been delivered with the baby?

Julie, Bird's wife; Cindy, Agile's wife; and Kate, Duff's wife, surrounded me.

"Have you seen the little one yet?" Cindy looked excited, like a baby fanatic. A tired fanatic. She had young ones of her own, and deep, dark circles under her eyes.

"No. I just got here." I wanted to see it—uh, her—sort of. Mostly I wanted to see Marilyn as a mom.

"Good luck tracking little Randi down," Julie's North Carolina drawl stretched out the words. "Dad's got her on his shoulder showing her off."

"Duncan loves being a dad." Marilyn nodded her head and smiled.

"How do you like being a mom?" I needed the truth.

She lit up. "Oh, it's—magic."

Maybe I looked less than convinced. Lack of sleep had left her eyes bruised and puffy. After kids came, did anyone manage to get a normal amount of sleep?

"I'm tired, I admit it. But Randi is so warm and sweet smelling and trusting and—" She shook her head. "What can I say? I'm a fan."

"And it helps that Donut is sharing the nightly feedings," Cindy said.

"You bet your sweet bippy, it does," Marilyn agreed.

"How does he do that?" Even I knew moms had the milk-producing apparatus.

Her face fell. "I couldn't make it work."

"Make what work?"

"Breastfeeding. Randi wouldn't, I couldn't. Even the La Leche League lady couldn't help. So we're bottle-feeding. God! I wanted to do it all the natural Lamaze way—natural childbirth, no drugs, and I ended up with a C-section—after twenty hours of excruciating pain,

98

mind you. Easiest way to feed a baby—mom's milk—and I can't even do that. At least now Duncan can feed her in the middle of the night without waking me."

Twenty hours of pain? I felt a bit dizzy.

Julie asked, "Can I get y'all a drink?"

"Um, a Coke?"

"Don't forget the rum and lime!" Marilyn said. "Marcia loves her Cokes with rum."

"No. Just plain Coke."

They knew. All four of them knew.

"Are you—?" Julie.

"It's so exciting!" Cindy.

"You are!" Kate.

Marilyn hugged me again. I wanted to cry. My face flamed red. Everyone joked about sex all the time, but now it was personal. Everyone knew I'd 'done it' at least once.

"What's all the excitement over here?" Merle, a new RIO lieutenant in the squadron, asked.

"Snatch and Marcia are going to have a baby," Cindy said.

"Oh. Good." Uneasy, the lieutenant turned away, ears burning brightly.

At last, someone who shared my feelings.

Julie smiled. "How far along are you?"

"Just six weeks."

"Funny. I'm just six weeks along, too."

"Julie? You and Bird?"

"Yes."

Both six weeks.

We said it at the same time, "Fallon." The single word held a volley of accusations.

Linda joined us, a sturdy strawberry blond, with pale skin and pale blue eyes. "What about Fallon?"

"Julie and I are both pregnant, and both six weeks along. It must have been when the guys returned from deployment."

Linda blushed, two spots of red on white, white cheeks. "I'm six weeks pregnant, too."

"Three of us!"

The young blonde Debby joined our laughing circle. "Three of you, what?"

We told her.

"So am I," she said.

"Pregnant?"

"Yep."

Suddenly I felt better. Four of us would be going through the whole thing together. I felt like a GDI who had joined a sorority—still reluctant and unsure if I'd get along with all my pledge sisters. Many of the unspoken rules of womanhood remained obscure to me.

"Damn those men. They're supposed to keep it in their pants." Janey walked up to the circle of women. "Did I hear there's something in the water?"

The boys in the other room had heard the news. The fraternity brothers were proud of themselves. Beers and sodas were raised, laughter and jokes about silver bullets, wondering why pilots and RIOs didn't aim that well at live fire target practice in Fallon.

"We saved all our best shots for our return."

"Once a Knight is never enough."

Ha ha. VMFA 314 guys were the Black Knights.

"Inspiration is key."

"It's all about having a worthy target."

"Hey!" Julie said. "I'm your wife, not a target."

Bird pointed his index finger at her belly and pulled an imaginary trigger. "Honey, all I can say is, 'Fox two.'" Just as if he'd locked on and fired a sidewinder missile at a bogey.

More laughter. More beer drunk.

Conversation about the upcoming deployment to Florida—College Dart.

"Don't get any ideas on your return from Florida," Cindy told Agile. "We have all the kids we're going to have."

"Then you might end up with a different gift from Florida," Kate warned.

"Oranges would be good." Cindy sipped her wine.

Kate's voice graveled with smoke damage, New England, and pissed-off wife. "Duff brought home a gift from the Mustang Ranch—*the drip.*"

Silence. Awkward silence. What could we say? What should we say?

"Are ya'll calling him names, Kate, or was thet his gift?" Trigger, the Texan calf-roper said.

Bird guffawed. "Duff, I didn't think you were in that room with your lady of the night long enough to do anything except have an air burst—much less catch the clap."

Guys obviously didn't worry about embarrassing a target; they fixed their sights and shot it down. And

101

Bird? Well, his ego's size demanded deflating any other sharing the same piece of sky.

Duff's already pink, freckled face brightened to fuschia; his flaring ears turned burgundy. He guzzled his beer.

Donut strolled in to stand next to Marilyn, baby Randi on his shoulder, and a welcome distraction. The women clustered around, oohing and aahing. They talked about how sweet she smelled, and how tiny, and argued about whether she looked like Marilyn or Donut.

"Nice wall décor, Donut," Agile said.

Donut grunted.

All heads turned to look at the wall. Front and center, a yellow-striped double loop hung at head height.

"What's that?" I asked Marilyn.

"A face curtain from Donut's ejection in Yuma."

Bird grimaced. "A face curtain from a dumbass accident that was a result of a dumbass decision by Unsafe-At-Any-Speed."

"Gee, Bird, Tell us how you really feel about him." Pops raised his beer to his lips, drank, then belched. "At least Unsafe had sense enough not to show up here."

"He's not known for sense." Donut patted Baby Randi on the back. "It might be I didn't invite him."

The tension in the room cut through the camaraderie. A face curtain from an ejection seat meant something bad had happened, something very bad with a lost airplane, but this time at least, no lost boys.

The Phantom F-4 came equipped with a Martin-Baker mkH7 ejection seat. Aviators flew planes. This was important to remember when discussing ejections.

An aviator without a plane to fly became just a Marine, not a bad thing—but not as good, either.

Aviators did not want to eject. But plane wings could fall off; engines inhaled birds through the turbine blades—something known as FOD—Foreign Object Damage; or equipment could malfunction at a critical point in flight, creating an unrecoverable airplane. Those were regrettable, but not the pilot's fault. A pilot who ejected in these circumstances and survived received sympathy and joined the Lucky Bastard Club—an unofficial community, as well as the Martin Baker Tie Club—an official honor and tie given to all pilots who eject from a plane with the aid of a Martin-Baker seat. Most of the time, ejection seats worked.

Unfortunately, too many things could go wrong with an ejection, not all of them dependent on the manufacture of the seat. First, the canopy had to be blown off. If not, the pilot or RIO would impact the thick plastic. The plastic would win. Then, an explosive had to explode under the seat to send it and the aviator up the rails, pulling ten to twelve G's. Elbows, knees, and shoulders needed to be tucked in or the force of the ejection would break, dislocate, or mangle. A rocket had to shoot the seat free of the plane. If the plane traveled at too high a rate of speed, the jet blast of air would hit the aviator like a brick wall. The jet blast would win. The parachute had to deploy properly and the aviator had to come down somewhere he could be recovered, preferably not in the fireball of his crashed bird.

Pilots thought paratroopers crazy for jumping out of perfectly good airplanes. So there was a corollary to

Rather Be Dead Than Look Bad At the Field: Airplanes Are Meant To Be Flown, Not Jumped Out Of.

The bright yellow and black loops, stained with smoke, glowed a warning like a venomous snake.

Marilyn answered my unspoken doubt, "Not my idea to hang it up there. Seeing it gives me the creeps. I almost lost my Duncan. Randi almost lost her daddy."

"What happened?" I asked.

"Unsafe-At-Any-Speed made a command decision that it was safe to fly with the air-refueling probe door tied down with safety wire." Agile explained.

"He's an idiot," Bird said.

Agile nodded. So did the rest of the men in the vicinity. "In the Yuma landing pattern, the jury-rigged door popped open, the fueling probe flailed out into the windstream, and then ripped off."

"Can't they fly without the fueling probe?" I asked.

"They could have if it hadn't punctured one of the fuselage fuel cells, which caught fire. That F-4, in an extremely short period of time, transformed from flying machine to flaming death trap," Bird answered.

"The Martin-Baker ejection seats performed as advertised. Donut had a new tie and a new wall decoration." Agile didn't look like that was a good thing.

"It shows he lived to fly another day, in spite of the idiot at the stick," Bird said.

"Donut's a lucky bastard." Pops took in the baby, Marilyn, and the friends surrounding Donut, all clapping him on the back, and laughing at his escape from the jaws of an incompetent front-seater.

Grins all around.

Randi started to cry.

"Wet diaper!" Donut whisked her off to the bedroom.

Later, the dinner portion of the evening over, groups formed: in the kitchen cleaning dishes and talking about school-age children, in the living room around the sofa with Marilyn talking babies and childbirth, in the family room with the young lieutenants and the CO talking flying with flat hands and animated voices.

I heard murmuring in the hall and moved into the doorway. Donut's silhouette held Baby Duncan, backlit by the glow from the bedroom, by the rumble of men talking about airplanes, and by the occasional clink of a glass or a bottle.

The baby squirmed and whimpered.

"Shh. Shh-hh. It's okay, little girl. Daddy's here." He hummed a bit of Rock-A-Bye-Baby, playing with the dark curls on the back of her neck. "Daddy loves you, and expects you to grow up sweet and beautiful—just like your mom."

A soft burp.

He chuckled and adjusted her on his shoulder, rubbing between her shoulder blades. "Well, maybe your mom's not so sweet. But you'll be feisty like your mom and sweet like my mom." He picked up her hand and kissed the tiny fingers. "You're loved, little girl. The world's a tough place, but it'll be okay. You've got your daddy. It'll all be okay."

I backed away, unseen. Perhaps I should have left sooner. But I hadn't been able to, hadn't wanted to. I needed reassurance as much as, if not more than, Baby

Randi. Even if I couldn't be the mother my babies deserved, I hoped Andy—like Donut—had depths underutilized as a military aviator.

Chapter 9
Tupperware Party

Although the guys needed no excuse to party at each other's houses or the O-Club, wives used practical reasons like kitchenware parties, baby or wedding showers.

Agile's wife, Cindy, was the hostess for my first Tupperware party. She answered the door and shepherded me into her comfortable, unassuming home.

I'd seen lots of Tupperware over the months since the wedding. Every potluck squadron party showcased some other plastic item essential to good housekeeping. I'd seen enough convenient cake keepers, pitchers, pie servers, flour, sugar, tea, and coffee canisters, and leftovers storage containers—all with the snap lock technology to keep food fresh. I walked in already sold, maybe even oversold.

A stay-at-home-soon-to-be-mom, I rarely went out shopping. Shopping meant buying, and buying was fraught with danger. Growing up, my father insisted there was little money to spend. To be fair, the food costs alone for six children must have been daunting. My mother liked to shop and she liked to buy. "Champagne tastes on a beer budget," she'd say. She'd buy anyway, hide purchases, using credit on the day after the billing period closed so it would be a month before it showed on any bill. Eventually, always, my father found out. His anger barked down our hallways late at night through closed doors, words unheard, a night monster with claws. My father growled and snarled and yelled, demeaning, dismissing. My mother remained silent. The few times I heard her, his anger escalated; loud voice pounding down her small voice. The control of money at home was a power game, a dominance game I now avoided at all costs.

I vowed to try to get to know the women and keep my purchases to a minimum.

Debby—my tallest sister in the sorority of pregnant wives—sat on the brown corduroy sofa. "Hi, Marcia." She patted the sofa cushion next to her.

Kate, not smoking for once, stood with a glass of wine in her hand. She lifted it in salute. "So, still on your honeymoon?"

I blushed, then grinned. "Yes, but he does have a tendency to wipe his shaving cream face on my towel."

"How is he about picking up his crap?"

"I do that for him. He's tired when he gets home."

Kate shook her head at me like she had some advice she'd share later. I liked her a lot, drawn to her blunt humor, sure she harbored no secret agenda or need to lord it over other women.

Mikki, Unsafe-At-Any-Speed's wife, almost disappeared into a blue tweed stuffed chair. She looked normal: brown hair, brown eyes, pleasant expression. I couldn't imagine being married to a man the other aviators openly despised. Maybe Unsafe had other redeeming qualities.

Linda, strawberry blond and already pudgy with her pregnancy, perched precariously on a rattan bar-stool at the bar dividing the kitchen and the living room. Julie, Bird's wife, sat next to her on another stool.

Dining room chairs had been pulled out for extra seating. Obviously more were expected. A grey, very fuzzy medium-sized dog slobbered on the sliding glass door from the outside. He scratched on the glass.

"Smoky! No!" Cindy clapped her hands at the dog. "Sorry. Can I get you some pop?"

"Pop?"

"Fizzy stuff. Coca-Cola. Bubble Up. You know—pop."

Oh. Soda. I must have still looked puzzled.

"I'm from Iowa."

I hadn't meant to laugh; it just came out. She looked like a Midwesterner: a bit old-fashioned and comfortably padded. "A Coke would be great. Thanks." Yep, and no wine for the preggo. I plopped next to Debby on the well-stuffed sofa.

Janey walked in. "Am I late? Didcha sell off all the goods already?" She commandeered one of the dining room chairs.

Cindy giggled. "We saved some for you to spend your money on."

I liked her giggle.

"You mean, 'Spend Chuck's money on'," Janey said. "I love to spend that man's paycheck."

Five minutes later, Sundy, Trigger's wife came in. She smoothed her frosted shoulder-length hair away from her face and settled with a small smile next to

Janey. For a Texan, she didn't talk much. She and Trigger had no children, only a small furry white dog they fed candy orange slices and spoke to in baby talk. Her reserve made me want to stand back from her—who knew what she really thought—but Andy liked Trigger, and I liked Trigger, so Sundy was my friend by marriage.

Janey asked for a soda. Guess she wasn't from Iowa. "Will you look at this group? Four of y'all knocked up from one deployment. Could the U.S. Census keep up if the guys keep deploying?"

"Four?" Mikki, Unsafe's wife, asked.

Janey nodded. "Yep. Snatch's wife—" She pointed to me. "—Julie, Debby, and Linda. That's four."

"Five."

"Nope. I counted correctly. My math skills might not be up to calculus, but I can count to four."

Mikki said, "Actually it is five. I'm pregnant, too, and it must have been after Fallon."

Well, the sorority just added a new member.

Not all the wives were there. Marilyn didn't want to bring the baby—and she had told me she didn't need more kitchen gear; she didn't even cook. The XO's wife, Margaret, probably stored food in china and sterling silver. Apparently, no obligation existed to attend a party meant for selling products.

I, on the other hand, wanted the magical Tupperware.

The Tupperware Lady was Cindy's neighbor. A well-coifed Susie Homemaker type, who probably ironed her sheets and pillowcases, she made everything look so easy and necessary. She passed around the plastic bowls

110

and pitchers. We burped the tops and ohhed and ah-hed.

Well, I did, at least. This was arcane domestic stuff from the mysterious society of married women. I didn't understand so much about being a squadron wife, but Tupperware? Tupperware was *useful*.

The other wives involved themselves to varying degrees.

Mikki and Julie spent most of the demonstration time talking about their pregnancies. Mikki was crazy about having her own baby. Julie had already been there and done that. She had two elementary age kids by her first husband, who'd been killed in Vietnam. So Mikki kept trying to get medical information out of Julie—much too detailed. Ask your Ob-Gyn, fergoshsakes!

She must not have been able to hear me screaming in my head, since she just kept asking gross questions. She asked about hemorrhoids. Was she nuts? Perhaps she matched well with Unsafe. Unsafe-At-Any-Speed married Unsafe-To-Tupperware-With.

I played with the pitchers and the marinating set and the measuring cups in harvest gold and burnt orange that all fit inside each other so you could fit them in the drawer. I practiced burping the storage bowls and thought how nice my kitchen would be with all these fine plastics—guaranteed for a lifetime.

Debby, the young blonde next to me on the sofa, and I talked about the advantages of various items. We filled out our order sheets. Strange bonding, but by the time Cindy passed out the homemade cheesecake, I liked Debby and wanted to spend more time with her.

Business done, the other women had broken into conversational groupings. Debby and I were the only ones on the sofa.

"So. How's married life treating you?" I asked her.

She laughed. She had heard that question fired at me during the squadron party at Bird and Julie's. "Waldo and I are almost newlyweds ourselves." She sobered. "His first wife divorced him while he was a prisoner, so we've only been married for a couple of years."

"A prisoner? You mean a POW?"

"Yes. In the Hanoi Hilton for a year and a half with Harley Chapman and James Stockdale." She twisted her napkin. "He doesn't talk about it."

"And his wife divorced him while he was a POW? Yuck."

"To be fair, she thought him dead for almost half that time. And they hadn't been getting along before he left. She hated that he flew. When he was shot down, it just reinforced all her fears." The napkin tore in two. Debby looked at the two halves for a long moment. "They were high school sweethearts. She never wanted to be married to someone in the military. A hometown kind of girl, she expected safe, sane, and keep the grass mowed."

We'd all like safe, sane and a nice lawn. My father mowed on Saturday. Dressed in Madras shorts—no shirt—he'd push the manual lawn mower with precision, each mowed swath barely overlapping the next until the irregular kidney-shaped yard had a darker, lighter pattern inscribed in parallel lines across the width of the grass. He mowed starting at eight in the morning and would finish by noon. When he was done, he knew he'd be mowing again the next Saturday and the Saturday after that. He worked at mowing like he worked at selling wholesale lumber, without joy.

As for safe and sane, the rest of my childhood was anything but. I remember dreaming often of flying, or of trying to fly—not in a plane but with a certain combination of hope, arm flapping, and running far enough to lift me up and away from the fears I lived with, dread of angry monsters. In my earliest remembered nightmare, I ran in footed sleepers from an unknown danger inside my house, and flew over the sofa to get away. The moments in the air were full of relief and delight at my escape and in the freedom of flight.

Of course I married a pilot.

I'd like to have safe and sane in my married life but I couldn't imagine asking Andy or my brother to stop flying. They were pilots. Pilots fly.

At least there wasn't a war on anymore. My chest ached, thinking about sending Andy off to fly while others tried to shoot him down.

The rest of Debby's and my conversation dealt with comparing which items we'd put on our order forms and laughing about what kind of mothers we'd be.

Cindy totaled my Tupperware bill. Everyone else handed her a check before they excused themselves and left.

I hadn't known to bring a check. Andy gave me cash whenever I left the house. Unfortunately, the forty dollars in my purse wouldn't cover what I'd listed to stock my kitchen with handy, convenient, durable plastic stuff. I looked at the total again. Andy might not agree we needed to spend that much on plastics, burpable or not. My gut started to ache.

"I don't have our checkbook."

"Oh, just send it to me in the mail."

"Okay." And like all things that made my stomach hurt, I tucked the need to write a really big check to Cindy, a check Andy might yell at me about, in my 'I'll think about that later' mind file—and forgot it.

But I couldn't forget or avoid my conversation with Debby. That night I told Andy what she'd said about her husband's first wife.

"So she expected safe and sane and keep the grass mowed." He shook his head. "That's not an excuse for disloyalty. Good pilots are safe. And when we're in the plane, we're sane. We keep our heads even '...when all about are losing theirs,' as Kipling would say."

"But what about Donut? He's a RIO. He doesn't have a control stick."

"Donut's a damn fine RIO. He's kept many a young and/or stupid pilot alive by staying sane." He saw my face. "Don't worry. I'm safe. I'm sane. So's Donut. So's your brother. We're all good at what we do."

He was sure so I had to be sure, too. Pilots fly—safe and sane. I'd never expected much from lawn mowing, anyway.

"I'm not worried—exactly."

But a teeny, tiny doubt inched into my heart and burrowed in.

Two weeks later, I sat talking in the family room with Mary, my neighbor from around the corner. She'd stopped in to talk after we met out on the sidewalk as I unloaded groceries.

"So your husband is an Air Force pilot?"

"No. Marine Corps." I didn't understand why civilians assumed pilots belonged to the Air Force.

"He flies helicopters?"

"No. Fighter jets. Phantoms."

"Oh. That makes sense." She nodded and her pale blonde hair shimmered in the filtered light from the bamboo shades. "My husband used to be a Navy JAG at El Toro. I never paid any attention to the military stuff."

A JAG was a Judge Advocate General—a military lawyer. JAG jokes were just as common and derogatory as lawyer jokes.

I changed the subject. She taught English at a Catholic school. I liked books and reading.

We were deep in a discussion of whether students should have to read Hemingway, she loved Old Man and the Sea and I hated the whole manly-man-sacrificing-everything-to-prove-he-could, when the front door slammed open and the sound of muffled thuds and rustling heavy plastic echoed in the entryway.

"Marcia?" Andy hefted three large plastic bags full of harvest gold, burnt orange and avocado kitchenware. "What's all this? Agile said it's ours."

"Tupperware. Isn't it neat?"

"Yeah. Sure."

I introduced Mary. Then I tried to interest him in how Tupperware worked with the seals and the lifetime

115

guarantee and how to burp the containers to lock in freshness.

Mary nodded and agreed it was wonderful stuff.

"Okay. Great. There's a Monday Night game on."

Mary said her goodbyes. I told her we'd have to get together again soon. She said she made a great pumpkin pie. I loved pumpkin pie. I liked meeting a woman from out of the military circle—no expectations.

Darn. I hadn't sent the check to Cindy. I hadn't told Andy I needed to send a check. And I especially hadn't told Andy how much the check had to be. My stomach hurt more.

So I left the explanation of the need for a check for another day and settled in to watch men run into each other.

The next morning, Cindy called. "Marcia? I'm so sorry to bother you about this, but I haven't gotten your check for the Tupperware."

"You haven't?" My face flamed hot. I felt dizzy. I couldn't tell her I hadn't sent it. "I sent it the day after the Tupperware party."

"I haven't gotten it. You better check with your bank and put a stop payment on it."

"Oh yeah. Yeah. I'll do that." I wanted to crawl into a dark hole and pull it closed after me.

"Okay, I'll talk to you later. Send the check in with Andy. He can give it to Jon."

"Okay."

But I didn't. I didn't even mention it to Andy.

Two weeks later he came home and said, "Agile asked me about the check for the Tupperware."

"Oh," my voice small. I hung my head.

I explained.

Most of the time, my Andy had an even temperament, but sometimes, upset with some event or someone at work, he transformed into an Alsatian, barking like a hackles-raised police dog. At those times, I cowered into my childhood; any yelling felt like my father's angry abuse.

Now I flinched, waiting for him to yell and be angry with me.

He didn't yell.

He said, "Did we really need all the stuff you ordered?"

"I'll use it all." Mice spoke louder than I did.

"Okay. I already wrote Agile the check. Next time just tell me."

A novel concept. I checked to see if the sky remained locked firmly above me.

I picked up the phone to call Cindy the next day.

I hung the receiver back on the hook.

I stared at the dial.

I dialed.

It started to ring on the other end.

I hung up.

Swiping my palms on my jeans, I quick picked the phone off the hook, and dialed.

This time I didn't hang up. Cindy answered on the second ring.

"Hi, Cindy. It's me, Marcia." Tears poured down my face and thickened my words with unsniffled snot. "I'm sorry. I lied. I never sent the check."

"Why didn't you just tell me?" She was so calm. Puzzled, but calm.

I couldn't explain my childhood of lying to avoid anger and punishment. I couldn't explain to her, but Cindy and my Andy had given me a gift—the truth really did set me free. The sky did not fall and my stomach returned to its now-slightly-rounded, gurgling, safe and sane self.

Chapter 10
The Third Deployment

"Hey, Kath. Busy?"

I always called before I went to my sister-in-law's. My parents thought nothing of popping in—although how they could think of it as 'popping in' when they lived over an hour away I didn't understand, and neither did Kathy. I appreciated precious private time. Andy and I took naps at all hours of the day when given the opportunity—and most of the time we weren't sleeping.

"The kids and I are eating lunch. Come on over."

Walking around the corner, I thanked the Fates for their hand in Andy's purchase of a house so close to Don's. I thanked all of them: Andy, the Fates, and especially my oldest brother. Just before Andy and I met, my brother had convinced him that a rich young bachelor needed to invest in real estate—and buy a house. Don wanted Andy around as much and as long as possible. He only let the realtor show homes within a two-block radius of his own.

Andy loved the crisp, clipped hedges framing the driveway. I loved the stylish shag carpet and the idea of filling its empty reaches with furniture and paintings of our choosing. I didn't love Andy's squishy, cabbage-rose-chintz-my-grandmother-would-have-loved-sofa. My new spouse didn't understand why not. He also didn't understand why I didn't want toothpaste mouth wiped on my bath towel. Luckily, he had compensatory charms that extended the honeymoon to weekend morning sleep-ins, long warm afternoons, and hot, sweaty nights.

Now, with Andy gone to Florida, having my brother and his family close by helped with the loneliness. The repainting of one bedroom and wallpapering with a forest photomural on one of the walls had taken me three days. My honey would be gone two weeks. Two weeks! I had over a week and a half more of feeling like I lost my left hand. I could get by without it since I was righthanded—but I didn't want to and it wasn't as easy as it sounded.

I walked to Kathy's house to breathe in the pixie dust of her home and her self and her attitude. Kathy was a believer: a believer in the magic of this world, a believer in love, and a believer in the goodness of the Fates. She even believed in babies. Most times I was a skeptic: No one I knew had ever been happy because of magic.

Except for Kathy and Don.

I knocked on the rough, dark brown wooden door.

"Come in!" Her voice sounded like a musical wind chime.

Our houses were twins: Madrid models built in 1967 by the Mission Viejo Company. Being at her house was like being at my home, but better decorated. She had flair. I did not.

Turning right into the family room and kitchen, my feet left shuffle marks in the burnt orange shag carpeting. Oops. "It looked so pretty until I walked on it."

Kathy stood in the entry into the dark wood kitchen, laughing. "I just raked the shag to impress you with my housekeeping skills. Silly me. There's no way with two kids it would last longer than five minutes. And I have no desire to be a housekeeper." She blew her blonde bangs out of her eyes.

"Your house always looks wonderful."

"Do you want a hamburger? Twenty-five cent hamburger night at McDonald's last night. Don stocked up."

"Sure."

She opened the freezer, took out a wrapped hamburger, unwrapped it, and dropped it on a stoneware plate. It clattered around like a hockey puck on the ice before settling down, silent.

She handed me the plate.

I stared at the frozen hamburger and back at Kathy.

"Oh. Did you want yours heated? We like them this way."

That's when I looked at my niece and nephew, blond heads bent, gnawing like hamsters on their lunches—the bun and patty obviously still rock hard.

Kathy picked up her burger and nibbled neatly on it.

"That's okay," I said. "You eat. I know how to work the microwave." Kathy was a warm, magic wife and mother. She just didn't like to cook. I had no problem with that. I opened the microwave, set the cook time to

121

a minute before closing the door and pressing "start". "Is Don at the squadron?"

She nodded. "MAWTS is working on a new slide-show on tactics. Toad and Manfred are helping him out."

I sighed.

Her green eyes, muted as beach glass, considered me. "Have you talked to Andy today?"

"No. It shows, doesn't it?"

"The sigh did it for me. I hate it when your brother's gone. Deployments are different than work. When they work at the squadron, they go off in the car, and then they're back to cuddle with at night."

"My bed's too big without him. I keep scooting over to find him and the next thing I know, I'm falling out of bed on his side."

"Oh. Ouch."

"It's okay. I usually catch myself before I crash-land."

Her gentle laughter invited me in to the world of girlfun. "Babies are tough when they're in our bellies and can survive much worse than a fall out of bed, but I wouldn't want you to hurt yourself."

"Thank you. When I told Andy, he just asked if the baby was okay. Any bruises I might have acquired didn't seem to faze him."

"Babies are miracles. Andy knows that. You will, too."

The front door opened.

"Hey. I'm home!"

Don. The amount of electrical energy in the air tripled. Kathy's face lit up. Kellen and Tim ran into their dad's arms. Tim spoke a mile a minute about Hobie, their kitten, and helopticopitors being overhead, popcorn from preschool, and lunch.

With his dark hair, swarthy skin, and eagle nose, Don's Cherokee heritage showed the most of all of us. I was a grown-up, married adult person, but my brother still loomed tall, bigger than life. A big man and a bigger presence.

Don swung Kellen up. "Here's my Peaches. Hey, sweetie." He ruffled the blond hair on Tim's head. "Slow down, Timoth. You may be able to talk about three or four ideas simultaneously, but your old man can only handle one at a time."

Still holding Kellen, with Timmy clutching his leg, Don gathered Kathy against his side, bending down to kiss her upraised face. "Missed you, sweetheart."

She stroked his cheek with her palm. "You need a shave."

Their smiles were incandescent.

I moved toward the door. "Well, I'll get out of your way."

Don ruffled his son's towhead, and bounced Kellen to squeals of delight. "No, don't run off. I've got some work to do on the slides. Stay and keep Kath company."

I checked Kathy's face. She smiled and nodded.

I stayed. I wanted to. I always wanted to.

Don folded his body into one of the bentwood chairs at the kitchen table. It creaked. He bounced in it a couple of times to highlight the creaking.

"Donald Stuart Jones!"

He laughed at his wife. "I'm procrastinating working on my training slides. Don't rat me out to Toad."

Kellen and Tim ran by, opening the sliding door to the backyard and slipping through.

Just before the door slid completely closed, it opened. Tim stuck his head in. "Dad, don't eat any of my popcorn." He pointed to a grease-stained paper bag on the counter.

Solemnly, Don said, "I won't. I won't eat your popcorn." His eyes twinkled.

The sliding door closed.

Don got up, reached in the bag, and took a handful.

The sliding door opened. Tim's hands fisted on his four-year-old hips. "Hey Dad! I *said*, 'Don't eat my popcorn!'"

By this time, Don grinned from ear to ear as he stuffed the handful in his mouth and spoke around the kernels, "I fwon't. Youf can trufst me."

My brother was twenty-eight going on eight. And he knew it and reveled in it.

Kathy and Don were my heroes. The two of them had been childhood sweethearts—since first grade by some accounts—and those clever Fates had brought them back together to marry, have kids, and love each other. I'd spent weekends at their house when Andy and I courted. Kathy's smiles and advice had been the dusting of magic that convinced me that I might be able to love and marry and live happily ever after.

Three days later, I called to see what Kathy was up to—actually I wanted to see if she wanted company. Leo the RIO, a bachelor friend of Don and Kathy's, answered the phone. Andy and I'd spent time at his girlfriend's house when we courted. Leo the RIO and Pops could have been twin brothers—both short, pudgy, balding and looking forty-seven years old at the age of twenty-nine. A buddy of my brother's, I considered him a buddy of mine.

Leo was house-sitting for the weekend. I'd forgotten the family had gone off on a trip to Santa Barbara.

"Why don't you come over?" I said. "It's lonely with my guy gone. We can drink some wine and you can tell me unauthorized stories of my brother." No need for both of us to sit in empty houses.

I had a bottle of Chianti I opened and poured a glass for both of us. My Ob-Gyn, an old Navy doc, had recommended a glass every day or so. He said relaxed mommies had happier babies.

Before long, Leo was well into stories about crazy stuff Don and Andy had done overseas.

"Bullet and Snatch deployed to Naha, Okinawa with a bunch of us lieutenants. That evening, as we all drank in the Air Force O-Club, the base CO's daughter celebrated her Sweet Sixteen birthday party in the adjacent room. Right in the doorway, in full sight of the bar one of those multi-tiered extravaganza cakes for two-hundred guests drew our less-than-sober attention. We pooled our funds to pay Worm, the youngest of us—whose first name really was Dick—to stick his dick in the cake."

He stopped the story. "Uh. Excuse me, Marcia, for saying 'dick'."

"No problem, Leo. What happened?"

"Worm looked at the hundred dollars we had scraped up and shook his head. He might be young, drunk, and stupid, but not THAT drunk and stupid. Instead, he backed up against the wall, took a running start, and bisected the cake with a full hai-karate chop. Cake flew everywhere."

"Oh no. That poor girl."

"Yep. I feel bad about it. I do. She cried. The AP—Air Police—arrived quickly and hauled Worm's ass off to the base jail. By eight the next morning, the Red Devil's Squadron Commander had flown into Okinawa and walked into the Naha Air Force base's CO's office to apologize."

"What happened to the lieutenant?"

"What could you do to a lieutenant? He promised never to do that again and returned to Iwakuni, one hundred dollars richer."

I drank another little sip of the Chianti. "Tell me more stories. Andy and Don never told me any like that one."

"Maybe I shouldn't either."

"Please do."

"Did Bullet tell you about the time they were chicken fighting by the benjo ditch?"

"Benjo ditch?"

"An open sewer full of piss and shit—excuse my language—and who knew what all."

"That's disgusting."

"That ain't the half of it. One of the pilots standing around watching pushed one of the fighting pairs in."

"Why would he do that?'

"Because he could. Because it was funny when they went headfirst in the shi—sewer."

I didn't understand everything about being a guy. I kept thinking about the diseases they could have caught, the smell, and wondered how far away the showers were. The fact that I would never ever do this to another human being, much less someone I worked with everyday, blended into my involuntary peals of disbelieving laughter.

"They got even with the lieutenant who pushed them in, though. That night they defecated in the sleeves of his flight jacket. The next morning was cold so he had put it on before he realized." Leo looked up. "I shouldn't be telling Bullet's beautiful little sister shit stories."

"Sure you should." Beautiful? Who was he kidding? "Have some more wine." I filled his glass for the fourth time and sipped my one measly little drink.

He smiled at me. Leo had hit on a theme. I didn't mind. I'd never hear these tales from my brother or husband.

I smiled back.

That encouraged him to go on. "One time your brother and JC were racing around on their 125 cc Yamahas. JC got to the stop sign ahead of him, looked back in victory while putting his right foot down to stop. Too close to the edge of the road, his foot hit only air. Don said JC's gloating quickly changed to 'Oh, shit!' as he toppled sideways into the benjo ditch."

127

I knew JC. He had a knack for putting himself in situations dangerous to his health. My brother loved that about him.

By now my cheeks hurt from laughing.

The phone rang. I looked at the kitchen clock. Six pm. "I bet it's Andy and they're done for the day."

Leo stood up.

"No, stay." I wasn't ready to end his storytelling.

He sat down and took a drink of his wine—more like a gulp.

"Hello." It *was* my honey. "Hi, sweetie."

"Hi. I miss you," he said.

I loved his voice. I hated the distance between us. Tyndall Air Force Base on the Florida panhandle was too far away.

"I just finished my hops for the day. Agile had to fly home in a C-130. He's got really bad stomach flu. Check in with Cindy to make sure he's okay."

Cindy. Yeah, sure I'll call the woman I lied to about Tupperware checks. Embarrassment still flushed my cheeks whenever I thought of it. She'd been forgiving. I couldn't forgive myself.

"What are you doing?" he asked.

"I'm sitting here drinking wine with Leo the RIO. He's telling me the best—"

Silence. Serious silence.

"What's the matter?"

Leo stood up again.

"Sit down. You don't have to go." I motioned him to stay in his chair.

Leo didn't sit down. He edged out of the kitchen.

I waved at him to come back.

"Who else is there?"

I'd never heard that tone of voice from my Andy.

"No one. Leo's house-sitting for Don and Kathy. I was here by myself and invited him to come over. We've been having the best—"

"Tell him to leave."

I didn't have to tell him anything. Leo waved unsmiling and hai-yakued out the front door.

"Bye!" I called out.

Leo didn't answer. The way he moved as he left, he must have been halfway up the street already.

"What's the matter with you? We were having fun."

"Nothing's the matter with me. You're the matter. I'm not home. It doesn't look right."

"It's Leo, fergoshsakes. Leo! Give me some credit."

What he gave me was ballistic in nature with lots of explosions.

He was jealous? I flirted all the time with cute lieutenants and captains and he didn't mind, but now—he was jealous? Of Leo? Leo who loved hot enchiladas that made him sweat from his baldhead down into his wife-beater shirt? Leo who looked like a disreputable gnome? Leo who told shit stories?

Leo avoided me from then on. No more wine drinking and stories of shit and my brother. When he saw me at a party, he edged away, eyes averted, as if I would blow up in his face instead of Andy. I'd always thought of him as an older brother or an elder uncle. Perhaps Andy had been closer to the truth of his intentions.

129

A lesson for me in the importance of the appearance of things. Sometimes things really were the way they appeared, whether I realized it or not. Being a military wife instead of one of the boys meant learning to make things be as they appeared to be. I had to fly within the envelope, even when I didn't understand the parameters or why I had to follow the lead plane's flight path.

I hated it.

Chapter 11
Ruptured and Repaired

The phone rang. I put my book down and rolled over to pick up the receiver next to my bed. "Hello."

"Marcia, this is Janey, Chuck's wife. Did I wake you? Gosh, I've forgotten what sleeping in until nine o-clock feels like." Janey put twenty words in a space for ten, the vowels colored with South Carolina. I felt breathless just listening to her.

"No. I was reading."

"I've forgotten what having time to read feels like, too. I'm calling officially as part of the calling tree, but you don't have anyone you have to call since you're the last on this branch."

"Calling about what?" My stomach twisted. The calling tree was for emergencies.

"Agile's in the hospital. He's pretty sick. Appendicitis, looks like."

For a moment I breathed relief. No planes down.

But Agile! One of my favorite men—in the hospital. "What do I do?"

"Well, we'll get meals over to Cindy. I don't know what she's doing with the kids while she's at the hospital."

She must be frantic. "I'll call her."

As soon as I hung up, I called and volunteered to watch Cindy's kids while she stayed with Agile in the hospital. Amazing what guilt will move a person to do. I'd wronged her by lying about the check. Now I'd help her.

Babysitting. Oh boy, my favorite.

Truth? Not my favorite. Small kids and responsibility. I had no SA—situational awareness—at all. Andy had explained SA protected pilots from getting into deep kimchi in ACMs—air-to air-combat maneuvers. Civilians talked about getting their heads lost in the clouds, but when it happened to pilots they looked bad at the field or, at worst, someone died.

I rubbed my slightly rounded stomach. Doubts about being a mother and taking care of my child blended with doubts about caretaking for Cindy and Agile's children. I worried my destiny involved looking bad at the field *and* getting into deep kimchi. I only hoped the small curtain climbers remained in the land of the living on my watch.

The kids were cute. Kelly was eighteen months old, Greggie almost three with a wide-open grin. They were both in their fuzzy, footed sleepers when I arrived to take over from the next-door neighbor.

The neighbor left, smiling, obviously relieved to return to her normal life.

I thought about telling her I'd made a mistake; come back; I had to leave.

Instead, I thanked her and waved goodbye, then looked at my watch—eleven thirty am—over eight hours until bedtime.

Panic hit. Eight hours! What could I do with two little rug rats for eight hours?

They could stay in their sleepers the whole day while we watched cartoons. That's what I always wanted to do as a kid. Worked for me.

Worked for them, too.

For lunch I fed them peanut butter and jelly, also apples cut up. That had worked for me as a kid, too.

Twelve-thirty. Would they take a nap? The neighbor didn't say and I forgot to ask. I'd wait to see if they became tired. Naps were for tired kids. Kelly and Greggie looked permanently wired awake.

I was exhausted, already. Too bad I couldn't take a nap.

Cindy called around two in the afternoon.

I turned down the volume on the Tom and Jerry cartoons. "Agile? How is he? What happened?"

"His appendix ruptured."

"I thought they told you it was the flu or gastroenteritis."

"They did. Then this morning he felt something burst inside."

"His appendix? He could feel it?"

"It wasn't his appendix. The surgeon thinks, because of the amount of infection, his appendix ruptured in Florida. An abscess formed around it, which probably saved his life since it contained the infection. Now, this morning, the abscess burst."

"Oh. Oh no. Is he—?"

"He's still in surgery. I don't know when I'll get home."

"Don't worry." I worried enough for the both of us. "I can feed them dinner and put them to bed. I don't have anything at my house except a crazy puppy in the backyard."

Cindy had to get off the phone to talk to a nurse.

I turned up the volume on Wile E. Coyote.

The phone rang.

"Hello?"

"Marcia?"

"Yep."

"Hi. It's Julie."

Bird's wife.

"How's Agile? How's Cindy?"

I told her what Cindy had said.

"I'm bringing over a meal for tomorrow night. I assume you're okay for tonight?"

"Sure." Sure I'd be okay. There was food in the pantry; I saw cans when I made lunch.

"Okay. Let me know what else I can do."

I didn't know what to do myself, but I refrained from saying so.

Julie's call was one in the midst of an avalanche of calls from Ernie, the CO's wife and other wives asking about Agile, food, the kids, and Cindy. I told them what I knew about Agile, bringing food over was a good idea, the kids were great, and Cindy sounded exhausted—of course. Fran Brinkley stayed with her in the surgical waiting room at the hospital. I'd let the calling tree know when I knew anything else.

The wives offered me any help I needed.

I felt needed, that I flew an important mission. Good to know if I crashed and burned others would come to pick up the pieces.

In between the third and fourth phone call, Kelly handed me her empty bottle. I asked Greggie what had been in it.

He pulled his blanket down from under his nose. "Tea."

"Tea?" For a one-and-a-half year old? The no nap in sight made more sense now.

He nodded emphatically. "Tea." He showed me the pitcher of it in the fridge. The blanket went back under his nose.

I liked tea. I poured myself a glass after filling Kelly's bottle. Sweet tea. Yum. What wasn't to like?

Around five-thirty, I went into the pantry. Didn't everybody have Kraft Macaroni and Cheese? Basic survival food. No mac and cheese. Hmm. Chef Boy R Dee Spaghetti-o's. That'd work. Canned corn and applesauce. Worked for me.

It worked for them, too.

Six-thirty and the kids still lived.

I put milk in Kelly's bottle after dinner. She took a pull, held the bottle at arm's length, looked at it fish-eyed, then put it back in for another pull.

Seven o-clock. Bedtime.

"Into your bedroom, Greggie." Tucking him in, I sang him a lullaby from Girl Scouts called *The Cowboy*

Lullaby. "Desert silvery blue beneath a pale moonlight. Coyotes yapping lazy on the hill—"

He didn't complain about my pitch problems. He just smiled and shut his eyes. I liked that about him.

Closed the door. Quiet.

Good.

Then it was Kelly's turn.

Same routine. Took Kelly into her room, lifted her into her crib. She stood at the rail and her eyes filled with tears.

"Don't cry. You're okay. Lie down and I'll sing you a lullaby."

She laid down. I covered her with a quilt, gave her the shreds of her security blanket.

A little girl might not like the coyotes, so I sang her a different lullaby from my Girl Scout days, *Bed is Too Small.* "Bed is too small for my tiredness, give me a hill topped with trees—"

Closed the door. Quiet.

Good.

For about the count of ten.

Then I heard, "Ba-ba. Ba-ba. Ba-ba! BA-BA!"

I opened the door.

Her insistence on a ba-ba turned out to be her bottle. I gave it to her with milk. Seemed like the right thing to do.

Same routine but without the lullaby. Closed door. Quiet.

Good.

For a minute.

Then the crying started.

I went in. Same routine.

Same result.

Boy, when Cindy got back, I would be out of there. Some other neighbor or wife who knew what she was doing should do the next shift. At least now I'd new respect for the deep dark circles under Cindy's eyes.

Finally, at nine o-clock, I gave up. Kelly and I sat up together, her with her ba-ba, me with my book on the sofa.

"Marcia. *Marr-shaa-a*." A gentle murmur. A warm hand on my shoulder.

"Wha—?" I opened my eyes, startled. Lights all on, Kelly tucked on the sofa with me; ba-ba had rolled onto the floor.

Cindy leaned over us. "Are you all right?"

"Yeah. Yes." I sat up careful not to joggle the finally sleeping child. Wiping drool off my cheek, I tried to remember where and what I was. Oh yeah. "Agile?"

"They finished the surgery. He's in ICU." She sounded as drained as she looked. "They—we—I don't know."

I didn't know either. A helpless feeling.

"All those years I worried he flew a high-performance aircraft and now this." She rubbed her hand over her face and grimaced. "They sent me home to get some sleep. You can go home, too."

Home. Sounded wonderful. Only responsible for myself. No sense of doing it wrong, of doing everything wrong. Home.

I imagined having my honey in the hospital fighting for his life. I knew I'd need to be with him.

"What time do you want to go to the hospital?" I asked. "I'll be back tomorrow morning."

What had I done? My smart self and my scared self had no intention of ever returning to this house for anything except maybe a squadron party, yet I'd just told her I'd be back tomorrow. Tomorrow!

My caring self said I had to. I'd survived the day. No kids had crashed and burned. Being needed felt good. I couldn't help Agile, but help his family?—that was possible.

Cindy hugged me goodbye. "See you tomorrow. Thank you. It helps so much to know Kelly and Greg are safe."

I could tell she meant it.

For the next few weeks, I spent most of my time at Cindy's, doing what I didn't do well, mainly because I could. The other wives had children or jobs and with the guys gone, they were on duty. I only had a golden retriever, Tawn. She'd dug partway to the Asian continent and chewed up all the shrubs in the backyard. The damage had already been done. I could leave her alone with a clear conscience.

Agile's survival was touch and go; multiple surgeries and fevers took a toll. His weight dropped from one hundred eighty-six pounds to one hundred twenty-five. He stayed in ICU.

The first day he'd been taken to Santa Ana/Tustin Community Hospital by ambulance. The military, in its infinite wisdom, wanted to transfer him to Long Beach Naval Hospital right after the first surgery. Military guys went to military facilities, end of discussion. His civilian doctors said they would hold the military personally responsible if they transferred their patient and then the patient died. The military let Agile be. Consensus in the squadron? The doctors saved his life twice: once on the operating table and once against the bureaucracy.

I trusted and admired the Marine aviators I knew—well—most of them. Now I wondered if I trusted the military itself. Was the Marine Corps on my side or not?

Squadron wives delivered meals to the house, did grocery shopping, took the kids on playdates to their homes, checked in with me regularly for updates on Agile's progress. Ernie Wadsworth, the CO's wife, had organized everyone and everything. She stopped by every afternoon between one and four so I could take a preggo nap in the bedroom. I liked her.

I liked being part of it, part of the support team. The wives were the maintenance department—they kept the families flying.

Andy flew in from Tyndall with the rest of the squadron and the planes.

That night the two of us went to the hospital to see Agile.

When we walked in the room two weeks after he'd been admitted, four surgeries later, I hardly recognized him. Half naked on the bed, his legs, abdomen, and arms uncovered—his modesty preserved by a casually flung sheet across his privates—he had IVs in the crook of each arm, in both hands, and on each side of his neck. His Betadyne yellow abdomen had a stained bandage running the length of it, and eight tubes—drains—four

139

on each side. Rail thin, fever bright, with hollowed-out dark circles under his eyes much worse than Cindy's ever were.

He saw us, but he didn't really know we were there. No smile. Agile without a smile seemed a shell of the person I knew.

The nurse bustled in and tucked an odd kind of baffled rubber pad under him—a water mattress to try to keep his temperature down while the infection raged through his body.

After a month in ICU, he spent several more weeks in the hospital.

He lived.

The docs said if he'd been less healthy and strong, he wouldn't have made it.

Agile's scar ran red and raw down his belly. He grew used to it—a badge of beating the odds.

Kelly and Greggie were like that, too. They were healthy and strong before I entered their lives. They were healthy and strong after. Survivors ran in the family.

In my own way, I survived too. My time with Cindy's children encouraged me to believe. I might be able to take care of this baby growing inside me, after all.

I'd gotten to know the squadron wives better, too. Instead of just being Snatch's young, naïve wife, I'd proven myself. I'd looked good at the field.

And the best part? Cindy. No longer embarrassed around her, no longer scared of her confidence. I counted her a friend.

And though she giggled at me occasionally, I could tell she counted me as a friend as well.

Worked for both of us.

Chapter 12
Search and Rescue

The guys had returned from Tyndall AFB. Agile still recovered in the hospital, but no longer in ICU. I recovered from a surfeit of responsibility. Today, when Cindy left for her afternoon visit, Debby had kid duty.

I curled in the curved cushion of the papa-san chair, a purple-covered romance novel balanced on my burgeoning belly. Trigger, the Texan calf-roper, liked to tease me about my reading matter. He said romance novels came in various tones of pink: the most romantic were baby pink—kissing and hugging and nothing else before marriage, moving through mauve with some euphemistic sex scenes, to purple covers full of steamy sexual hydraulics. I'd started using his rating system to choose my next read. This one hadn't gotten to steamy yet, but it gave every indication of moving in that direction.

The phone rang. I rolled myself out of the half-circle cup of the chair and ran into the kitchen. "Hello."

"Hi, honey." Andy sounded odd.

"Are you okay?"

"I'm fine. Just wanted you to know I'm fine."

"You don't sound fine."

Silence. "We lost a plane today."

"A plane?"

"They haven't found the crew." Silence. "I didn't want you to worry if you heard anything."

Worry. That word.

"Who?" I thought of the guys I'd laughed with at the club and at the squadron parties. I thought of my pregnant sorority sisters and of Donut with his new baby. I thought of all the wives I knew.

"Phil Lahlum and Mike Maher. But that's not for public dissemination."

I knew Mike, barely. I'd seen him at the last squadron party. I knew Mike's wife, Diane. Sort of. Not well enough to go over there,but I knew them. Who was Phil? Both the pilot and RIO worked in 314 with Andy, flying the same planes as Andy. Diane. Something tore inside me.

I wrapped my arm around my stomach, not sure if I protected myself or restrained the need to be sick.

"Marcia? You there?"

"What happened?"

"I can't talk about it now. The crews are still out where the plane went into the ocean."

The plane went into the ocean. There had to be questions to ask, but I couldn't think of the right ones. I couldn't think.

"Should I call anyone?"

"Don't!" His emphasis lingered.

"Not even Cindy?"

"Not even Cindy. That's how rumors get started. I gotta go. I'll call later. When I can. I might be late tonight."

I sat down with my book. Couldn't concentrate. Got up and made a cup of tea. Extra sugar. Sat down with sugared hot tea. Rubbed my belly just above the shoestring tying Andy's jeans together. Reminded myself of my determination to stall buying clothes meant for preggos. Frumpy housefrocks for fatties. Tried to read. Felt like I'd swirled into a dark hole.

I picked up the phone. He said I shouldn't call and start rumors. But I needed to talk to someone. He didn't understand. He was at the squadron. He had all the guys to talk to. Kate was older, settled, a straight shooter. She'd have heard. She'd be able to talk to me about the accident and what I should do for Diane.

"Kate?"

"Yeah?"

"Hi. It's Marcia."

Her graveling voice warmed. "Hey. How are you?"

"Has Duff called you?"

"No. Why?"

Now I didn't know what to say. I wasn't supposed to call anyone and I was certainly not supposed to talk about the accident.

How could Kate help me if she didn't know what had happened?

I took a deep breath. I needed to talk to someone and I could trust Kate. She wouldn't start any rumors. "Andy called me and said there'd been an accident—not Duff. Duff's fine."

"Wouldn't figure I could get him off the face of the planet with anything convenient like an accident. He's a Warrant Officer. Doesn't fly."

145

"Oh yeah. Uh—" Kate's relationship with her husband confused me. Why stay married? "Andy said Mike Maher and Phil Lahlum's plane crashed."

"Did they eject?"

"I don't know. They don't know. They're still looking."

"If they'd ejected, they'd know. Sounds bad."

It all sounded bad. "Should we call anyone else?"

Kate huffed on the other end of the line. "As Tonto said when he and the Lone Ranger were surrounded by Indians, 'What you mean *we*, keemosabe?'"

"Should *I* call anyone? Shouldn't someone be with Diane?" Mike's wife. I felt guilty that I was safe, safe from losing my husband. Andy and my brother flew their own planes and flew them well. Mike was a RIO. RIOs and RIOs' wives risked their lives and safety on another's skills.

"I'm sure someone is with her besides the chaplain and another officer from the squadron. The boys don't like to deal with sobbing women, or stunned women for that matter. Chat doesn't come easy to them and neither does unhappy silence."

"So?"

"So don't call. We'll know when we know." Kate paused. A long pause. "Start cooking. No matter what, they'll need to eat when he's rescued or when he's not."

"Oh. Good idea." I hung up.

I didn't want to cook.

I went back to the papasan chair. Picked up the book. Turned pages. More pages. Realized I'd no idea what had happened to the heroine or the hero. That was the problem with today. I didn't know what had happened. If I knew, I could figure out what I needed to do, how much I needed to worry.

Worry.

I worried about the boys floating in the ocean, not being picked up by Search and Rescue. I worried about them not floating on the ocean, but stuck in their plane too deep in the dark sea. I worried about them being torn apart by crashing into a concrete ocean. I worried about Diane being alone. I worried the wrong people were with her, though I'd no idea who they might be. I worried about Phil's parents, far away from the squadron, being told the news and waiting, waiting for joy or anguish. I worried about any girlfriend Phil might have who wouldn't even have the call or the company or the news until it was okay or too late.

I worried about me.

Even though Andy hadn't crashed, the bargain I'd made when I'd married into the fraternity of Marine aviators made every plane mishap about Andy and me and our marriage. Nothing fit into safe and sane. I needed a reason why it wouldn't be Andy. Why it wouldn't happen to my brother.

I called Cindy. Kate might be my brash truthteller, but Cindy was my mom, my older sister. Kate gave me unvarnished brass. Cindy wrapped me up in her warm heart.

"Hi. Cindy? It's me, Marcia."

"I know it's you. I know your voice. What's going on?"

"Did Agile call you?"

147

"Yes. He said not to call anyone."

I paused. "Uh, so did Andy. But I—"

"There's a reason why not to call when not much is known. Wives say things wrong to the wrong people. Things are repeated wrong. Marcia—"

So my mom also scolded me sometimes. I'd forgotten Cindy was a rule follower. My face flushed with guilt.

I needed her to understand. "But I don't know what to do. I tried to read, but I can't. I can't sit. I can't stop thinking about the guys and the planes and Diane. This isn't like waiting for the calling tree to let me know what I should bring to the potluck."

"No it isn't. Is it?" Her voice softened. Cindy in hug mode. "Don't cry, honey. We wait until we know what we can do to help."

I swiped at cheeks and sniffled. I needed a Kleenex.

"It's one of the hard parts of our job," she said. "And too often, we can't really help at all."

They held the memorial service in the Base Chapel at MCAS El Toro six days later.

Andy's hand heated my back as he walked with me along the sidewalk to the entrance. Sun-blinded from the bright whiteness of the chapel set against a blue, blue sky, I entered the double doors blinking, trying to see. My irises widened, focused on the rows of pews, the high open ceiling, the clusters of people sitting in dark clothes against white walls, the white flowers on either side of the altar framing large photos of Mike Maher and Phil Lahlum.

No caskets. This was a memorial, not a funeral. No bodies had been recovered.

Andy took a memorial booklet from the usher. We sat on the hard wooden seats, somber. I opened the booklet. The faces of Maher and Lahlum smiled back. I closed the booklet.

I looked around, trying to be unobtrusive. Most of the squadron had already been seated. Agile and Cindy slid into the pew with us. We slid over to make more room. Nodded.

Diane came in the side door, older people following. They took their seats in the front pew. Her parents? The pilot's parents? A young woman. A couple of young men. I wondered who they were.

I fumbled in my purse. Found a tissue.

The minister began with a prayer for Mike and Phil, for their families. A young woman read a passage from the New Testament.

I opened the memorial booklet to see the order of events. The photos with the life story seemed like the Change of Command Ceremony programs—but without the celebration, just a change—a sad, grievous change. The survivors were listed. Mike Maher survived by his wife Diane, a sister, and his parents. Phil Lahlum survived by his parents and brother.

I twisted in the pew, trying to get comfortable. My hipbones ached.

My heart ached more.

The booklet said Mike's sister read from the bible. A young man read a different passage. His last name was not Lahlum or Maher—a civilian friend of Phil's?

Trigger stood up and spoke of Mike, a fellow RIO, his qualities as a friend and a professional.

I wondered if his widow wanted to be reminded of what he was doing when he died.

Her shoulders remained straight, still.

People dabbed at eyes.

I tried to blow my nose without making noise. I made noise. A couple of people turned to stare at me.

A young lieutenant spoke of Phil, the person as well as the Marine aviator, in Training Command—his transition from helos to F-4s. Warm, funny stories. It sounded like Phil had been a nice guy.

Would everyone sound like a nice guy at his own memorial? Would Unsafe At Any Speed?

An older woman in the front pew bent her head against an older man's chest. Phil's parents? He wrapped an arm about her.

I looked away, down at the words. Read nothing. Handed it to Andy.

He opened it. Closed it. Reached out and squeezed my hand. Let go.

A woman sang.

Someone read a poem about slipping the surly bonds of earth. I knew that poem: *High Flight*. A pilot's poem. My brother had a calligraphy copy of it on his wall at home.

The chapel grew quiet. From the back, a trumpet sounded *Taps*.

The hairs on my neck and arms stood on end.

150

We had always sung *Taps* at the end of a Girl Scout campfire in the evening before we filed silently to our sleeping bags and to sleep.

Day is done,
Gone the sun,
From the lake,
From the hill,
From the sky.
All is well.
Safely rest.
God is nigh.

But this trumpet in the back of the El Toro Chapel sang no words of comfort, just announced piercing loss. The end of two lives.

I cried at my own loss—for I hardly knew them.

Chapter 13
The CO's Wife

I cooked and baked the next couple of weeks after the accident, delivering casseroles, snickerdoodle cookies, baked chicken, and boysenberry pies—the only way I knew to contribute. I fed Diane's in-laws and her visitors who tried to give comfort to the uncomfortable. My cooking and baking did not help Diane. Each time I saw her, her face had paled further, her arms wrapped tighter around her body. In the accident, she'd lost her husband, and now from the look in her eyes, I saw she had lost herself.

And as I baked and drove and delivered and left, worry nibbled at me. It ate at me until I wanted to punch and hit and kick at the world.

Phil had been transitioning from helicopters to Phantoms. Did his reflexes fail him at a critical point—helo reflexes instead of F-4 reflexes? Why hadn't Mike helped save them both? He'd been a great RIO with lots of experience. Andy always said RIOs helped save pilots in bad situations. And I'd heard a whisper about something falling off the plane. Why hadn't they ejected?

No one would tell me anything.

The first of December, Andy sat at our kitchen table thumbing through the mail, throwing most of it on the floor next to his chair. "The CO and Ernie are having the holiday squadron party at his house to welcome the new XO. Hanley and his wife are being transferred and leave before Christmas. It's a Hail and Farewell party."

Wait. A party?

"And you're to bring a dessert or an appetizer."

"A party? We can't party. Phil and Mike are gone."

"Phil and Mike are gone, but we're still here. Squadrons get together at parties. Calm down."

"Calm down?" My voice escalated. "I'm not going to calm down! Diane—she's—."

"Don't cry."

"Don't 'don't' me." I wiped my palms down my cheeks. "And I'll cry if I want to. No one knows anything, and if they know, they won't talk about it and I don't understand and I *need* to understand." I'd turned into a blithering, hiccupping idiot.

"It's an active investigation."

"'Active investigation' means diddlysquat to me."

"Now, Marcia."

"Now, yourself. Investigate as actively as you need to but tell me what happened. How do I know you're safe if a totally senseless accident can happen and I have no pieces to put together to make it fit anywhere?" I blew my nose, loudly. "Just tell me—I'm your wife."

He sighed. "You can't talk about it to anyone. Not Cindy or Kate or Debby."

"I won't bring it up if they don't bring it up."

"You can't talk about it *at all* because you might hurt Diane, or Debby or Cindy. You could wreck my career if you talk about it. I mean it."

"Why is it so secret? How could it hurt anyone to know the truth?"

A deeper sigh. "Accident investigations are not to help everybody feel better by letting them know what happened. Usually the opposite happens. People feel worse when they know someone screwed up, or the maintenance wasn't done correctly, or the plane broke. People look for someone or something to blame other than the loved one they lost. Accident investigations are held to prevent the accident from happening again. As aviators, what we don't know can kill us. And if the military had to worry about being sued, they might cover things up that could prevent a repeat."

I hiccupped. "Okay. I won't say anything to anyone except you."

"No one but me." Andy stared at me.

I nodded.

He sighed, from deep in his chest. "The hop was briefed as a two vee four ACM—a two fighters versus four other airplanes Air Combat Maneuver—over the ocean against some F-106s. Phil piloted one of the F-4s; Mike sat in his backseat. Lots of planes were in the sky. They were maneuvering for position when Phil and Mike's wing came off."

One part of that I understood. "The wing came off? Do wings come off? That doesn't sound—"

"Marcia."

I shut up and listened. He didn't say to, but I knew that's what he meant.

"With the loss of the wing, the plane snaprolled the opposite direction, whipping the tail off. Everything happened fast, at a high rate of speed. No chutes were seen even though there were five other planes in the sky."

"But after the services I overheard the family, Phil's family, mention something about abandoning them in the ocean too soon. They were talking about currents and where they might have floated."

"The family was unhappy they called off the search because one of the F-106 guys saw a deflated raft, or a piece of a raft, in the water. Rafts can't get out of the plane unless the ejection seats are also out—they're in the seat pan underneath. The family thought that meant one of them had ejected. Martin-Baker experts—who make the ejection seats—surmised the snaproll had thrown the seats out of the plane—probably after crashing against the canopies."

Guys I'd met, strapped in ejection seats, and flung into hard plastic.

He looked at my face. Paused. "It would have been quick. Everything indicates a lot of g-force. We don't know because by the time the helo came, all the debris had sunk."

Gravity held me in my chair in the kitchen. Debris—the plane and the aviators in it.

"Why would the wing fall off?"

"We don't know. We've checked all the wings for cracks. The pilot might have overstressed the airplane trying to change direction too quickly."

"It was the pilot's fault?"

"No one knows. It's one explanation."

"I thought an accident investigation wasn't about blame."

"Somehow, the powers-that-be prefer to blame a dead pilot."

A dead pilot lost in the ocean.

I didn't know where to put the information Andy had given me. I didn't want to think about wings falling off, bodies smashing into plastic, pilots—who couldn't defend themselves—being blamed. I didn't want to think about Andy flying without a wing, unable to eject, being blamed. Being debris.

"Marcia. Believe me. It was a freak accident. I'm safe. Your brother's safe."

I wanted to believe him. It wouldn't do me any good if I didn't. So I did. Andy flew. I had to believe he knew what he was doing.

Andy and I got to the CO's house right on time. No one answered the door. Testing the knob, finding it open, Andy swung it wide, stuck his head in, and called out, "Isn't there supposed to be a party here?"

Ernie's voice drifted through the house, "I'm in the backyard! Come on through."

She knelt next to a partially completed brick wall, trowel in hand. Wooden stakes and blue string delineated the shape and structure of the project. She slapped mortar on a brick, inverted it before laying it in its place, and scraped off the extra like she had done that same task a thousand times before.

"Your husband lets you work on his walls?" I asked.

"My husband wouldn't know what to do with a brick if it hit him between the eyes. We all have our

157

strengths. Mike flies high-performance jets; I know how to lay bricks."

"Where is Wads?"

"I sent him to get the ice and beer."

After washing the mortar from her hands, she directed us to put the pie in the kitchen, get out the paper plates and plastic forks and spoons, bring the beer bucket to the back porch. By that time, Wads had returned from the beer and ice run, so he and the lieutenants who had arrived helped chill the bottles and cans.

I chatted with Ernie in the kitchen and stirred the onion soup mix into the sour cream.

"Oh. There's the door. Would you get that?" she asked. "I don't think Wads can hear it."

On my way to the front door, I spotted Wads in the backyard with a beer and a couple of lieutenants hanging on his every story. The CO could tell a good story.

Debby and Waldo.

Debby hugged me. I hugged her back and tried not to cry. She lifted a plate of brownies. "Do you know where I can put these?"

"Yep." I pointed her toward the kitchen.

The doorbell chimed again. I greeted Kate and Duff, started to close the door, saw Janey and Groove heading up the walk, decided to leave it open.

It was good to see everyone, but it seemed wrong somehow to carry on craziness as usual. All the wives gave extra long hugs. The guys drank beer and ate Ruffles and onion dip, corn chips and salsa, carrot and celery sticks in ranch dressing. They drank more beer.

158

Hanley, the outgoing XO, and his wife, Margaret, never showed. Something about packing for the move. Probably buying cotton batting for the silver and antiques.

Budman had a new girlfriend, Laura. She wore a crocheted dress, filling out the neckline. Actually, she overfilled it. Duff never looked at her face, but he followed her around, panting. I hadn't known that when a freckled man got flushed, his freckles showed as negative light spots against bright red.

Budman liked the stir she caused.

I met the new XO and his wife: lean Marine flying machine and calm sweetness. Actually, Bash, the XO, had a warm smile but he was all about the flying. Patty had a quick feminine laugh that seemed to catch her by surprise. I wondered if it was surprise at what she'd heard or surprise that she'd found something to laugh about.

There was plenty of good stuff to eat. I loved potluck.

Ernie rushed here and there taking care of all of us. Ernie organized her family like she was the CO and treated the squadron like we were family. Always busy, she was never too busy to take charge or help out.

"Aren't you eating?" I asked her.

"No," she said. "I'll get something later. My stomach's been bothering me. A touch of indigestion."

After dinner, Kate, Debby, Marilyn, and I sat on the sofa, balancing paper plates of dessert goodies on our knees. Cindy and Julie perched on upholstered chairs facing us.

The guys had moved out to the patio.

"Anyone talk to Diane lately?" Julie asked.

Cindy patted her lips with a napkin. "She's not answering the phone."

"Someone should go over," Julie said. "She shouldn't be alone."

Julie would know. I remembered her first husband had been an Air Force pilot killed in Viet Nam.

"I dropped a casserole over at her house last week," Marilyn said. "She said to tell the squadron wives thanks, but since the family and friends were all going home, she'd cook for herself."

Debby finished a bite of cookie, swallowed. "She told Waldo, who's her Casualty Assistance Officer, that she'd be moving out of housing just before Christmas."

"Where's she going?" I asked.

"Far, far away. That's what she said."

The guys moved back inside and started refilling from the dessert-laden table.

Waldo said something about the accident investigation findings.

Bird looked at Unsafe, then said, too loudly, "Not to speak ill of the dead, but damn, I hate it when incompetent pilots kill good RIOs."

"Uh oh." Julie stood up.

So did Mikki, Unsafe's wife.

Bird put his plate down. "Donut, don't you just hate trusting your life to *unsafe* pilots?"

Donut reached out and gripped Bird's arm. "Hey. This isn't the time or the place."

"There is no right time or place for a good guy like Mike to be totally fucked over and dead." Bird slugged down his beer. He twisted the cap off another, raised it up. "Here's to the good ones." He drank. He belched. "And that's for the ones who can't fly worth shit, like Unsafe here."

Unsafe-At-Any-Speed's face turned bright red. "Not everyone has the ability to be a totally-right-all-the-time asshole like you."

Mikki tried to pull him away. "I don't feel so good. Could we go home?" She placed a hand on her belly.

He shrugged her off. "No. Let's stay and socialize with more self-righteous pricks."

The CO joined up on Unsafe's other side. "That's enough. Time to take your wife home and get some sleep."

Wads walked him to the door and out.

Ernie put her arm around Unsafe's wife and led her through the house. "Too much beer. Too much testosterone. They'll all be over this tomorrow. Monday, they have to work and fly with each other."

Julie pulled Bird out back. I could see her through the plate glass window, chastising him, pointing her finger like an angry schoolmarm. Bird's head hung low.

The party had never really started. Now, it ended in shreds.

We gathered up our dishes, told the new XO we were glad he was aboard, thanked Ernie—oh yeah—and Wads, whose contribution was keeping ice on the beer, and left.

Three days later, Cindy called me.

"Marcia?"

"Yep."

"Ernie just got the word she's got cancer. It's bad."

"How bad?"

"They said she has just weeks left."

Wads flew high performance aircraft—a dangerous job. The CO's wife stayed grounded, making a home for her kids and the boy she'd married—but that did not keep her safe. It wasn't fair.

I wanted fair.

I wanted a miracle.

Ernie built her own brick walls around her patio. Maybe she'd build a miracle out of this. I didn't want to go to another funeral. I didn't want to hurt anymore. I wanted safe and sane and keep the grass mowed. I had an urge to run out front and make sure my grass was green and neatly shorn.

Chapter 14
From The Sky

No miracles. Ernie was gone by late January. The new XO, Bash, took over most of the CO's duties—at first because Wads was too busy taking Ernie to the doctor and then, too quickly, because he sat with her at the hospital. After the funeral, Wads mentally checked out and Bash managed the day-to-day decisions of the squadron. Patty took over holding the wives' coffees, as well as organizing the feeding of the CO and his four kids.

I told Wads at the funeral I was sorry and I'd miss Ernie. I was sorry and I would miss her. But I didn't do anything to help. I didn't bake or ask if I could watch the kids. I held a hand against my belly and avoided all of it. There were plenty of other wives who knew Ernie better—who knew Wads better. They'd take care of it.

Grieving hurt. I'd had a surfeit of it. It couldn't be good for the baby. I used my pregnancy shamelessly as my excuse not to do anything I didn't want to. And I couldn't think about Ernie without crying.

Wads wandered through his life like a lost boy without his mother. The squadron had an art auction for Navy Relief—a military charity—in early April. The most expensive print up for bid was a huge, signed Miro.

Andy asked, "Why would anyone let chickens step in red, yellow, and black paint and then run all around on the paper?"

"And why did they frame the chicken droppings?" Agile wondered.

The bidding began.

Wads teetered on his bar stool in the O-Club and, egged on by the drunken element in the crowd, topped each bid made.

Game on. A contingent of there's-no-way-in-hell-we-would-buy-that-painting-but-let's-see-how much-we-can-get-the-CO-to-put-out kept bidding and encouraging Wads to defend his manhood by not letting the wusses win.

How drunk was Wads?

Pretty drunk. Yee haw.

Squadron rumor mill had it that Wads woke up from his hangover the next morning, looked at the painting, and wondered who played the practical joke on him. He said it was the ugliest damn picture he'd ever had the misfortune to see. When they told him he'd paid twenty-two hundred dollars for it, he almost puked right there in the ready room.

The guys loved to tell that story.

Something always twisted inside me when I heard it. Something sad. But I knew I couldn't save Wads or myself from Ernie's loss.

The next two weeks I holed up at home, reading a lot of pink and purple romance novels—bubble gum books. They were fun and easy to chew, though they held no nutritional value except a temporary bit of sweetness.

The phone interrupted love's first kiss. I rolled my-self off the sofa to answer it in the kitchen. Got there by the seventh ring.

Andy. "Hi, honey."

"Hi."

"I'm fine." Long silence. He cleared his throat. "There's been an accident. Donut's plane went down."

My legs folded under me. I sunk to the kitchen tile floor and wanted to throw up. "Willie?" I stared through the woven woods at a beautiful blue sky. The house finches had just started making nests. I could hear their high-pitched chirping.

"Yeah. I'm talking to the helo guys who are trying to find them."

Them? Oh. F-4s had a pilot and a RIO. "The pi-lot?" Dread at the answer. I knew most of them.

"Jim Bassett, a new lieutenant. He just attached to the squadron a couple weeks ago."

I didn't know him.

"Is there—? Could they have ejected?" Donut had to have gotten out. He was one of the best.

"We don't know. I'll let you know as soon as I can." His voice said he didn't think so.

"Call me at Marilyn's. I'll be there. I love you." I hadn't the slightest clue whether it would help Marilyn to have me near. I hoped it would, but I knew I needed to be with her. Even though I'd had my fill of grieving, being alone with worry and loss was worse.

A pause. Then, "Yeah. Same."

Ohmigod. Ohmigod. Ohmigod. A prayer, swear words—I didn't know. The litany ran through my brain the whole way to Tustin.

Agile answered the door at Marilyn's, still gaunt from his ordeal, his face revealing little.

I hugged him; glad again he was alive, no longer in the hospital, not in the Phantom that had been lost. I whispered, "Any news?"

He shook his head.

Marilyn sat on the sofa, her face and eyes red and swollen. Cindy sat next to her. Marilyn clutched her hand in a grip so tight their entwined knuckles looked white. Cindy patted her arm at random intervals. A chaplain I didn't know sat in a straight chair. No one spoke to him. Another couple stood in the kitchen talking quietly to each other.

I sat on the other side of Marilyn, levering myself down with one arm on the cushion below. Nothing graceful about being seven and a half months pregnant.

She realized I was there. "Hi Marcia. Do they know anything yet?"

"Andy said he was talking to the helo guys. They'll call." I didn't know they'd call, but of course they would. If anyone needed to know about Donut, Marilyn did. Andy said he'd let me know.

Marilyn started talking about what she and Duncan had done that weekend and how Randi had just started to crawl and how she looked like her daddy when she smiled and when she did something she wasn't supposed to do, Duncan said she looked like Marilyn.

Then she cried.

I handed her a Kleenex from the box on the coffee table.

She wiped her eyes and blew her nose. "Duncan would be so upset with me for losing it like this."

Marilyn asked about the pilot.

I told her Andy said he was a young lieutenant fresh from the training command.

She talked about how she had called Duncan's parents and her parents and they were on their way and had I met Oren and Sherry? They'd just checked into the squadron so they'd come with the chaplain and they lived just around the corner practically and Sherry had met them out in front of the house so there'd be another wife here. Agile had been off flying status still, so he'd come over, and Cindy had just gotten here. Did I want a drink of something?

I heard Randi fussing down the hall.

Cindy jumped up first. "I'll get her."

I let her. I wasn't in any shape to jump anywhere.

Marilyn turned to me. "Thank you for being here. I don't know what I'd do without my friends. I don't know what I'm going to do without Duncan."

"Don't say that. They'll find him. He'll be okay."

She dropped her voice. "I had a dream last week that Duncan died in a flying accident. In my dream, the doorbell rang and when I looked out the peephole, I saw two men in uniform standing on our porch. Today, when they came, the doorbell rang, I looked out the peephole and there were two men in uniform standing on our porch. They told me his plane went down in the water and an aircraft carrier looked for them. But I know. I know he's not coming home."

Then she hugged me while I cried.

We played with Randi, put out food. No one ate more than a bite or two.

Marilyn talked about Donut: how they met, what his parents had thought of her, what a good daddy he was. "Randi's going to miss her daddy."

Then she cried.

Other wives—Debby, Patty the XO's wife, and Kate—came and stayed as well.

Marilyn kept thanking us for coming and for being there.

She didn't understand. It helped me to be there.

The chaplain spent time talking to new arrivals, but mostly to Patty. Maybe Patty took pity on him.

Around eight that night, the chaplain stood. "I'll be going now." He leaned over and took Marilyn's hand. "Child, I will pray for you and your William. Call me if I can bring you comfort. God loves you."

She nodded and extricated her hand.

He left.

Andy called. I took it in the kitchen.

"They've found Donut's helmet," he said, "but didn't find him or the pilot."

"How long will you search?"

"We're calling it off for the night." He cleared his throat. "Marcia, it doesn't look like there'll be any rescue. I'm sorry, honey."

"So'm I." I said fiercely, "I love you."

He whispered, "I love you, too."

I hung up the phone. Reported the search had been discontinued for the night.

Marilyn nodded. She wasn't surprised.

Marilyn's parents arrived around nine. Donut's parents got there around eleven. Each time, Agile repeated his solemn brief on the known facts and how a SAR was conducted.

We ran out of tissues in the coffee table box. I found more in the linen closet in the hall.

At midnight we left Marilyn and her family to themselves and their grief.

When I got home, Andy sat at our maple butcher-block table, his head in his hands.

I wrapped my arms around him from behind, tucking my chin against the top of his head. He'd lost Donut, a good friend. I didn't know how he stood it. Taking the seat next to him, I leaned on his shoulder.

Silence stretched. I had a million questions, but none I could ask.

"We found the helmet. There were sharks in the water. Donut's gone."

"Had he ejected and—?"

"No. The plane must have flown straight in. The sharks came after the pieces."

I made it to the bathroom before I threw up.

Now I understood why wives and widows shouldn't be told everything.

I sat in the pew in the white chapel at MCAS El Toro and cried. I cried for my loss and my husband's. I knew Donut too well. I knew Marilyn's loss too closely.

169

I knew Randi would grow up without her daddy. I knew my Andy had lost one of the good guys.

And I cried because I felt guilty that I was glad my Andy hadn't died.

Don and Kathy sat next to me. Kathy tucked Kleenex after Kleenex into my hand.

Numb to the words of the chaplain, I looked up at the white beam crossing the width of the ceiling and saw Donut sitting on it, swinging his legs.

Then I knew he was okay.

Wherever pilots go when they die, they're up above us all, looking down, golden, and grinning from ear to ear.

A bugler played Taps.

Chapter 15
Two Births

Marilyn coped with her grief by rarely being home. Oren, known as OJ, and Sherry adopted her into their very active family. Whenever I talked to her she was on her way out the door to a barbecue or waterskiing or out to dinner. OJ and his wife had just checked into the squadron, so they hardly knew Donut. I'm sure she found them easier to deal with. The rest of us were an additional burden: our words and tears reminding her of our loss and reflecting her own.

Andy dealt with Donut's loss by not talking about anything. When he wasn't at work, he watched TV: movies he'd seen a hundred times, old football games on videotapes, and inane sit-coms. Don came over and watched with him. They didn't talk about much, certainly nothing to do with the accident.

I asked Andy questions about what hops he had each day. He answered, usually, but not in the detail I needed. Just, 'I'm flying with the CO over the desert,' or 'I'll have three hops today, don't wait dinner,' or 'I'm taking a plane down to North Island for repair.' I wanted to know who he flew with in the backseat, whether the plane had had maintenance problems, how complicated the air combat maneuvers would be. I wanted reassurance he'd have a safe day, but I couldn't tell him that. I couldn't say, 'Because Donut died, I need you to tell me you won't. I need you to tell me everything you are doing and thinking and all the maintenance problems because I am afraid.' I didn't want to jinx him. I didn't want to jinx our life. So he thought I was only a caring wife who listened well, who wanted to know when to fix dinner, and which buddies he'd be hanging out with.

I wanted to talk. Sometimes, my heart hurt and beat so hard I thought I was having a heart attack.

I couldn't go to my brother's wife for solace. My sister-in-law, Kathy, avoided ugly things. Death in a plane crash had nothing to do with magic or miracles. She believed in babies but she also believed talking about bad things gave them power and could make them happen. Good thoughts brought good things.

So I spent a lot of time during the next weeks with my sister from the pregnant sorority, Debby. Married to a RIO, she wanted to talk about the accident, too.

She blamed the young pilot. "Something probably went wrong with the airplane, or the young pilot lost where he was in the sky and then lost it. I've told Waldo he's to fly with the experienced pilots. We're going to have a baby. I need him around to help."

She helped me stay semi-sane and also semi-excited about my impending motherhood. I found comfort in her enormous roundness and internal creaks and external moans. Misery loves company.

Debby angled her tall frame into the chair across from me at my butcher-block kitchen table. "I'm counting on the baby helping Waldo."

"What can a baby help a RIO with?"

She smiled, only tilting up half her mouth, rueful. "Sometimes he just goes away even though he's still in the room with me."

"Andy does that. It's called, 'I'm not listening'. It's a guy thing." I pushed down on my baby's heel to keep it from cracking my rib from the inside.

"No. With Waldo it's different. I think it's from when he was a POW. I think he survived within himself and he doesn't know how to deal with the rest of the world anymore."

"How can a baby help with that?"

"Julie says babies demand attention. They have to be fed when they're hungry or the parents hear about it. She says it will be good for Waldo if I make him take care of the little one while I go to the movies or go shopping."

Mm-hmm. My father-in-law bragged he'd never changed a diaper. Wonder how Andy would take to being left for periods of time with an infant. Somehow I doubted it would improve his listening skills during our conversations. But Debby knew Waldo better than I did, so I smiled and nodded and agreed it would be a good thing for a new daddy to do.

Debby went into labor two weeks early.

Janey, my calling tree buddy, let me know. They had no children, so the wives' consensus was to let Waldo take care of feeding himself. Time enough to bring meals when Debby had the little one at home.

I went to the mall to look for a baby gift in green or yellow. No one knew if it would be a boy or a girl, of course, and they were safe colors.

I'd been told walking could bring on contractions.

You couldn't prove it by me. I walked the length of that mall three times. Nothing.

Debby called the next day in tears.

"Are you okay?" Stupid question. I could tell she wasn't okay. "Do you have a baby?"

"It's a boy. A little boy. I named him Michael Wallace after Waldo. But—but—" She couldn't speak through the sobs.

Were these happy tears?

"Something's wrong with him. With his brain. He's anacephalic."

My stomach lurched. "What's that?"

"His skull is full of fluid, so his brain didn't develop. They're doing surgery on him right now to put a shunt in to try and drain the excess fluid out so his brain can grow." She blew her nose.

Poor Debby. Poor Waldo.

"Pray for little Michael."

"I will. Of course I will. Is there anything else I can do?" I held my belly tight.

"No. He can't have visitors. He's too sick. I—I just needed to talk to someone."

"Is Waldo there?"

"Yes. He's right here. We're waiting to hear about the surgery. He's been wonderful."

"I'm glad Waldo's there. I'm so sorry, Debby."

"Oh, Marcia." She sobbed as she hung up the phone.

Debby called me daily with updates. The shunt surgery was successful, but the brain didn't grow. Her IUD had damaged the fetus in its early development, so the heart pumped and the lungs breathed in and out just enough for Michael Wallace to stay alive. Without a suck reflex, he had to be fed through a tube into his stomach.

She went home two days after little Michael's birth, but returned daily and spent hours sitting by his incubator holding his tiny, flaccid hand.

The day the doctor told Waldo and Debby that Michael would never be a normal baby, wouldn't survive more than a few months, Waldo stopped going to the hospital.

Debby believed Michael needed her.

Waldo believed Michael might as well be dead. He grieved and compartmentalized his loss—locked it away where it would no longer hurt. He wanted Debby to be at home when he came home. He wanted everything to return to normal.

Debby hurt for the both of them. Then she grieved that Waldo couldn't be a daddy to the little scrap of themselves.

Then Waldo got angry.

She told me he screamed at her, "Let him go! He's dead."

"He's your son," she said.

"I have no son."

Then she got angry.

Soon, they had no marriage. Waldo moved out. Debby spent every day in the neonatal ward at Mission Community Hospital.

I thought babies were magic. I thought they were miracles. I prayed for a miracle for the two of them.

And I worried.

Then I let the worry go. I didn't use an IUD for birth control, after all.

Our baby would be fine.

I had to believe it, so I did.

———————

By mid June I was past ready to get the annoying, rib-stretching, enormous alien invader out of my body. I'd pat my stomach and say, "Time to go."

Of course the baby didn't listen to me—I was its mother.

Trigger and Sundy had a squadron barbecue mid-month. Hungry, I waddled out to the Weber charcoal grill. Three men rubbed my belly as I passed. Only two of them were guys I knew. How was a pregnant woman like a Buddha?

"Trigger, what are we having for dinner?"

"I'm cooking up a mess of burgers now. Y'all wait another ten or fifteen minutes and these will be just right."

They looked done to me, already.

They had been.

The charcoal briquets Trigger called burgers were as hard as my sister-in-law's frozen cheeseburgers, and as black as hockey pucks. I gave Andy a mission to put new burgers on for us, and make sure to cook them more medium rare than charred.

Linda, Mikki, Julie, and I found seats.

Julie groaned. "My feet are so swollen."

Bird passed by our sorority, "That isn't all that's swollen."

We threw corn chips at him until he went away.

"Been going to our Lamaze classes with Andy," I said. "The La Leche League woman came to talk. I'm not looking forward to getting up every two to three hours at night."

Linda smiled serenely. "I won't have that problem. Marty will be sharing the nighttime duties with me."

"You're not going to breastfeed?" Julie asked.

"No. Why should I? This way I'll know exactly how much the baby's getting and I won't be exhausted. I think that will make a much happier baby."

"Don't have to warm up breast milk," Julie said. "Comes prepackaged. No sterilizing bottles."

Julie had good points.

Linda shook her head in disagreement. "You're going to have to worry about what you eat so the baby doesn't get colic."

"What's colic?" I asked. "I thought horses had to be put down when they got colic."

Linda snorted. "Don't you read books about babies?"

"I'm too busy reading about being pregnant to worry about what happens after."

"My oldest had colic." Julie looked at me with pity. "Marcia, I hope you never have to find out for yourself."

"And it is—?"

"An upset tummy," Mikki explained.

Julie laughed. "That's like calling a tsunami a wave. Colicky babies are guaranteed to destroy marriages, sleep, and sanity—though not necessarily in that order."

MARCIA SARGENT

I murmured, "Babies are miracles. Babies are magic." Didn't they know I'd enough to worry about? Now my stomach hurt—maybe I had colic.

After a few minutes, I stood up. "This kid is like carrying around my own space heater. Too bad it's eighty degrees outside instead of the temperature of a New England winter. I'm going to take a swim to cool off."

Trigger had a large pool, which seemed a contradiction since he didn't swim.

He dreaded swim quals. Raised in inland Texas, comfortable on horseback, roping calves, and comfortable training pilots from his rear seat in the airplane, he could barely manage to keep his head above water even in a pair of swim trunks, much less in a flight suit, g-suit, seat harness and flight boots.

Pilots and RIOs were required to pass a swim qualification—recreating what they'd have to do if they ejected over water and their life raft failed to inflate properly. Aviators had to jump into the practice pool fully clothed, take off their flight boots, and tread water for a period of time without drowning. Since the military invested a lot of time and money on aviators by the time they got to swim quals, there were rescue divers in scuba gear in the pool watching to save any who might be in trouble.

Taking off his boots required the longest time with Trigger's face underwater, so he thought he'd outwit the hardest part by loosening the laces until they barely stayed on his feet on the pool deck.

The aviators jumped in.

Unfortunately, leather became sodden and sticky when wet. Trigger tried to remove his boots without submerging, only gasping on the surface, his lower lip barely clear, while tugging frantically. He must have struggled too much. The ever-helpful rescue diver on the bottom of the pool came up and helpfully tugged on the boot as well, pulling Trigger's lower lip and head under. He gasped in a lungful of chlorinated water. He clawed his way to the surface, his eyes the size of altimeters.

He did not pass that round. Rumor had it he took three tries before barely succeeding.

Trigger was even less fond of the parachute drop. A motorboat would tow the aviator up in the air over the ocean—think Acapulco parasailing—and then disconnect the parachute and aviator from the towrope. The aviator would then float to the sea, and into the sea, where he'd practice disentangling or cutting himself from his parachute without drowning.

As much as Trigger disliked the intimate contact with water, he feared what lurked beneath the surface more. He knew, just before his toes touched the water, a great white's open maw filled with razor sharp teeth waited. He called the parachute drop, 'Trolling for Sharks'.

I put on my swimsuit, waddled past the barbecue and my pregnant sorority, and executed a perfect racing dive. At least it would have been—if only I hadn't had forty extra pounds in a basketball in my belly. Most of the water in the pool displaced onto the deck. On surfacing, I heard the gasps from the audience.

Unfortunately, it didn't work. I didn't go into labor that night, either.

Linda did—on *my* due date. Her little boy was born by C-section eighteen hours later. Seven pounds, six ounces.

They lived around the corner from us. I volunteered to deliver a meal at the end of her first week home.

I knocked on the door.

"Come in! I'm in the kitchen."

"Hey. I told you that you didn't have to cook. I've got your dinner right here."

There wasn't a clean, empty space anywhere on the counter. Linda had a pot full of pinkish brown muck she poured through cheesecloth into a one-quart Pyrex measuring cup. Empty baby bottles lined up. Linda used a clean wrist to brush her strawberry blonde wisps out of her face.

I put the lasagna into the refrigerator. "Directions for heating it up are on a card I taped to the foil."

Wails echoed from the living room.

"Uh. You want me to go get him?"

"No. He's hungry. I'm making the baby formula. It's almost ready."

"What are you doing again?"

"He's allergic to every formula manufactured or available in the United States, so I have to make his from strained lamb meat and vitamins and—oh! This is a mess." Some glopped on to the tiled counter.

The wails increased in intensity.

"Are you sure you don't want me to—?"

"Would you?"

I scooped him awkwardly out of his bassinet. Red hair, pale skin. Well, it would have been pale if he weren't oxygenating his blood and dilating all the vessels with his screaming. Poor kid. A redhead. Only my mother loved them. And maybe his frazzled mother in the kitchen.

Holding him didn't calm him down. My holding him didn't, anyway. He almost flipped out of my arms arching his back to gather breath for another frenzy of crying.

When I left Linda's formula factory, I walked straight to my sister-in-law's house.

She opened the door.

I burst into tears. I felt like I'd been crying for months. "I thought babies were magic and miracles."

"Babies are magic. What's the matter?"

She made a pot of tea, brought out the honey bear for sweetening, sat me down at the table and listened.

I told her about Debby's baby in an incubator and Linda's redhead allergic to formula and who didn't like me to hold him. "That's two out of the five. How do I do this, knowing how badly it can all turn out? And even if my baby is okay, what if he doesn't even want to hold him?"

Kathy handed me the box of tissues.

"Your baby will be okay. You have to believe. It's not good to get upset. Your baby knows when you're upset."

"But—?"

181

"Your baby knows you already and loves you. I think babies' souls choose their family. Your baby chose you. You'll see."

"What baby's soul would choose me? I don't even think I like babies."

She got a dreamy look on her face and stared off over my shoulder, smiling. She turned the look and smile on me. "There's magic that happens when you hold your baby for the first time. You're going to be a wonderful mother, you'll see. It's meant to be."

I had to believe her. When it came to babies and being a wife, I found the magic of Kathy impossible to resist.

Chapter 16
Three More Babies

The next week, Unsafe's wife, Mikki, and Bird's wife, Julie, gave birth, both to boys.

Four out of four. Andy and I felt confident our little one would also be a boy. We started calling him Alex, short for Alexander, Andy's maternal grandfather's name. A good name. A strong name.

We planned a visit to the new arrivals, but by the time I'd walked the mall for two more presents and wrapped them, Mikki and Unsafe had already left the hospital with their youngest family member. Considering his disdain of Unsafe as a pilot, Andy was okay with just seeing Julie and Bird's little guy.

Four other squadron mates and their wives crowded into the room.

The nurse looked harried. "There are too many in here. New mothers need rest."

"She isn't a new mother." Bird said, grinning and bouncing the little bundle in his arms. "Julie's an old hand at this. Look at her. She likes us in here. And so does my kid. He's a party animal."

Julie's cheeks glowed. Her smile shone.

Julie looked good and she looked happy.

The guys took up a lot of space in the room and they weren't showing any signs of leaving. The wives koochie-cooed and oohed over the baby.

The nurse gave up trying to shoo away unshoo-able aviators.

I stuck close by Andy who deflected inadvertent elbows from my protruding belly.

Nothing deflected Duff's gaze at my burgeoning breasts. I doubted he knew the color of my blue eyes. He hadn't looked above my chest since my pregnancy bloomed.

The baby started fussing.

"Let me have him. He probably needs a diaper change." Julie deftly unwrapped the burrito of a baby.

"Wait until you see his package." Bird commented to the guys. "He's got a set of balls on him a bull would envy. Takes after his dad."

Julie opened the diaper.

Groove backed away from the bed. "Gross, Bird! If he takes after his dad, his dad's full of shit. Is that what you meant?"

His wife, Janey, hit him on the shoulder. "Be nice. There are ladies present."

Bird folded his arms. "Wait until he's cleaned up. You'll see."

Agile nodded. "I see he takes after his dad all right."

The baby's dad beamed.

"He's got skinny little knobby-kneed legs just like you."

Bird sputtered.

"Guess he's gonna be Baby Bird."

General laughter. Nothing better than giving grief to the one who usually dishes it out.

Didn't stop him from showing off his Baby Bird to each new arrival.

Bird's ego sometimes got in the way of friendly relations in the ready room, but no one doubted he loved and was proud of his little guy.

Even Bird believed in babies.

———

I believed my belly would pop before I went into labor. Ten days after my due date, I was still due.

Unsafe and Mikki invited us to see their baby boy and for drinks. Sorority sisters and their spouses had obligations. I had the baby gift I hadn't delivered to the hospital, and honestly, welcomed any diversion. Andy indulged me by going along.

Chips and dip rested on the coffee table alongside an enormous photo album.

Unsafe busied himself in the kitchen getting the drinks.

Mikki saw me eyeing the photo album. "Take a look. We just got all our baby pictures put in."

Impressed at their speedy assemblage, I turned to the first page ready to pretend the newborn W. C. Fields or Winston Churchill was a handsome devil and looked just like his daddy.

He had dark hair like his daddy—and that was all that could be seen because the photo had been shot from the foot of the bed straight toward the vee of Mikki's thighs. Full crotch shot. Oh my.

I looked up quickly. Andy choked.

Mikki beamed with pride. "Bill did such a good job of getting every moment of our little boy's arrival."

185

Andy leaped up and mumbled something about helping Bill with the drinks.

"Take your time, honey," I told him. Yes. I was a good wife and did not believe both of us should be tortured.

I turned a number of pages in one clump, hoping to get to the baby pictures where a pink or red-faced scrap of humanity slept through the flash of the camera.

"Oh no, go back! You missed a bunch of pictures."

I tried distracting her by asking to see the new baby, but he slept and she did not want to wake him. I tried to get her to open the baby present we'd brought, but she wanted to wait until Bill could watch so why didn't I finish looking at the pictures?

Not only was Unsafe's wife Unsafe-To-Tupperware-With, she was definitely Unsafe in many different areas.

Mikki scooted next to me and helpfully turned the pages, pointing out each bit I should pay attention to: not only the crotch shots, but the cord cutting, the dirty diaper changing, the swollen balls from about six inches away and the circumcision. Did I mention the breast-feeding pictures with her whole chest exposed?

"Bill thinks a breastfeeding mother is as beautiful as a Madonna."

Okay. Good to know, but nipples are not for public disclosure.

A nightmare. The hardest part? She and Unsafe were so nice in their sharing of too much information. Their excitement about their baby boy and the experience of parenthood was genuine.

186

They were nice; we were appalled. Andy and I'd never been in a labor and delivery room. Now I wondered even more what I'd gotten myself into.

Thank the good Lord, Unsafe did not own a movie camera.

Much later, Andy helped me into the car.

"No camera in the delivery room," I hissed. "None!"

Fate had a sense of humor. Two weeks after the due date, Andy flew three hops—two during the day, one night hop. Three in one twelve-hour period was a lot of flying. Andy staggered home ready to collapse on the bed. I met him at the door, eleven at night, suitcase in hand.

"Time to go."

"Time to go?"

I nodded. "Time to go."

"Are you sure?"

My inarticulate groan as a labor pain hit convinced him that someone, somewhere, was sure.

None of my pregnancy books mentioned back labor. Back labor was excruciating pain in the lower back, caused by an inverted baby's skull pressing with each contraction on the mother's spine. The only solution, other than drugs, was counter-pressure applied by strong and determined hands. For the health and well being of my child I'd studied for weeks how to give birth the natural way—no drugs. Failure of the objective was not an option.

Please note: Counter-pressure could not be applied by a snoring husband. Also note: elbowing deeply

187

sleeping husband did not encourage cooperation or sympathy.

They say you forget the pain after the baby's delivered. Maybe so, but I wouldn't forget Andy's dereliction to duty for a very long time—if ever.

At six-fifteen in the morning, the newest member of our family arrived—a girl. A perfect little girl.

"A girl? Are you sure?" Andy peered at the messy red thing the doctor held aloft.

The doctor smiled. "Pretty sure. After twenty years of doing this, I know one when I see one."

"But we don't have a name for a girl," Andy said.

"Yes, we do. Remember the name on the wall in our Lamaze class? Brooke?"

"Uh yeah. Sure."

He didn't remember. "Brooke. And Elisabeth for her middle name, after my grandmother."

"I thought your grandmother's name was Glaydus."

"Exactly. So we are naming her middle name after my grandmother's middle name."

———

After Andy helped me from the mandatory wheelchair into the passenger seat, the nurse handed Brooke to me.

I'm not sure what my expression revealed, but I'd just realized Brooke did not come with an instruction manual. I knew I didn't know what to do, and the only person who seemed competent to care for a baby handed the baby off to me.

The nurse smiled at me and said, "Don't worry. She'll teach you everything you need to know."

———

Doorbell.

"Coming!"

My brother, Don, loomed in the doorway. "Hey. I came to see the new rug rat." He wrapped me in a big brother hug.

"Shh. She's sleeping in the living room. And she's not a rug rat yet—more of a squirm worm."

"Oh. She's sleeping. Okay. You know what they say?"

"What do they say?"

"Let sleeping babies lie."

"I thought the quote was about sleeping dogs."

"Dogs and babies. If they're sleeping, let them lie."

I shook my head and smiled. "Do you want a Coke?"

"Sure. Just cold—no ice."

"You're in luck. I'll get you a cold one out of the fridge."

I got out the can and turned around. Don hadn't followed me into the kitchen. Where'd he go? "Don?" I whispered.

Turning the corner into the living room, I saw him at the bassinet.

He looked at me, put a finger to his lips for quiet, and went back to tickling Brooke's pudgy baby feet and grinning.

Let sleeping babies lie, except if you were Don and wanted them awake. Breaking rules and getting away with it was part of the fun.

———

I don't know how guys learned to fly fighter jets with all their gadgetry marked with acronyms and numbers, but in the weeks following Brooke's birth, I decided tak-

189

ing care of a tiny infant had many similarities. She had nothing printed on her, but the variety of things that went wrong seemed much like a jet going hundreds of miles per hour on a 2 v.1. In a jet, the pilot risked his life. As a parent, when things went bad, the baby suffered for it—and then the baby made the parents suffer.

The cry of a baby irritated. The cry of my own child was an agony akin to having my ears flayed alive— a Phantom afterburner fifty feet away had nothing on her wails. I'd do anything to get her to stop. Andy would do anything to get me to get her to stop. Confidence and talent as a pilot did not translate to confidence and talent as a parent. I'd not yet left my husband alone with Brooke for longer than fifteen minutes.

At least I'd little time or energy to worry about anything other than the demanding one. Even grief took a backseat to baby care.

Now, two months after Brooke's birth, I rocked in the bentwood rocker, feeding her and reading a fuchsia-covered paperback.

Breastfeeding enclosed us in a bubble, excluding worries and the rest of the world until Brooke had had enough and needed burping. I treasured those minutes for their peace. Peace with a baby had proved elusive.

Brooke stopped sucking and grinned up at me. I still didn't think babies were all that cute, their features unbalanced and pudgy, like old men, but the smile, Brooke's smile said, 'Gee, you're wonderful. You take care of me and I trust you completely.'

Babies might not be cute, but smiling, mine was the most beautiful baby I'd ever seen.

I closed the book.

And burst into tears.

Kathy was right. Babies were magic and miracles. I realized I'd kill for this little drooling one. I'd die for her.

Ohmigod. I was a mom.

Chapter 17
Marine Corps Ball

My friends, Kate, Cindy, and Janey surrounded me at Bash's house, showing off their gowns and admiring mine. The women sparkled with beading, metallic thread, and excitement. Even this pre-Ball party promised to be fun.

I smiled and laughed, but felt the weight of the year before. So much had happened: Phil Lahlum and Mike Maher's accident, Agile's hospitalization, Ernie's death, Willie Duncan's accident, the five babies. Diane Maher no longer lived nearby. Wads had taken the MAG—Marine Air Group—XO job. Agile had been back on flight status for several months now. Marilyn declined an invitation to the ball. She said without Duncan it wouldn't be the same. It wasn't the same without him. Truth was, it wasn't the same without Marilyn, either. Waldo had resigned his commission and returned to his hometown in Connecticut to be a mortician. A mortician! Debby moved into an apartment in Laguna Beach and visited little Michael Wallace every day.

My eyes filled. So much to grieve.

I blinked them away. If I started, I'd never stop. Mascara and tears were mortal enemies. Tonight I'd focus on my friendships and the future. Everything had to be better from now on. The worst had happened.

The other four babies had been left with grandparents or reliable babysitters. I'd driven Brooke up to my mother's this morning.

I missed her, but planned to enjoy being a wife and dancing with my honey.

Andy looked very fine in his dress blues standing next to Hombre, Trigger, Fish, and Bash, the XO. Too bad they kept checking their sixes and grimacing.

"I think I have a chunk missing from my ass," Bash said.

Andy hadn't explained what had happened this afternoon at the base to have the upper echelon of the squadron, one captains and three majors, abashed and annoyed. I listened in shamelessly.

My Andy, a captain and the squadron maintenance officer or AMO, rubbed his rear. "I'm pretty sure mine is totally gone."

"Da-amn. Terrible Ted knows how to chew," Trigger, another major and the squadron operations officer said.

Fish, a major and the logistics officer, lean and dark, nodded. "Terrible Ted knows how to chew, swallow and spit out the bones."

Agile joined them. "What's with you four?"

They all looked around.

"Where's the CO?" Hombre asked. A worried expression replaced his normally goofy smile. A new captain in the squadron, Hombre always looked up to no good and having fun at it.

"He's in the other room," Agile said. "Why?"

"You know the cake ceremony at the hangar?" Hombre asked.

"Yep."

"Normally the Marine birthday daytime celebration is a squadron affair and only the troops and the officers know what goes right and what doesn't. This year the group CO waited to present the squadron with the safety award. Our CO wanted everything to be like a well-oiled machine to show his boss how well he ran the squadron. Unfortunately, only some of the troops stood at attention ready to cut the cake, and we didn't have the youngest troop there to do the honors." Bash added.

Hombre grimaced. "The CO turned white, red, then purple and whispered in Trigger's ear like a snake that he better get that troop there and get him there five minutes ago."

"And it wasn't five minutes," Andy said. "Trigger had to drive to the barracks and drag him out of bed, throw him in the shower, and get him dressed in his blues. Apparently, the youngest Marine in our squadron had stood duty the night before."

Trigger looked glum. "I'd feel sorry for the poor bastard if I hadn't been the target of the CO's displeasure."

"You weren't the only one standing at attention in the CO's office while Terrible Ted yelled and bit and chewed." Andy shook his head. "Damn. A couple of planes had gone down because of maintenance issues after their last hops. My troops wanted them up and flying, so they had them in the pits with the engines running doing a last check when the ceremony was supposed to begin."

"Shit. The sound of turbines turning a couple hundred feet away would not make the CO happy," Agile said. "Especially not with the Group CO listening in."

"We broke the number one rule: 'Never make your CO look bad'." Bash said.

Janey broke away from our ladies' group. "You boys done admiring your asses?"

"Our definitely-the-worse-for-Ted asses?" Hombre asked.

"Y'all need to focus on a more important part of your anatomy." She turned back to ask us. "Do you know why men name their penises?"

Okay. Janey had had a couple of drinks already.

Cindy giggled.

I said I'd no idea why.

Kate wondered if Duff actually had one, if so, it hadn't made an appearance in awhile.

The men groaned. Fortunately or unfortunately, Duff wasn't around to hear Kate's remark.

"Ooh. Shot down." Hombre.

"In flames." Bird.

Janey waited until the boys were quiet. "Men name their penises because they don't want ninety-five percent of their decisions made by a complete stranger."

We women laughed—a lot.

The boys waved us off. They had important stuff to talk about.

196

They clustered in corners talking. I caught snippets of conversation about flying hops and ways to avoid getting their asses chewed by the CO.

We women sat on the sofa and chairs in-between and talked about children, childbirth and men. I enjoyed getting caught up on my sorority sisters' children and lives of the women I'd grown to know so well. I added a few Brooke stories into the mix.

Sarah, Terrible Ted's wife, mentioned that either in February or March she'd be hosting a squadron party at her house. A friend stationed on the east coast had volunteered to fly out a squadron's worth of Maine lobsters on a cross-country.

Sundy, Trigger's wife, drawled, "We'll need a lot of pots. If everybody comes, that's seventy or so lobsters."

Sarah smiled. "Oh, no problem. I have enough room in my dishwasher."

Blank stares at the CO's wife.

"I cook the lobsters in the dishwasher. It works great."

I couldn't help asking, "With soap?"

Sara shook her head. "No one wants Cascade-flavored entrees."

No one wants lobster-flavored dishes either. Eww.

"We could just throw some lemon in with them," Janey smiled slyly. "It would get them sparkly clean and fresh."

"No streaks on the crustaceans." Kate's gravelly laugh.

We groaned.

"Ladies, let me tell you how to cook for large groups the easy way," Sara said.

I leaned forward to hear better over the men's flying stories.

"The washer works well to spin dry lettuce."

My mind turned to lint and Downy softener—neither I wanted to taste on my salad. "You just put it in the center basket?"

"Yes, but in one of those bags for washing pantyhose."

Our faces said it all.

"A *different* bag. Not the one I use for my own pantyhose—a clean one."

By this time we were all laughing, either from amazement, disbelief, or grossed out admiration.

Cindy wiped her eyes. "Sarah. You should tell them about Friday nights."

"What about Friday nights?" Janey asked.

"Happy Hour. Ted likes to go to Happy Hour, but his often lasts until all hours."

We nodded. Some guys were like that.

"But Ted wants a home-cooked meal every night. So I make him the same one every Friday: meatloaf, baked potato and green bean casserole. I put it in a three-hundred fifty degree oven so it will be ready for when he gets home at seven."

"Seven? But—"

"Yes, ladies. I know. He doesn't always return home by seven. I just let it keep cooking until he does get home."

The thought of meatloaf and baked potato left two or three extra hours in the oven cracked us up. Sarah knew how to get her point across with no yelling and no drama.

I liked her. I admired her. CO's wives were people too. Good people. Terrible Ted had good taste, even if his Friday dinners rarely tasted good.

Hombre came and sat down with the women. We ignored him. We were having too much fun to care if he listened in.

All of a sudden, Hombre groaned. Loudly. "Oh. The pain!"

All eyes turned to him.

He leaned back in the chair and brought his knees up and out. "There I was, dilated to three and I needed to push, but that idiot doctor—"

Snickers.

Susan, Hombre's wife, had moved in on the men's corner. Her hands flew through the air. "I was inverted at 30,000 feet, the pipper locked on the bogey at my 12 o-clock, when suddenly my RIO screams out, 'Bingo fuel. Bingo fuel!'"

Outright laughter from the men's corners and the women's group.

Hombre groaned again. "I had to push. Oh Jesus, Holy Mary, Mother of God! Give me some drugs. I need drugs!" He pointed a shaking finger at Susan and then at his crotch. "You are never getting any of this again, you bastard!"

Susan spoke again in a faux deep voice, "I told him, 'Bingo fuel? You're full of bullshit, RIO. We've got time for another sortie.'"

Trigger snorted. "Are you channeling Snatch? I know I've had this conversation with him off San Clemente Island. He always thinks he has enough fuel for another 1 v. 1."

Loud laughter.

"Now we have your attention—" Hombre and his wife stood and bowed to applause from the assembled.

"Patty and Bash say it's time to move to the main event." Julie said.

"Susan and I *are* the main event." Hombre grinned at her.

"Only in your dreams, Ego-boy."

I thought about how much we laughed whenever the squadron aviators and wives got together. Life was serious. Being an aviator and an aviator's wife was serious, but laughter lightened the dark corners and reminded us we were not alone in the room.

"Shh. They're starting."

I craned my neck to see.

Marines stood at attention in the doors to the ballroom of the Anaheim Convention Center. Hundreds of officers in Marine dress blues and their dates sat at banquet tables all around me. The loud hum of talk calmed then faded to silence.

A captain in the group at the door called out, "Fall In!"

Two Marines with stars on their shoulder boards stood up from the head table and went to the front of the room. Generals.

Damn, generals looked old.

A Marine at the podium announced, "Ladies and Gentlemen, the Commanding Officer 3rd MAW, Major General Davis, and our Guest of Honor, Lieutenant General Les Brown, FMFPAC."

Guess the Corps let old guys keep working.

"Sound Attention."

Ta dah, ta dah!

Then the Adjutant's Call. I'd grown to recognize the bugle notes that straightened shoulders and quick-paced my heartbeat.

The band played *Semper Fidelis*—upbeat 'aren't we grand?' music about being Marine, being alive, being here surrounded by friends, with the guys looking so good in uniform.

Andy stuck his index finger in the front of his collar, stretching it away from his Adam's apple, and grimaced.

Okay, he looked good but the uniform thing didn't feel so good.

"Ladies and Gentlemen, please stand."

The bugler played. Marines marched in with the American flag and the globe and anchor flag of the Corps.

"The Star Spangled Banner" sang out in notes of brass and percussion. Piercing patriotism filled my ears and vibrated in my chest. A Marine band playing indoors made music as tangible as my heart pounding blood through my body.

A narrator said, "It is a tradition to read General Lejeune's Birthday message from 1921 on November 10th of each year:

"'On November 10, 1775, a Corps of Marines was created by a resolution of Continental Congress. Since that date many thousand men have borne the name "Marine". In memory of them it is fitting that we who are Marines should commemorate the birthday of our Corps by calling to mind the glories of its long and illustrious history.'"

I thought about my own memories of Marines. Too many weren't here. Would never be here again.

Cindy smiled at me and tucked her hand in the crook of Agile's arm.

Some *were* still here. I smiled back, listening again.

"'...In every battle and skirmish since the birth of our corps, Marines have acquitted themselves with the greatest distinction, winning new honors on each occasion until the term "Marine" has come to signify all that is highest in military efficiency and soldierly virtue.'"

Honorable, loyal, and brave, my Andy signified all that was highest in soldierly virtue. I grinned at him.

"What?" he asked.

"Nothing."

The narrator talked about how the Marines' reputation was earned by the others who went before. He said that as long as Marines stay true to the spirit of the Corps, they'd be worthy successors to the men who served as 'Soldiers of the Sea.'

I wondered about the wives of all the men who had served over the years, and about the widows who had carried on raising the children of the 'Soldiers of the Sea' both as mother and father, civilian and Marine.

Marines in a variety of historic uniforms lined up on stage.

"This ceremony illustrates the uniforms that Marines have worn in the past, from those of the Continental Marines and those worn fighting Barbary Pirates to the modern day utilities and service alphas."

The narrator told about the accomplishments made during each era of each uniform.

No mention of the wives, but the shadow of their women stood behind each Marine in uniform. I saw them wearing the dresses of the Revolutionary War, the Civil War, the two World Wars and the Korean War. Fran Chapman smoked her pipe behind the Vietnam soldier. The smoke curled around the room and drew me to her side, to all the women who waited on home ground and so served as well. Served all of us well.

The bugler played, *Ta dah, ta dah!*

We all stood.

The band played *The Marines' Hymn.*

The men stood straighter, the colors glowed stronger, the brass shone brighter. Tenor and bass voices swelled and echoed as the Marines throughout the enormous ballroom sang along with the band. They weren't required to, but the music pulled them to join in. *"From the Halls of Montezuma to the shores of Tripoli, we will fight our country's battles on air on land and sea. First to fight for rights and freedom and to keep our honor clean. We are proud to claim the title of United States Marines."*

A long silence.

I loved being a part of this.

I hugged Andy.

An enormous cake was rolled to a position in front of the generals.

"Ladies and gentlemen, please be seated."

The narrator read the General's Birthday Message, then the Birthday Message from the Commandant of the Marine Corps.

The guest of honor mumbled his way through a speech.

The oldest and youngest Marines moved to the left side of the cake cart and near the generals.

The generals advanced toward the cake.

The captain stepped forward, and presented the sword over his left forearm, handle in front, to the guest of honor.

The band played, "Auld Lang Syne."

Should auld acquaintance be forgot and never brought to mind.

The words echoed in my mind. Semper fidelis. Always faithful. Always faithful had a corollary: Never forget. I promised Donut. I promised Ernie. Semper Fi.

I cried. Andy took my hand and squeezed.

I was part of the Corps. A Marine wife, I was a Marine in my heart. I knew my place now. I was a member of the sorority of the grounded: the women who took care of the homes, the children, and the hearts of our guys so they could keep flying. I belonged with the women.

Peter Pan and his lost boys needed Wendy. And Wendy never stayed for long in Never Never Land.

Cindy caught my eye and smiled. She patted Agile's hand.

"It is traditional that the first slice of our Corps Birthday Cake be presented to the Guest of Honor, and the next piece to the oldest Marine present, followed by the youngest Marine present."

Tradition. A sweet tradition. The Marine Corps kept the *esprit de corps* more than most by keeping to their traditions. I'd come to honor Marines. Their birthday, but cake for me, too. I was a Marine wife.

General Davis cut all three pieces of cake and placed each piece on a plate, with a fork, provided by the captain. The pieces of cake were then presented, in order, to the guest of honor, the oldest Marine, and the youngest Marine.

General Davis returned the sword to the captain.

"Ladies and gentlemen, the first piece of cake is being sampled by our Guest of Honor, Lt. Gen. Brown."

"The oldest Marine present tonight is Lt. Col George Feeney, who was born on January 16th, 1912. He entered the Marine Corps on January 16th, 1941. Col. Feeney is currently retired."

"The youngest Marine present tonight is Lt. Allen James who was born on November 18th, 1953. He entered the Marine Corps on January 2, 1974. Lt. James is currently serving in VMFA 531."

Each took one bite from their cake and returned the plates to the captain who placed them on the cake cart.

"Detail, Forward, March." The escorts each took one step toward the cart, halted, then, automatically and in unison, turned to face the exit.

"Forward, March."

The escort, the youngest, and the oldest Marine departed the ceremony area with the cake cart. Shortly, waiters would serve pieces of cake to each place in the enormous ballroom.

"Ladies and gentlemen, please rise for the retiring of the colors."

"Retire the Colors."

"Forward, March."

The band played *Semper Fidelis* again. The Marines with the flags marched in front of the generals, executed a counter march, and then exited the ceremony area.

The generals marched out.

The captain and the other Marines exited the ceremony area.

The band quit playing.

"Ladies and Gentlemen, this concludes our ceremony for the evening."

It concluded the ceremony, but only began the festivities.

The band started to play a slow oldie, *Smoke Gets In Your Eyes.*

Andy and I stood to dance. During the year, we did a lot of kissing and hugging and horizontal rumba on our double bed, but only at the Marine Ball on November tenth, we danced together upright, on purpose, to music.

Kate and Duff walked toward us. They must have sat at the other end of the banquet table since I hadn't seen Duff yet.

He looked straight at my chest—eye level for him. A long look. His face crumpled. Then he looked up at my eyes; his dismay plain. "Where'd they go?"

They. My pregnant breastfeeding boobs. I hit him on his shoulder. Hard. "You're a worm."

"Ow. That hurt!"

Kate nodded. "Good. You are a worm." Kate raised her eyebrow in my direction. "Told you."

No argument from me.

Andy just shook his head and laughed. Later he said, "Don't be so hard on Duff. He's a good Marine."

And a bad husband.

Grateful for my friends, grateful for my husband, I was also grateful I married someone who was a little shy around other women, respectful enough not to stare at anatomical parts of other wives, and who always wanted to come home to me, forsaking all others. Semper fi.

Chapter 18
New Year's Eve Party

Ten o-clock on New Year's Eve.

I checked myself in the full-length mirror. Makeup perfect, short slinky dress, shiny curling brown hair—I looked good, darn good. Earlier, I'd dropped Brooke off at my mom's for the night, leaving me free of parental responsibility for the second time in six months. I had plans, big plans having to do with drinking, laughing with friends, and sex at the end of the evening with my sweetie. All followed by a tumble in the sheets again in the morning.

Unfortunately, my main man had not yet arrived to take me to the squadron party. I checked my watch again. Ten-o-one. What was he doing? Well, I knew what he was doing; I just didn't know why he was taking so long.

My husband—who never went drinking with the boys and rarely drank even a beer—had called me four hours before to say he and some of his buddies were stopping in at Reagan's Irish Pub for a beer on their way home.

I told him to have fun.

He hadn't come home yet.

Perhaps I should have been more specific.

MARCIA SARGENT

He'd better be ready to leave the moment he came in the front door. I hated being late to a party—and the party had started an hour ago.

The front door banged against the doorstop and then crashed closed.

"Honey! I'm home!"

"You're late. Get changed, quickly." I walked down the hallway toward him.

He wore his flight suit and the stupidest look on his face: a goofy, lopsided grin and half-closed eyes.

Drunk?

He staggered toward me, hitting the walls on either side.

No, I was mistaken. Not just drunk, absolutely schnockered.

"What—?" The shock of it made me laugh, but not for long.

"We dran' shom beers."

"How much did you drink?" I'd never seen him even slightly lit, much less totally blasted. I still couldn't believe this was my sober Andy.

He leaned on the wall, slipping down slightly, then catching himself. He held up two fingers, "Two beersh."

Two beers did this?

He brought his fingers close to his face and peeled up one more. "Three. Three beersh."

"Three beers?"

"Not beersh. P-pitchers. I dran' three." He put his fingers right in front of my nose and tried the lopsided stupid grin again.

210

I started to drag him into the bedroom to help him get dressed. "We've got to leave." His aberrant drinking could not be allowed to wreck my evening.

"I'se got to liesh down. I don' feel so good."

He staggered to the bedroom and fell face down, spread-eagled on top of the bedspread.

"Later," he mumbled, drooling.

I shook him. "We've got to go to the party!"

Before he became completely comatose, I managed to roll him over and pour—in my brother's opinion— the eighth wonder of the world, Alka-Seltzer, down his gullet, and then I stomped into the living room to fume.

Cindy drove up with Agile and parked in Jaime's driveway at the same time Andy and I did. We got out of our cars and shook our heads at the stumbling derelicts we brought as dates.

"Agile drank at Reagan's today, too?"

"What was your first clue?"

The time? 11:45 pm. My big plans, minus the sex with my honey, needed to take off.

Everyone in the squadron—wives, girlfriends, and aviators—was three sheets to the wind by the time Cindy and I arrived. We needed to catch up—in fifteen minutes.

I'd rarely had champagne. I split the bottle with Cindy. Chugging the bubbly tickled and made me burp, loudly.

"Marilyn!"

Marilyn hugged me.

I swayed into her, then righted myself. "Where's Randi?"

"Randi's with Duncan's parents. It's great having them to count on and they love spoiling her."

"I miss him. I wish he were here." My eyes filled.

Her own eyes reddened. "Don't you start. If you start, I'll start, and my mascara will run." She smiled. She understood.

Eight months since Donut's accident. More than eight months. It might have been a lifetime, or only the day before. Sometimes the pain of it, the unfairness, would hit me hard and I'd burst into tears or—more often—wander around the house straightening pictures and magazines, putting order back in the only way I could.

I picked up my glass of champagne.

Jaime came out of the family room and swiped a cloth across the coffee table. "Otherwise it leaves a ring."

I swallowed it down in two gulps. "Unlax. It's New Year's Eve. Have a drink with me, Jaime." I hugged him.

"Behave. Go play with Snatch." He lifted my arm off. "I've got to do my host duties."

"Why should I behave? It's almost midnight and I am bound and determined to have fun when the glittery ball drops."

Jaime caught Andy's eye and pointed his finger down at my head.

Andy leaned on a wall in the corner with Agile. Both looked green around the gills. I lifted my empty glass to Andy and smirked. He shook his head and continued slumping with his hung-over buddy.

"Ten! Nine! Eight! Seven! Six!" The crowd watching the TV yelled from the game room.

I moved over toward Andy for my New Year's kiss.

"Five! Four! Three! Two! ONE! Happy New Year!"

"Happy New Year, honey!"

He kissed me, but he didn't kiss as well as at home. Chickens pecked better. What was with the public performance anxiety? Okay. My guy was shy. Damn. But he was also good. Definitely liked him good at the field rather than *trying* to look good at the field.

OJ and Bird tried to kiss all the women in the room, whether they were married to them or not. No pecks on the cheek for them. Oh my. OJ had a lieutenant's wife bent over backwards. I maneuvered behind Andy. Flirting was a different kettle of fish from lip locks.

Agile turned from kissing Cindy and kissed me on the cheek. "I'll help protect you." He stepped in between me and the two kissing fools.

"Thanks." I listed too far to the left. "Whoops!" I clutched his arm for a moment to steady myself.

Okay. I was okay. I stood up straight.

Jaime moved around the room picking up empty beer bottles and wiping off tables.

"Oops!" Pops had spilled his beer on the rug in front of the bar.

"That smell will never come out! I'll get some soda water." Jaime bustled behind the bar. He came out with a rag and the soda, crouched down. He sprinkled and rubbed, sprinkled and rubbed.

A vision of Jaime as a blond bullfrog wearing an apron like June Cleaver played in my brain. I giggled.

213

Then I couldn't stop giggling. The room started to wheel around first to the left, then to the right.

Andy smiled and wrapped an arm around my waist. "I didn't tell you my news—our news."

I tried to bring his face into focus. "News?"

"I just accepted orders to Twentynine Palms. We won't have to leave the West Coast." His face went in and out of focus.

I squinted at him. The words sank in. "Twentynine Palms? Twentynine Palms!" My voice had escalated until I shouted across the suddenly totally quiet room. "I've been to Twentynine Palms!"

"It's a good deal. I'll be the Air Officer and I'll still be able to fly."

"And I'll still be in *fucking* Twentynine Palms!" I flinched. It was the first time I'd used an Anglo-Saxon swear word. I'd been around Marines too long and their idea of what passed for acceptable language, but in this case I'd used the right word. Twentynine Palms was in the middle of the high desert, miles from anywhere and anyone I cared about.

The room undulated.

I felt nauseous. The champagne, the orders, my shock at my language, all contributed to a reeling of my view of my world and myself.

"You don't look so good." Cindy swayed in front of me.

"I don't feel so good." I hiccupped.

Andy looked at my face about the same time Agile inspected Cindy's. "We better get you out of here before

Jaime gets upset at you tossing your cookies on his well-vacuumed rug."

"Tossing my—?"

"Blowing chunks," Agile grabbed Cindy's arm under the elbow and hustled her to the front door. "Hey Jaime, Pops. We're out of here with our drunken wives."

Drunken? They were the ones who had come home drunk. Cindy and I were just trying to catch up. The cold air felt good, until it didn't. The elm tree spun. The cars in the driveway jiggled.

Andy poured me into the front seat of the Volvo and started to shut the door.

"I think you better—" I pushed the door back open.

Bleah. I puked on the driveway.

Cindy gagged from her car, followed by the unmistakable sound of throwing up.

Oh gross. But kind of funny. We both had thrown up, in tandem.

I felt better. I chuckled.

Cindy giggled.

Female bonding.

My best friend in the whole world. "I love you, Cindy!"

"I lo—" She retched. "Love you too."

"Is Marcia all right?" Agile asked.

My least favorite husband said, "She'll be over all of it in the morning."

I'd never be over it. Twentynine Palms!

Bullet

Wedding
Don Jones, Mary Jean Jones, Stuart Jones, Rheta Jones,
Marcia Jones Sargent, Andrew Robeson Sargent II,
Ignatius Sargent, Frances Moffat Sargent, Michael
Sargent

Naval Aviator Wings

Mission Viejo House

Wadsworth to Berwald Change of Command VMFA 314
Back left side (saluting) Ted Berwald and Mike Wadsworth
Front row (with swords) Duane Wills, Bobby Rogers,
"Fish" Mel Johnson, "Snatch" Andrew Sargent

MARCIA SARGENT

Change of Command

Change of Command Cake

Shepard and Snatch

Donut, Randi and Marilyn Duncan

MCAS El Toro Chapel

MARCIA SARGENT

"Donut" Willie Duncan

Andy, Brooke and Me

Lt Col. "Scorpion" Ted Berwald and Maj. "Trigger" Bobby Rodgers

F-4 Cockpit

VMFA 314

Back row L-R: John McLeod; "Mutt" Steve Mutzig; Harv Hegstrom; ? ; "Budman" Gordie Taylor; "Beamer" Bill Beam, Tom Campbell; ? ; Mel Johnson; Vasquez; "Karnack" Mike Karnath; John Robinson ; Terry Bradley; ? ; WO Duff Alger

Middle L-R: Rick Ward; Doug Thrash; "Snatch" Andy Sargent; ? ; "Yosemite Sam"; 'Groove' Chuck Hoelle; Dave Schnack

Front row L-R: ? ; OJ Riddell; 'Trigger' Bobby Rogers; "Terrible Ted" Berwald the CO; 'Bash' Duane Wills; 'Agile'; Stu Mosby in blue cover; 'Donut' Willie Duncan.

Lt Col. John Ressmeyer, Maj. Andy Sargent, Major
Beau Wiley, Nittany Lion fan, "Yucca Man" Bob Haber,
Lt Col. Bob Liston-Wakefield

Christmas Picture from Beaufort
Don, Kathy, Timothy, Kellen and Toburn

VMFA 531 Flightline El Toro MCAS

Chapter 19
Death in Desert Camouflage

Twentynine Palms was even less wonderful than I'd anticipated.

"Andy, take the boots off!"

He had clomped in the front door greeted by Tawn, our big golden retriever, squeals of joy from Brookie, and me—barking at him to get his polished black boots off before they added more dark marks on the white linoleum floor. Turkey Breath, our Siamese cat, wove in and amongst the chaos. Turk saw himself as an island of Asian intelligent calm in the mayhem of our family.

Andy sat at the kitchen table, and unlaced his boots. "Sorry. I forgot."

I loomed over him, hands on my hips. "It's just this floor and this place. Today I opened the kitchen door to throw the trash out and almost stepped barefoot on an baby sidewinder."

He pulled me down for a kiss. "I missed you."

Good kiss.

He pushed me away. "Whew. You stink!"

"Thanks. I love you, too."

"So you played bridge today?"

"Yes, and they all smoke. I can't figure out which is worse, staying home with Brooke and going stir-crazy, or playing bridge at the Club with the O-wives and smelling like a pack of cigarettes when I get home."

"Right now, the pack of cigarettes is worse."

"Remember we have bowling league tonight. I'll shower first. You watch Brooke."

"Yeah. She doesn't mind sweaty desert Daddy." He scooped her up under her arms and swung her through the air. "Flying lady!"

She chortled. He needed no more encouragement to fly her around in the other direction. Too high. Too fast. I resisted the urge to snatch her to safety.

———

Jim Sparks, the 3rd Tank Battalion CO who lived next door lent us his daughter, Susan, to babysit—at a price. Instead of having to pay a sitter, I should have been paid to bowl—to make a total fool of myself. I was the comic relief act. No one bowls an eighty-six—on a good night—who is over the age of nine. I did have a great handicap—if only I could bowl higher than my qualifying score. Eighty-six seemed to be my personal best at the start of bowling season, and I went downhill from there.

"Marcia! Andy! You're here!"

If there had been anything else to do on a Tuesday night in Twentynine Palms I'd have been there instead.

"Hi, Sue. Hi, Ken." The Flanders looked like part of a relay team, both angular, leanly muscled and under five foot seven. Sue looked like Little Orphan Annie, curly strawberry blond hair and all. She even had blank blue eyes like the cartoon character.

I wondered sometimes if Sue took drugs to keep her super-charged, high-energy enthusiasm going all the time. I became exhausted in five minutes, listening to her spiel through her running routine, her kids playtime and her gym workout. Are weights and the number of repetitions something that needs to be shared with a social acquaintance?

Lucky me. They were our bowling teammates.

I bowled a seventy-seven. Andy bowled a one-eighty-six. I won the raffle for a new bowling ball, bowling shoes, and bowling bag. Yippee.

If looks could kill, the battalion CO's wife, Mrs. Betelmann, would have had my hide flayed and stretched out to dry in the next day's brutal sun.

I should have given my prize to someone who wanted to bowl, but dammit—I'd earned a reward. Bowling ranked right up there with picking at a hangnail. Something to do to pass time until something else happened—like other orders to other places.

A couple of weeks later, Andy called to tell me he'd invited men home from the Expeditionary Air Field, the EAF, for a home-cooked meal.

I didn't mind. The poor guys spent most of their deployment living in tents in the heat, the dust, and with snakes—all to give them practice under real desert conditions. Their meals were C-Rations, called C-Rats, food eaten when out in the field. No one considered these canned meals particularly appetizing. They came in a box the guys would dump out on the ground upside-down so no one could pick and choose. Dinner by lottery draw. After the blind choices were made, trading began. Andy said the hot dogs, "Beans and baby dicks", were gross. The meatballs were gross. The boned chicken was pretty good. Ham and lima beans was "Ham and motherfuckers". A home-cooked meal looked good.

I went all out: a big green salad, fresh artichokes with homemade hollandaise, long grain and wild rice, Rolled Chicken Washington and boysenberry pie for dessert.

The Marine officers who came to dinner were very appreciative.

But none showed their appreciation quite like Ray. He complimented Andy on his incredibly gorgeous wife. He thanked me in a soft drawl for welcoming him to such a beautiful home. He commented on how lovely I looked and how charming our little Brooke was.

Then at dinner, with each bite into his mouth he mmm-mm-ed and ohh-hhhed at the taste, the texture, and the excellent preparation. He said how lucky Snatch was to have married such a talented cook.

The rest of the conversation over dinner was a typical flyby of funny stories about funny aviators: aviators extracting themselves from situations with grins all around or situations immersing poor bastards in deep kimchi. Then, just as I stood to clear the plates and serve dessert, someone at the far end of the table mentioned Col. Profane.

"Did you say something about Col. Profane?" I sat back in my chair. "Who is he anyway? I've heard about him for a long time, but never met him."

Ray leaned forward to look the length of the table at me. "Why ma'am—"

Chortles from around the table.

Ray ignored them. "—You want to know who Col. Profane is?"

More snickers.

"That's me, ma'am. I've been real well-behaved to-night, haven't I?"

And he had been, and he was. I never heard a word of profanity from the colonel that night or any other.

In the right company, with the right incentive—no matter how outrageous their behavior with each other—some members of the fraternity of pilots knew how to behave as officers and gentlemen.

———

Today was to be a very special day—according to the major's wife who had called me.

I looked out my back window. Yep. The buzzards were back and breaking the branches off the smoke-trees at the edge of our lawn. Dumb birds didn't realize fifteen of them couldn't perch on one spindly excuse for a tree. They flopped to the ground with a squawk and a flurry of dust and feathers, then awkwardly flopped and flurried to stand and flap to another tree with too many buzzards perched on it.

But Buzzard Days weren't held until the spring when the birds returned from their southern migration.

Today was special because it was the Wives Tour of the Live Fire Exercises Day. Our tax dollars and hus-bands at work. The theory was we wives would be hap-pier living in the hellhole of Twentynine Palms if we understood what our husbands actually did for a living in the godforsaken desert.

I stood on the hill with four other wives and looked in vain for a hint of green. Plenty of sand for a beach, but hundreds of miles away from the water. Hundreds of miles away from my squadron mates, my friends.

Millie standing next to me was nice enough—actually I felt sorry for her. A second wife, she'd married only last year, so the whole military thing was far beyond her personal experiences. I couldn't imagine the difficulty of marrying into the Marine Corps and becoming an instant colonel's wife. I'd just started to understand the requirements of being a captain's and now a major's wife.

The other wives were married to grunts—ground Marines, not aviators. They took everything so seriously—rank, protocol, and social obligations. I knew from prior interactions that every one of them had a card case with calling cards inside the small clutch purses tucked neatly under their arms. As far as I could tell, no one present knew how to party. They looked too concerned that something they would say or do would interfere with their husbands' chances for advancement.

I returned my attention to the valley of booms, explosions, crashes and bombs. The tank rounds were impressive. A *kaboom!* echoed off the sides of our hill and back to the far hill, returning three times. The projectile flew from the gun of the tank faster than my finger could track from my right to my left and exploded a tank into bits.

Our escort, the captain, assured us the targets were all empty of personnel. Then he laughed. "But two motor homes with retirees had to be escorted off the range this morning. They'd set up lawn chairs to catch some rays out in the desert. If they hadn't been found, they would have caught something else—like some five hundred pounders when our friends from El Toro arrived."

A rumble in the distance moving nearer.

"Here they come now."

An F-4 Phantom flew in low and dropped three bombs. Thud. Thud! THUD!

Another jet, and the center of the range in front of us exploded into black oily smoke and flames a hundred feet in the air.

Millie asked, "What was that?"

"Why ma'am, that's napalm."

"What's that used for?"

"It's an antipersonnel weapon, ma'am."

"Antipersonnel? You mean they drop that on people?" Her face whitened, then turned a pale shade of green.

Where was she during the newscasts of the Vietnam War?

My mantra might be 'Make love not war', but I paid attention.

The doorbell rang.

Mrs. Betelmann, her fist clenched in the collar of my dog, its belly swollen to beer barrel proportions.

"Tawn! Are you okay?" I took her collar from Mrs. Betelmann. "Thank you so much. I didn't know she had gotten out." I smiled.

She didn't.

Apparently, my dog had eaten a twenty-five pound bag of dog food out of her garage.

She lectured me for several minutes about how close the houses were in military housing and since I was a major's wife, I needed to act like it and consider the possibility that my dog might inflict his bad manners on a lieutenant colonel wife's dog food. I must learn to act proactively.

She may not have used exactly those words, but the meaning was clear. I needed to keep my lower rank dog from eating her higher rank kibble.

She and Margaret Hanley had a lot in common. However, the years had toughened me up. Mrs. Betelmann didn't intimidate me. I just didn't like her.

Slamming the screen door, I reminded myself to avoid bogeys. When Andy flew air-to-air combat maneuvers, he worked at avoiding the bad guys trying to shoot him down—without live ammo. As I pursued homebase missions here in this wasteland, I had to watch my six and avoid those determined to make me look bad at the field.

I sat on our leather sofa and listened to the whooshing of the swampcooler.

Lost in the desert with strange people, I wanted to return to the familiar.

I missed Agile and Cindy who had moved to Hawaii when we'd moved to the desert. I asked Andy why he hadn't requested an Aloha Land assignment. He ignored the question. Anyway, Cindy would have giggled at my walking barrel of dog food retriever. Then she'd have worried that he might die or get sick from eating so much.

The dog survived. Would I?

The cooler air settled on the floor. I kept my bare feet on the linoleum, hoping to chill the rest of my body. My brains felt braised. I wanted to lie down on the white floor and soak up relief from the oppressive stillness. I wished for elsewhere with other friends.

Debby called me now and then, but she lived in Laguna Beach as a single person, so we had little to talk about other than shared friends and past experiences. She always asked about Brooke, but her anacephalic baby, William, had died at eleven months old and I didn't know what to say that wouldn't hurt. She said Waldo kept calling, trying to get her to move back to Connecticut and give him another chance. She said sometimes it sounded like a good idea.

Now the sun slanted through the aluminum blinds. I closed them, shutting out the grayish brown desert. I sat back down in the half gloom.

Kate and Duff were getting a divorce. No surprise but I worried about their kids. I worried about Kate. Her job had been Mom and homemaker—the pay was abysmal. I hoped Duff took care of them financially. Julie and Bird had been transferred to Quantico. Groove and Janey took orders to the Pentagon and then they were to go to a squadron in Beaufort, South Carolina. The rest of the squadron prepped to go out on cruise—a six-month deployment to the Pacific.

Even when we went back to the squadron, it wouldn't be the same. I knew this, but I ached for the

MARCIA SARGENT

ties of friendship and the laughter that made all the rest of the military life bearable.

I missed my brother and sister-in-law. They'd moved to Beaufort. We'd spoken at Christmas, two weeks ago, but this first night of the New Year I wanted my brother to make me laugh, wanted to hear stories of the kids, wanted to be reminded that life and marriage—even in the dry sun-seared furnace of Twentynine Palms— could be magic if I thought of it the right way.

I dialed, tapping the tile counter while I waited for the phone to be answered.

"Hello?"

"Hi, Kath. It's me, Marcia."

A laugh. "I know."

Another way to say my voice was distinctive.

"I miss you."

"I miss you, too."

Okay. I said nothing while trying to say everything. I wanted a hug and a cup of tea. I tried again, "How are things?"

"Good. Really good. We went out in Don's Boston Whaler last weekend with friends. They caught fish and cleaned them. We got to eat some—and I didn't have to cook, either. Don's been taking Tim crabbing off the dock whenever he gets home early enough from the squadron, which is fairly often. Kellen has a friend who lives right across the street in housing, so she's happy. Sometimes I have two darling girls here and sometimes I don't see her all day."

The children and Don and their regular life. I was so glad I'd called.

242

Andy waved to me from the doorway and held a phantom phone to his ear. I nodded.

"So is Don there, now? Andy wanted to say hey if he could, after we get done chatting."

"No. He's flying tonight, but should be landing anytime now. He usually calls from the ready room right before he leaves for home."

"Oh. It'll be too late by then for us to call. I think Andy just wanted to talk boats."

She laughed. "You know your brother; he'd love to talk boats anytime, anywhere."

"How's the little guy? I hardly got to know Toby before you moved."

"He's a sweet boy, but he knows what he wants and when he wants it. Stubborn."

"We both know where he gets that from, and it's not from your side of the family, Kath."

"Good thing I love your big lug of a brother. Otherwise he'd be impossible to live with."

"Uh huh. Sometimes I don't like Andy at all, but I love him like crazy."

"My heart still beats faster when Don enters the room. Has ever since we were in sixth grade together."

"It's love."

"Yeah, it's love. That's a good thing."

Magic.

I fell asleep smiling. Everything would turn out okay. I could get by without green, with buzzards, playing bridge and bowling. My exile would end. Kathy and Don were only a phone call away. Friends were friends no matter how far away they were.

———————

I surfaced from a deep, deep sleep into a heart-pounding panic state. It was dark. The phone was ringing. Andy answered in his best military guy I'm-going-to-pretend-that-I-wasn't-asleep serious voice, "Yes?" He handed the phone to me. "It's your dad."

I looked at the clock. Six-fifteen in the morning. Why was my dad calling at six-fifteen?

Dad said, "Don's plane is lost."

Lost? Someone better find him.

"They're looking for him now."

Looking. Lost. My brother. The phone slipped from my fingers.

Chapter 20
Lost in the Swamp

Andy lifted the phone from where it had fallen. "You still there?" he asked. A pause. "What happened?"

Don. I closed my eyes. Nothing could have happened to him. He was safe, like Andy. He had to be safe. I just needed to wake from the nightmare. Wake up.

I opened my eyes. Filtered morning light slid through the Venetian blinds.

Andy still on the phone. "I'll call the squadron in Beaufort."

I heard the rumble of my dad's deep voice from the receiver. Couldn't understand the words. I didn't want to. Nothing to understand. Couldn't be. Shouldn't be.

"Of course, I'll let you know anything I find out. I'll put Marcia on a plane as soon as I can get her a flight out of Palm Springs."

Don flew planes. He had to be all right. Dad had it all wrong. They'd find him. Don was lost, but SAR would find him. I pictured Don waving from the life raft, grinning his wide, white smile in his dark-bearded face. He'd have a five-o-clock shadow by now. He'd need a shave.

Andy hung up, reached to me, his eyes reddened. He held me and told me what he knew even though I hadn't asked and the words buzzed around my brain like wasps, stinging.

"Not Don."

"Shh. Shh, honey. They're out looking."

"Don's a good pilot, a good stick. You said he was safe. Don's okay. He has to be okay. Kathy would be—"

Lost.

Andy held me and we cried.

My brother.

His friend.

Everything else blurred.

Next thing I remembered, the doorbell rang.

I stood up from the sofa in jeans and a t-shirt. I must have dressed. Where was Andy? Where was Brooke? Someone knocked on the screen door.

Odd how thick the air—how hard to move through. So tired. I opened the door.

Who?

The woman said something I didn't hear. Should I know her? My eyebrows and my head hurt and I continued staring at the strange woman at my door. Go away. I don't want to talk. I don't want to—

"Don's plane is lost." I shared it with the woman at my door, but I stood in front of her, not wanting to do anything else. Now that I stood in the door, I'd stay in the door.

"Blah blah blah," the woman said. Then, "Marcia."

"Marcia? Don's my brother. He's lost. They're looking for him."

The woman pushed past me, grabbed my arm, and pulled me toward the sofa.

Ohmigod my brother. My brother could be floating and waiting in a raft. I stood up, refusing to sit on the cushion. I had to go somewhere. Where? Where Don was. Silly me. Of course I had to go search for Don. "I have to go now. Don is lost."

"Marcia, are you all right?"

How could I be all right?

The woman sat on the sofa and tried to pull me down. I pulled back, trying to break free from this stupid woman who did not realize I had to leave.

Suddenly, everything crystallized into a question. Why was Stella Betelmann, the battalion CO's wife, whom I could not stand, sitting in my living room holding my hands?

"Mrs. Betelmann?"

"Call me Stella."

I wanted to call her Mrs. Betelmann and get her out of my house.

"Marcia, I'm worried. You don't seem like yourself. When Bill told me you were all alone here at the house and your brother was dead, I knew I had to be here for you. Can I get you a drink of water, my dear?"

"My brother's not dead. He's lost. They'll find him soon."

She wouldn't let go of my hands.

Blah blah blah blah blah. She wouldn't stop talking.

Her eyes watched me. Greedy black eyes searching for me to—what? Break down? She wanted me to stop believing and cry. I wouldn't cry here for her, now or ever.

Blah blah blah? She asked a question. Blah blah blah blah? Another question.

I didn't answer. I couldn't answer.

I watched her lips move and sounds thudded against my eardrums. Nothing made sense. Stella Betelmann never made sense. She didn't like me either. Why was she here?

Hours. She stayed hours—hours of annoying kindness. I wanted to leave. I wanted her to leave. Trapped in her words, trapped by muscles and brain without will, I sat. Sat and believed Don would be okay because Don had to be okay. If Don weren't okay, nothing would be all right again.

Andy had told me once of a pilot flying out of Iwakuni, Japan. The lieutenant had a night hop over the Sea of Japan. Next thing he knew, he was being picked up out the freezing water by SAR—Search and Rescue. He remembered nothing of a crash or ejection, but his plane had disappeared. Pilots hate mysteries. What they don't know can, and often has, killed them or others. With any accident, there is an Accident Investigation to figure out the cause of the mishap.

In an unusual step, they had the pilot hypnotized. Under hypnosis, he remembered going to join up on lights below him, but instead of his wingman's lights, they must have been reflections on the water. His plane flew into the sea before he realized he needed to eject. He came to, in absolute Stygian darkness, in a cockpit filling with icy water. He tried to manually open the canopy, but the pressure outside wouldn't allow it. The ejection handle wouldn't have helped; the water would have held the canopy on and he'd have been rocketed into the plexiglass. So he waited in the black cold until the cockpit filled, then he opened the canopy and swam up to the surface, one hundred feet above the plane. He kept his cool to live to fly another day.

Don always kept his cool. I thought of him in the dark waters.

Everything turned to gray.

<hr>

On a plane. A man sat next to me.

"Are you all right, Miss?"

His tie lay neat and blue on his crisp and clean, striped shirt.

"No. No, I'm not all right." I blew my nose. I caught my breath. Had I been crying? Yes. I remembered. I waited until I got on the plane. Andy already felt so bad. When the plane lifted off, I cried. Andy wouldn't know I cried.

"Do you need me to get the stewardess?"

I looked at his face. He seemed kind. "My brother's plane is lost. I don't think the stewardess will be able to help with that."

"Oh. I'm sorry."

"Me, too. I'm sorry, too. He's a Marine pilot like my husband. They're looking for him. When they find Don, I'll be fine." I wanted him to not look so stricken, but I wanted to say my brother's name more.

"I hope they find him soon, Miss." He looked uncomfortable and sad, but still kind, not impatient.

I was impatient. South Carolina existed on the other side of the time continuum. "Thank you."

MARCIA SARGENT

"If I can help at all, let me know."

"Thank you." He couldn't help me get to Beaufort any faster.

Please God. Please take care of Don. Take care to find him soon and get him back to his family—to Kathy, to Kellen, Tim and Toby. I wanted to see him again. Talk to him. Be with him. Get him back safe.

I cried. My mind fell into the litany of prayer and begging and bargains.

The stewardesses served a meal somewhere over the Grand Canyon. I didn't eat. My stomach had twisted into a small hard knot of if onlys and maybes and please God this can't be trues.

The man reached over me, put down my tray table, and set a Coke on it.

Did I ask for a drink?

"You should have something. The sugar will help the shock."

Shock. It was all a shock.

"Thank you."

"Where's your brother? Where are you flying to?"

I appreciated his using the present tense. Kathy and I knew that magic requires belief. Mrs. Betelmann had Don dead already. I didn't like her. I liked this man of the gentle voice and kind eyes. "Beaufort, South Carolina. But I have to fly to Savannah and drive to Beaufort. Can't fly there. Funny. Can't fly there, but that's what my brother does—he flies."

"Do you want to talk about what happened?"

I did. "My husband spoke to the squadron. Don, my brother, was on a night hop, flying intercepts. They were under ground radar control until they closed on each other. So they knew where both planes were up to a certain point. But the ground radar lost the signal and lost radio contact as well. My brother's a very good pilot. He'll be okay."

"Maybe the radios broke."

I nodded. I'd thought of that. "Maybe they had to eject. It takes time to find rafts in the ocean."

I worried about Don ejecting. What could go wrong, would go wrong. A guy Andy knew in the training squadron, Jack Hartman, was on the catapult to launch on the USS Saratoga. The bridle connecting his jet to the cat broke on one side and the catapult flung him and the plane from zero to two hundred miles per hour in six seconds—twisted sideways with one wing forward. He knew the plane would never fly, so he ejected successfully. His plane crashed in front of the carrier. He floated down to the sea surface directly in front of the bow of the ship going twenty-five knots.

The aircraft carrier ran over him. The last thing he remembered while underwater was the sound of the screws, with blades twice the size of a Volkswagen. No one could figure out how he was spat out by the wash without the parachute or parachute cords tangling in the blades.

It wasn't always enough to be good—sometimes an aviator had to be lucky.

Don needed to be lucky.

"Is he married? Kids?"

"He has the most beautiful wife. They were child-hood sweethearts. Three kids. Great kids. He's thirty-three. He has to be okay."

"I'm sure he's okay."

"Yeah. It'll be so great when I get there and he's home and I'll get to have time with him and he'll laugh about what a lucky bastard he is and how idiotic it was the umptyfratz broke and they had to jump out." God. I sobbed. Too much. Don has to be okay.

The man squirmed in his seat. "Sorry. I'm sorry."

"No. It's okay. I keep thinking—it's just my brother. He spent a lot of time when we were kids teasing me and ignoring me, but now—well. He's my husband's best friend. He introduced us. I wouldn't be married to Andy without him."

I closed my eyes. They hurt; they were so swollen. "I'm going to try to sleep."

I didn't sleep. I knew I wouldn't, but I didn't want to talk anymore. I wanted to picture Don happy and smiling and with his family. Tears leaked from under my lids and down my face. They tasted bitter.

Driving through the cypress swamps from Savan-nah to Beaufort seemed to take longer than the flight from California. The trees grew out of the water, their fingers of prop roots twisting into dark oilyness.

If he had parachuted into the swamps it would be hard to see him. He might be hanging in a tree, hurt, not able to get down. He might be in the dark water, not able to call for help. He hated swamps. Boy. He'd be mad when they finally found him.

I peered between the trees into the midday gloom. No sign of him. No sign of anything.

———

"Breakfast, Marcia? I've got eggs and bacon, pancakes?" Donna, a neighbor of Kathy and Don's in housing at Beaufort was putting me up at her house. Not enough room at Kathy's, the neighbors in base housing had divvied Don's family among themselves.

"No, thank you. My stomach can't—won't—"

"Toast?"

I guess the expression on my face said it for me.

"At least drink this." She pressed a glass of orange juice into my hand. "And take these."

Pills. I started to push them away. I didn't want any drugs to falsely calm the pain or make me sleep away the waiting.

She smiled. "They're vitamins: a multi-vitamin and vitamin C. They'll help your body deal with the stress."

I swallowed them with a glug of juice. Then I drank the rest of the juice before handing the glass back. "Thanks."

She tucked her dark hair behind one ear. "Of course. I wish I could do more."

So did I.

I walked across the rolling green lawn, across Banyan Drive and into Kathy's house. People milled around, speaking in hushed voices.

The kids seemed muted, as well. Kellen sat on my mom's lap. Tim wandered from person to person. Toby leaned into each of his runs from one end of the house to the other, but said nothing.

"Where's Kathy?" I asked as I hugged my mom and kissed Kelly on the cheek.

"She's in her bedroom talking with her sister. We've haven't seen her this morning."

I hadn't seen her yesterday because she was talking with her sister. I walked down the hall. Knocked on her door. "Kathy?"

The door opened a crack with Val, her sister, blocking it. "What?" she whispered.

"Is she sleeping?" My voice matched hers.

"No. But she doesn't want to see anyone right now."

I could hardly hear her. "Oh. Okay. Tell her I'm here."

"I will." The door closed.

I walked out to the living room. My other older brother, Charly, stood at the dining room table leaning over a sheet of paper and talking to a big guy I knew, a good friend of Don's.

"Slug!" I hugged him.

"Marcia. Where's Andy?"

"We could only swing one ticket. He volunteered to watch Brooke." My eyes filled up. "So good to see you."

"You'll be seeing a lot of me. I'm the casualty assistance officer."

"I'm glad it's you."

"Just trying to help. Don is—"

—A friend.—One of the good guys.—A good stick.

Slug shifted his eyes back to the table.

"What's that?" Then I saw it was a map of the South Carolina coastline.

"We're looking at where they're searching," Charly said.

"The radar track from the ground radar put them about here—" Slug pointed to a spot over the ocean. "—when they lost the signal. The intercept was briefed to be over this area." He traced out another space.

"And the currents?" Charly asked.

"The wind blew from the southeast and they'd briefed that they'd be between thirty and fifty thousand feet. So the chutes could have blown anywhere in this direction. The currents move easterly away from shore toward the Gulf Stream, which moves north-northeast. The wind could have pushed them closer to the shore, but all the currents would have moved them farther away. The SAR guys and the squadron have been briefed where to look."

The phone rang. It was for Slug. I watched his face. It collapsed before he turned away. Not good news.

He took his time coming back to the table.

"What did they say?"

"A commercial jetliner, thirty thousand feet lower in elevation and fifty miles away from where the planes were, observed an explosion that lit up their cockpit at the same time the two planes disappeared from radar."

I tried to think of a big explosion that wouldn't involve my brother in anything catastrophic. "Could they have fired a missile inadvertently?"

"They didn't have any missiles loaded on the planes. There's more. NORAD has a tape of the two planes. It's fairly conclusive they collided."

255

Collided. Collided with explosions lighting up cockpits far away. "But they could have ejected."

His face said he thought it unlikely.

"Where's NORAD?" my brother Charly asked.

"In Florida."

"What's NORAD?" I asked.

"It stands for the North American Aerospace Defense Command. Its job is to keep an eye on the sky for threats. The planes weren't a threat, but the radar is lit up all the time for anything flying off the coast."

Charly straightened. "Can I talk to them?"

Slug shook his head. "I don't think they'll talk on the phone to anyone but the squadron."

"They'll talk to me in person. I'm driving down there."

"It's an eight hour drive."

He wouldn't be back until tomorrow. "That'll take so long," I said. "Shouldn't you stay here?"

"What's here? Better than waiting around."

I could see his need for action, any action. I wanted to take action, but not if I had to leave. Don's family, information about his accident, and mourners centered in this house. I'd stay.

Slug nodded. "I'll call them and tell them you're coming."

"Will that help me see what I want to see?"

"I'll make sure the squadron CO talks to them, too. Other than that, I don't know."

Charly left.

Slug told me what else he knew. It hadn't been only Don and his young RIO, a new first lieutenant in the squadron named Steve Kapitan, "Kap".

Another plane with the squadron XO, Major "Suitcase" Bill Simpson and the MAG-31 XO Lieutenant Colonel Fred "Razor" Schober was missing as well.

Missing. I didn't want to think about what the reported explosion probably meant. "What job does my brother have?"

"He's the Ops Officer."

One accident, and the Group XO, the Squadron XO and the Ops Officer were all missing. Only being in a squadron gave me a sense of the enormity of the tragedy for MAG-31 and VMFA 333—the enormity of the loss for the community of aviators here in Beaufort.

Slug explained the planes were traveling fast. "Maybe they didn't see each other and ran into the same piece of sky."

"But they could have ejected."

He looked sad—as sad as I felt inside. "We're still looking. We want them to come home, too."

Over the next hour, the room filled with another group of visitors milling around, asking questions, talking to my parents, and playing with the kids. There were too many people around I didn't know and didn't have the energy to get to know.

I wanted to talk to Kathy. She'd always been one of my touchstones. I wanted to share with her, lean on her, talk about Don. But I knew my grief would be a burden.

So when her sister continued to isolate her in her room, allowing no one in, I didn't argue. I didn't beat on the door.

I found no comfort in my own family members.

My brother Charly wanted to get the real answers from the military; convinced after his time in the Navy that the military served only to lie about all that they did. Charly's military was a vast conspiracy.

My father, struggling under the stress of losing his first born most beloved hero of a son, yelled often at my mother, "Mary Jean!" for everything she said or question she asked. His sub-text was: 'You idiot woman.'

My mother retreated into knitting and hugging the children.

My military family had taught me about truth and gave me strength. I missed Cindy and Agile, Janey and Kate. I thanked God for my husband and my child, the family I'd created. I hated being apart from them. To-night. I'd call Andy tonight.

Food kept arriving.

I knew what to do with food. I dedicated my day to putting casseroles in the freezer, in the refrigerator, in the oven. I tossed salads, put out cookies, cakes, and pies. I filled plates from the prepared food. I made sand-wiches from the cold cut trays. I offered food to every-one as they came to the house, or sat in the house, or as they were leaving. I washed dishes. I put them away. I filled more plates.

Every time I moved to the fridge, little Toby in his stocking feet would appear from nowhere, slide across the kitchen floor, and jam himself against the refrigerator door, blocking me from opening it.

Toby's size belied his mass. I could move my stubborn eighty-pound golden retriever more easily than push Toby away. Besides, my heart wasn't in it.

Because once he truly wedged up against the door, he'd grin. His dad's grin.

More wives and squadron mates dropped by. Kathy wouldn't see them, but they spoke to my parents and played with the kids.

They didn't know me. They didn't know they should know me. I was just the sister, or even less, Kathy's sister-in-law.

The voices and people blended into a loud buzzing like grasshoppers click-whirring across dry grass.

I mourned the lack of my military family, and hated being apart, not a part of things.

I felt a warm touch on my arm.

Slug. "Marcia. Are you okay?"

I shook my head.

He walked me outside.

I put my head on his chest and cried. I cried until I realized the tenseness of his muscles. His hands shifted to my shoulders, awkward.

I ducked my head and wiped my face. "Sorry."

"We all thought it couldn't happen to a pilot like Don. I—" Slug had deep circles under his gray eyes. "If it can happen to Don, it can happen—" He choked up.

To anyone.

Slug had tried. He wanted to comfort, but he had no comfort in himself. The unexplained killed pilots.

Sometimes it wasn't enough to be good—a pilot had to be lucky.

Charly arrived back at the house at nine the next morning without a copy of the NORAD track. They had shown it to him, explained it to him, but refused to give him a copy to take with him. He drew it on a pad of paper.

The drawing showed one plane descending from fifty thousand feet and another plane ascending from thirty thousand feet until the two planes intersected at sixteen hundred miles per hour of closure. Then they disappeared.

They called off the search. No beacon was activated by a seat ejection. No debris was found on the sea surface. No oil slick. They theorized that the jet fuel and oil burned up in the blast. Everything pointed to an explosion caused by two planes flying into each other going very fast.

Kathy didn't believe it. Ray Sanford, Don's childhood buddy, hired a plane and went out with Kathy searching the coastline for two days, looking for the raft, for Don, for magic.

Nothing. The sea, the sky, or the swamp covered any trace, every trace.

I didn't want the military theory to be true. I wanted him to show up, grinning. The radar track and the jetliner seeing the explosion were facts. The military collected data and drew conclusions. Don would have wanted me to listen to the facts.

So I did.

I remembered Marilyn telling me she had known Donut wouldn't be coming home. At the time I worried she had given up too soon. Now I knew why she had accepted the truth her heart told her. Without a body to look at, to touch, to convince my warm fingers of the coldness of the skin, it was too easy to think Don still lived—and somehow had chosen not to come home.

I listened to the facts and my heart. I knew he'd come home if he could.

I wondered if Kathy believed that.

———

"Andy. It's me." The phone weighed too much. I leaned my elbows on the table to prop it up to my ear.

"Hi, honey. How are you doing?"

"Not good." I couldn't imagine life ever being good again. "Have you been talking to the squadron?" I asked.

"Yeah. Pete's been telling me how the investigation is going. I'm sorry. I'm really sorry."

"My brother, your friend. I'm sorry, too." Sorry I wasn't with him and he wasn't with me.

"Yeah." The silence stretched.

I explained I still hadn't seen Kathy except on her way out the door to go look for Don in the prop plane. "Mom and Dad feel left out of the loop, but Kathy's the one who's not seeing anybody or talking to anybody except her sister and Ray Sanford and Robbie. She's more out of the loop than anyone except her sister, Val."

"Robbie's there?"

261

"Yeah. He says Don really helped him when his dad was killed in his P-51 last year. He just wants to return the support however he can."

"When are you coming home?"

"The memorial service is the day after tomorrow."

"Three more days?" He groaned. "I miss you. Brooke misses you. You've been there four days already." He sounded frazzled and lonely.

A high-pitched scream in the background.

"I don't know how much longer I can deal with Brooke without you."

His lonely touched my lonely across the country.

"The memorial service is on Wednesday. I guess I could come home the next day."

"Do you have to stay for the service?"

What? Of course I'd stay for the service.

Guilt bit at me. Andy had lost his best friend and I left him alone. I left him alone except for our hell-on-wheels one-and-a-half-year-old daughter. I'd thought I needed to be here for Kathy, but Kathy didn't need me. Andy needed me.

I needed him, too. "I'll see what flights I can get out on tomorrow."

Chapter 21
Buzzard Days

I flew out the day before the memorial. I didn't want to hear Taps played for my brother. I wanted, needed to be with my Andy. If only I could get home, everything would be okay.

Andy's hug at the airport felt good. Tears filled my eyes.

He handed Brooke to me. I hugged her. "Hey sweetie. Did'cha miss Mommy?" My arms felt like lead. I worried I might drop her. "Honey, I'm tired." I handed her toward him. "Go to your daddy."

She squirmed. Cried. Flailed her arms and legs.

He grabbed my bag instead. "I've got the luggage."

I'd been on a plane for hours. I wasn't even home yet. "Can't you take her? I can carry my bag." I couldn't deal with anyone else's emotions, not even an eighteen-month old's.

"I've had her by myself for five days."

He expected me to calm her down.

We reached the car. I put her in her car seat. She wasn't happy.

Neither was I. Nothing felt right. I didn't feel right and Andy wasn't the bulwark against the world I wanted.

Brooke wailed. "Want out. Want out!"

"You have to stay in your car seat." My head hurt. I couldn't breathe. "Did you bring a bottle for her?"

"No. I worried about getting both of us to the airport. She ate lunch."

"Bottle! Want bottle!"

"Now you've done it," he said, putting the car in gear.

I wanted to cry. I wanted to yell at him, but it didn't seem worth the effort it would take.

He looked over at me. "I'm sorry. This isn't the homecoming I wanted for you. I love you."

I was tired. Not mad, just tired. "I love you, too. Are you okay?"

He kept his eyes on the road. "Sure. Better now you're here."

I tried to soothe my young daughter, tried to tell her it would be okay. Nothing worked. My words lacked the conviction needed. Nothing would ever be okay again.

Andy and I gave up trying to talk over the wails and whines and sobs in the backseat.

It was a long drive back to Ocotillo Heights in Twentynine Palms.

My home looked like a stranger's. Had I been gone only five days? Sand, smoke trees and spiny ocotillos defined the boundaries of my yard in yellowish-brown, gray-green, brown, and gray. Inside my head the same colors swirled. Dull, duller and dullest. The buzzards hadn't returned yet.

Getting out of our station wagon, the world spun. I steadied myself. Too much time on planes, not enough to eat or drink today.

"Marcia?"

"I'm fine."

But I wasn't. The next morning I woke in a pool of sweat, my body burning up. My arms and legs might as well have still been asleep—I couldn't move them. Grief did strange things to a body.

By the afternoon I could hardly lift my head off the pillow. My next-door neighbor's teenager came over to watch Brooke. Maybe I just needed to sleep.

The day after, every movement required effort and my head and body felt like I lay in the midday desert sun baking.

After dropping Brooke off at the base childcare, Andy called to check on me.

I'd decided to go to the dispensary—Twentynine Palms's version of a military medical clinic. The closest actual military hospital was at Pendleton, a four-hour drive on a good day.

"I've got a live fire exercise with jets and helos from El Toro and Yuma."

I assured him I could go to the dispensary myself.

Good thing it was only ten minutes away. The road wavered and fogged as I drove. Once I pulled to the curb until the dizziness passed and my vision cleared. A good military wife didn't bother her husband when he had important work to do. He'd already spent five days watching Brooke. I could do this.

"I'm sorry, ma'am. You can't see the doctor. He is busy. Tell me what's wrong." The nurse spoke with a heavy Pakistani accent. I tried to read her nametag. Day-rit. Nurse Dayrit.

"I'm really sick. I just got back from my brother's funeral." None of her business I didn't stay for it.

"Ohh-hh. Your brother died?"

"Yes. In a plane crash and I—"

"Stress will make anyone feel bad." She patted my arm.

I didn't like the way she patted my arm and spoke to me as if I were three years old.

"Now just go home and take a nap and you'll feel better soon."

"I've been sleeping for two days! I'm sick. I think I have a fever." Tears ran down my face. I wiped my nose with a Kleenex.

"You're not a doctor. Trust me, I would be able to tell if you are sick. You are just sad."

She didn't even take my temperature.

I drove home and called Andy at work. He said he couldn't leave the field, but to go back and not leave until they gave me some medicine.

I went back, signed in, and sat in the waiting room for two hours. Nurse Dayrit ignored me. Finally, I staggered up to her desk, leaned on it for support and said, "My husband, Major Sargent, said I am to stay here until you give me some medicine." Pulling rank went against my nature, but miserable desperation drove me.

She stomped off down the hall without a word. I went back, sobbing, to my seat.

She stomped back five minutes later with a prescription for tetracycline, an antibiotic. "Here, crybaby. Take these. But you don't really need them." She turned her back and walked away.

She still hadn't taken my temperature.

Bed felt good. I didn't.

I took the first dose of antibiotic.

Half an hour later the pill and the little I'd had to drink came right back up.

Hysterical, I called Andy again. He left the field, came home in uniform, and took me to the dispensary. Five minutes and I was in an examining room seeing the doctor. Even the quality of medical care was dictated by rank and uniform. He took my temperature, listened to my lungs, took blood and urine, and said, "You have double pneumonia. Since you are also pregnant, it's a good thing you threw up the tetracycline. It's counter-indicated in pregnant women. I'm going to prescribe—"

Pregnant?

The rest of the conversation blurred. I was sick. I was pregnant. I was pregnant and Don was dead.

Three weeks later, the pneumonia had run its course.

I was still pregnant.

My brother was still dead.

———

I'd forgotten how Andy had grieved for Donut. He grieved the same way for Don, but worse. He had no one to sit on the sofa with him and watch TV. So he didn't talk. He worked. He ran long runs in the desert—training for a marathon, he said. He watched TV—a lot of TV.

I reclined on the sofa, reading. About nine pm, he looked up from the sitcom. "Hey, honey. I'm driving to El Toro tomorrow."

These days I hated when he left for anywhere. "What's at El Toro? A meeting?"

"I've got a cross-country. It's great the squadron lets me fly, even though I'm stationed here, but I have to drive to where the planes are."

I didn't care about the driving; I cared about the flying.

"When I get back, maybe you and I could have a date since you're feeling better." He double lifted his eyebrows Groucho Marx-style.

'A date'. He meant nookie, boom-chicka-boom-boom, in other words—sex. "Yeah, okay." Inside, not a flicker of warmth or interest. Maybe the hormones from the pregnancy had temporarily flicked a switch. And my whole body was tired. Still too tired.

And annoyed. Annoyed was a new feeling. I didn't want to worry about having to do anything. Not even making love with my husband.

By the time he returned from—oh God—flying, I might feel like wrasslling in the sheets with my Andy. I'd always liked that part of our marriage. He made me feel good and I loved making him feel good. In fact, the last three and a half weeks was the longest stretch we'd gone without since Brooke was born.

I remembered, before Brooke's birth, when my ob-gyn had told me to abstain from sex three weeks before my due date to four weeks after.

In shock, I'd asked Kathy whether I should listen to him.

She'd said yes.

I'd gasped in dismay. "That's seven weeks without sex!"

She'd paused, blushed, and said, "There are other ways to satisfy your husband."

"My husband? I don't care about my husband," I'd said. "What about *me?*" In the end, my hubby and I rumpled the covers together right up until the birth, and started up again as soon as the doc let us—or maybe the week before that.

I shook my head at my younger self and went to bed. Only enough energy remained for Louis L'Amour and Zane Grey westerns.

In the morning, Andy packed his green flight bag with a pair of skivvies, a clean t-shirt, a pair of Levis and his toothbrush.

"You don't have to go." Leaning on one elbow, I watched him. A dark hole had opened inside me. Only Andy could save me: save me by staying with me, connecting me to Brooke and the smoke trees and even the buzzards.

"This is a great deal. I get to fly all weekend."

"And I get to stay home and watch Brooke all weekend." I spread sarcasm as thick as I could. My desperation widened the dark hole.

"You can go visit Ann next door and read all day and night without me telling you you're in a rut."

"Don't go. I need you here." His face blurred as if I looked through rain droplet covered glass. I swirled toward the black void.

"You'll be okay while I'm gone." He zipped up his bag.

"No. No, I won't be okay. I may never be okay. You promised." My voice raised. "You promised and it was a lie."

He looked up, confused. "I promised what?"

He *should* know. "You promised you were safe and Don was safe." The blurring rain overfilled my eyes and ran scalding hot down my face. "Don wasn't safe."

He came around the bed, sat down and wrapped his arms around me. "Shh. Shh. Don't cry. It was a fluke—an accident. I'll be fine. Trust me."

Not an accident. He flew fast fighters on purpose. I pushed him away. I didn't trust him because I didn't trust Fate. "Please don't go." I wasn't a child to be told there were no monsters under the bed. I'd met the real monsters and they threatened everything.

He ignored me. He went.

The door closed, softly.

I flung myself across our bed, breathing in sobs without air, drowning in a vacuum.

Damn him. Damn him and damn the airplanes he flies.

I only thought it.

No. I didn't mean it. Oh God.

I'm sorry. I take it back. Do overs. Please watch over Andy and let him come home again.

I'd little faith in a kind God. A kind God wouldn't take Donut and Ernie and Don. But maybe he'd bargain with me. A fickle God would bargain. What was a bargain but a bet God couldn't lose? Did God have control of who lived and who died and when?

I regretted being such a religion mutt. My father was Presbyterian, but never went to church services after he left for college. My mother was baptized Catholic, but my grandmother divorced my grandfather. Neither went to church. I went to church and catechism classes with my best friend at the Episcopalian Church until I was twelve and my father refused to let me be confirmed in my friend's religion. He said I wasn't old enough to make that commitment. I think he saw all churches as propaganda machines. The Catholic priest at my wedding had sprinkled holy water on our car before we left—and when I mentioned I hadn't been baptized, he'd made sure I got a good sprinkling, too.

I wished I'd been raised in a structure of church and faith and the comfort of doctrines.

I believed in God. I believed in trying to be good. There were many people I looked forward to seeing when I went to Heaven. I believed in Heaven.

On the other hand, part of me believed in karmic fate. Kathy believed we lived the life and died the death that was needed to move us on our journey to being a better soul, a better person. Too many good people died young. Was their death a lesson for those of us left behind? If so, I wished the learning didn't hurt so much.

Maybe it wasn't about God at all. Maybe it was just luck. Don had always been lucky—lucky and good. Then he lost his luck. Did luck run in families—if you had good luck as a family, was it conferred to all? Bad luck for one—bad luck for all? Would I be unlucky? Would Andy be unlucky? I couldn't gamble with my life or his. I had to be very, very careful and keep my side of the deal.

God? Do you hear me? Keep Andy safe. Keep me safe. And I'll be good.

Andy flying. My stomach flipped, departed controlled flight, and augured into the ground.

Andy called that night. I heard clinks of glasses, laughter, men's voices, more laughter. "Hey honey! I'm in Yuma."

"*Where* are you? I can barely hear you."

"Sorry. I'm at the O-Club in Yuma."

But he didn't sound sorry. He sounded happy. How could he be happy? I'd been making deals all day to keep him safe—and he's *happy*. If he'd been closer I would have kicked him, hard.

"We're going to Chretin's for dinner and I knew it would be too late to call afterward."

"Have fun. Goodbye."

"Wait!"

I disconnected.

He tried to call back. I didn't answer. I had no answer. No answer for him, no answers from God.

I wasn't one of the boys. I couldn't be a part of their fraternity of aviators. I didn't want to be. There was no safe place for me with them. They supported each other by downplaying the possibility of something going wrong. They partied and drank and laughed and smiled—because they had cheated death another day. And I couldn't join in because the lives they gambled with belonged to my friends, to my children, and me.

Chapter 22
A Friend in Need

Twentynine Palms didn't get any better. Dusty brownish sand stretched to the horizon. When the wind blew icy cold in the winter, the sand gritted in my teeth. Spindly smoke trees in shades of gray hid in depressions. I stepped out my kitchen door to dump garbage in the outside can and just missed stepping on a scorpion with my bare foot. Joshua trees raised their spiky arms up to the heavens like aliens praying to be saved from the desert—or in surrender. I knew how they felt. I missed suburbia. I missed green. I missed real trees and wanted pine-covered mountains instead of rock piles.

When Andy returned from the cross-country, we had sex. Well, he had sex. I was somewhere else—in the same bed, but not with him.

"I'm tired," I said.

"I'll make it good for you next time." He meant it.

It didn't get better. Somewhere a connection had been cut. All the feeling in my body, all my hollows and buttons and strings Andy excelled at licking and pushing and plucking and strumming to glorious warm life, turned off.

He didn't give up. We still made dates to have marital relations. I dressed in sexy lingerie and put on perfume. He showered and scrubbed his teeth and put on my favorite aftershave. The hydraulics were there. The pieces and parts still fit. I might as well have been asleep. Maybe I was asleep and living a nightmare.

Making love became work, futile work. Sometimes I just wanted to say, "Get that thing away from me." But we were married. For better or worse, for richer or poorer, in sickness and in health. I wanted better. I wanted it *good*. So I tried and I cried and he held me. After awhile, we'd try again. I knew he cared.

I didn't. I wanted to, but I couldn't summon the energy for it.

I called Kathy to talk after all her family and friends—the comforters—went home. Kathy remained uncomforted. She frothed with anger. Carter, a flight surgeon and a pilot, told her he went up and followed Don's briefed hop and it scared him shitless. He implied Don was to blame. Blame a dead pilot. Always try to blame a dead pilot.

"He risked his life. He risked our lives! Why would your brother risk everything flying crazy?" she asked.

My only answer: he wouldn't.

She wouldn't listen to tales of the Don we knew. Fear, sorrow, and rage twisted her memories of him into a monstrous chimera: selfish, reckless, uncaring.

Carter tried to comfort Kathy by hitting her up for sex, making his motive for the previous comments suspect, but Kathy held on to her anger. "Don died and left me alone and at the mercy of lowlifes." Even widows blamed dead pilots.

Andy blew up when I told him; he matched and exceeded Kathy's rage. "Carter wasn't scared shitless, he's full of shit. Messing with widows." His jaw muscles jumped. "None of us want lies told to our wives if we die in an accident. Don *hated* those worms who disturb widows. Respect the dead and respect the grievers of the dead."

I still believed in the magic of Don and Kathy's marriage, but Kathy dug its grave a little deeper everyday. She buried the love under regret and fierce anger and deep sorrow.

Every time we spoke, I sank deeper into the black hole of unending dread. Dread of what, I didn't know and didn't want to think about.

A month after my return from Beaufort, Mrs. Betelmann arrived at my door. "Hello, Marcia. I thought I'd drop by for a cup of coffee and a chat." She sidled past me into the family room.

"I don't drink coffee."

I moved back and watched her sit down on the leather sofa. She scooched back to sit straighter and patted the cushion beside her. Ignoring the invitation, I sat in the bentwood rocker across the width of the Navajo-patterned rug.

"I'm concerned about you. You haven't been to a Wives' Club meeting since your brother's unfortunate death."

"No. I haven't." Don. Dead. I knew that.

"Well, I've been understanding since you *have* been sick, but—"

"I had double pneumonia and a temperature of one hundred and four."

"Yes. Well. There is that, but it's time you return to your responsibilities as a major's wife. You can't expect

275

the rest of us to do everything, can you?" She smiled sweetly as a rattlesnake before the strike.

"It's only been—" My sense of time was shot all to hell.

"A month. I know. But he was only your brother after all."

Suddenly all air left the room. I couldn't breath. Red gathered at the edges of my vision, then turned grey, then black.

Anger filled me, stiffened my knees, stood me up, and moved me to the door. Gritting my teeth, I managed to say calmly, "Thank you for your concern. You need to leave now."

On her way out the door she said, "Remember. We're a family in the Marine Corps. We all pull together to help each other through these little bumps in the road of life."

If she was in my family, she was hateful Aunt Agatha who commented on facial blemishes, wondered what had happened since the others in the family were beautiful, recommended a dermatologist for those unsightly spots, and enlisted help cleaning out her garage on a Sunday in the summer.

No one brought me food. I wasn't a widow. My pneumonia cured, sympathy and casseroles went to others. I didn't care. Hunger became a stranger. I ate when I'd nothing else to do and Andy put food in front of me.

Mrs. Betelmann tried weekly to come in my house on her rounds to comfort (!) the sick and the sad. I told her to go away. Sue came by to ask about bowling. I shook my head. Millie offered to watch Brooke. No. I clutched my child tighter. When Millie left, I sat with Brooke in front of Sesame Street. Bright colors, easy lessons, humor—why couldn't life be like that?

Isolated in the desert with the sidewinders and scorpions, I watched the wind carry sand from here to there to nowhere. A neighbor killed a bull snake because of its size and his fear of rattlers. Bull snakes weren't rattlers or poisonous. They ate rattlers. I tried to tell him that. He wouldn't listen. A senseless death. He deserved to have more snakes in his yard filled with venom.

I hated the desert where Andy and the military put me. Some days I wondered if I hated Andy and the military as well. I thought about leaving. I thought about leaving Andy, if only I'd the will to pack a bag and drive anywhere.

———

Rheta Lyn, who had been my matron of honor, came to visit a few weeks later. She'd been married to my brother, Charly. He divorced her and I kept her, in spite of her insisting she should fade away from the family entirely. For the past six months, she'd dated a Marine colonel to whom we'd introduced her.

Now, whenever she came to see John, she stopped in.

I knew she meant well. I hoped she'd leave soon.

"Marcia. You haven't dressed yet?"

"Pajamas are comfortable."

"Let's go out to lunch."

"I'm not hungry. I already ate."

"At ten-thirty in the morning?"

"Breakfast. I already ate breakfast."

"Then you need to eat lunch. Brooke's at preschool, so you're free. We'll go to that Mexican restaurant in town and have a margarita and some tacos."

"I—"

"Ai ai ai! Get dressed. We're going."

An hour and a half later, I watched the salt slide down the outside of my glass and stirred the lime slice deeper under the ice.

"You're supposed to drink that, you know." Rheta Lyn sipped hers.

"I hate it here," I mumbled.

"What?"

I looked up into her concerned brown eyes. "I hate it here. I hate the desert. I hate the buzzards and the smoke trees—which aren't even proper green trees— and the snakes and the scorpions and Mrs. Betelmann. I hate being any part of the Marine Corps. They didn't issue Andy a wife but I resign my commission."

She slapped a hand on the table.

I jerked back in my chair.

Her west Texan drawl hardened, "Well, poor little baby. Isn't this a pity party for Marcia? What do you want? We all wish we could all live in Hawaii for our entire lives, but that's not going to happen. What did you *expect*?"

She was so mean. "I'm sad."

"We're all sad. We all wish we could get Don back. But we can't. Your husband was his best friend and room-mate for almost five years. Don't you think he misses him, too?"

I fumbled in my purse for a Kleenex.

"You're allowed to be sad and to grieve, but you have to be a wife and a mother. You have to keep going."

"I don't want to keep going and even if I did, I wouldn't want to keep going *here*."

"There's beauty in the desert, and if that doesn't impress you, there are life lessons. Plants like ocotillo and Joshua trees grow here in spite of the summer heat of a hundred and seventeen degrees. They've adapted and thrived."

"Goody for them."

"Petulance looks ugly on you, Marcia."

"I feel ugly, as ugly as this desert."

"You're strong as this desert, whether you admit it or not."

"No." I dreamed of freshly mowed green lawns.

She reached out and covered my hand on the table. "We aren't given any promises, you know. I could leave this restaurant and get hit by a truck. Knock on wood; it won't happen." She rapped on the tabletop. "Life is precious and we are not in charge. The only thing we control is how we react to the hard times and to the good times."

"Good times in Twentynine Palms are few and far between."

"Living in Twentynine Palms has its advantages."

I looked at her disbelieving. "Like the forty minute drive to get pizza?"

"Millie showed me yesterday how much easier it is to clean up after her dogs. The poops dry right away and then she scoops them up with a baggie over her hand."

"Millie, the colonel's new wife?"

279

"Yep. She even let me help."

My smile escaped.

She laughed. Her laughter hurt my heart. No one should be laughing.

She sobered. "How's Andy?"

"Quiet. He runs for hours."

"Aviators don't deal well with death."

"No one deals well." I started to realize I didn't deal well, hadn't been dealing well.

"But the pilots and RIOs have to keep flying. They can't if they focus too much on the risk."

Risk. My Andy flew. I always thought I was safe from disaster, from death. A realization of the truth. As long as Andy flew, the possibility of losing him remained unacceptably high.

I took a real swallow of my margarita.

"That's my girl. Here's to us."

"And here's to you, my friend." I lifted my glass and clinked it against hers.

God bless Rheta. God bless her for whomping me upside the head. I had a lot to think about. It was time I stopped swirling toward the drain and made some decisions.

———

Turning the heat down under the rice and checking the chicken breasts in the oven, I waited for Andy to get home for dinner. Brooke played in her room. I waited and mulled over my options.

My friends—my Marine Corps wives friends—supported me and kept me sane. Not so much the guys—who were funny and cute and caring in their own way—

but the women, they took me into their heart. They might have to move away or I might have to live far away, but being there for each other didn't require geographical proximity. No matter what, in an unsafe world, they cared enough to fly at my wing.

I refused to be a Mrs. Betelmann. The structures and strictures of Marine Corps tradition, though often admirable and exemplary, did not define *esprit de corps*—something Stella remained incapable of understanding. The Marine Corps asked too much of me and mine. Let the demands of major's wives be forever unfulfilled. Leave me be. The Marine Corps regulations and expectations couldn't replace Donut or my brother, couldn't soothe Marilyn's loss or Kathy's or my own.

I sat at the kitchen table, the round butcher-block maple table I'd often sat at with Andy and sometimes with my brother. I laid my head down and pressed my cheek to its cool smooth surface.

Andy flew fighter jets just like my brother. If he died, I'd be lost. Lost like Diane Maher. Lost like Donut in the ocean.

I stroked my palms across the tabletop, then tightened my fingers into fists.

The front door whooshed open, letting in the smell of heat and dust before slamming shut. "Hey, honey! I'm home!"

Andy.

Brooke ran down the hall. "Daddy!"

Swooping her up in his arms, he tickled her and twitched her nose. "How's my little Brookerdoodles tonight?"

She was fine. She laughed and babbled about her day. I thought how much they looked alike, jaws and noses a match.

Later, showering, I let the hot water run on my tight neck, down my back and between my breasts. Soaping my hills and valleys, my palms remembered the cool flatness of the table, the cold reality of my brother's death, and Andy still flying the kind of plane my brother died in.

Suddenly, I realized what had happened in our between-the-sheets marital sorties. I'd distanced myself from Andy, from sex and love with him, to protect myself from the pain of his loss. If it hurt so much to lose a brother, it would hurt so much more to lose my Andy, my lover. So I'd cut myself off. Cut myself from caring and feeling.

The shower door opened. "Got room in there for a smelly, horny husband?" Naked Andy.

I didn't know if I did. "Um, I'm just done."

"I can make it worth your while to stay." He stepped in and pulled me toward him, tight against his enthusiastic guy parts.

"No! I—uh—" I backed away, backed into cold tile shower wall. Squirming, I opened the door and left him.

He deserved better than what I could give him. Maybe I *should* just leave, divorce him, and start over with a normal guy in a normal job.

I cringed at the thought.

Wrapped tight in the covers, my back's bone-blooded wall toward the bathroom, I heard the water stop, the shower door open. Andy's wet feet slapped lightly on the linoleum floor. The bed sagged on his side. Smell of warm damp man. My man.

"Are you all right? I thought we could—you know—make some whoopee. Brooke's asleep."

"No. I'm not all right." I couldn't tell him all my doubts and worries and dreads. No matter what, I needed to help keep him safe. My doubts, worries and dreads could distract him at a critical moment in flight. "Aren't you tired of propositioning your wife? Aren't you tired of working so hard to have sex?"

A hand on my shoulder. He rolled me over to face him. I couldn't face him. I kept my eyes down.

"Look at me." He tilted up my chin.

I shook my head.

"I love you. None of this is work. You are so *beautiful.*"

I looked in his eyes, then. He meant it. He meant all of me, inside and out.

I could ask him to stop flying. He loved me enough to do that. Maybe.

My mood lightened. Yeah. We could be normal people. He could get a normal job where the most serious danger is a paper cut or a headache from the boss yelling at him.

Andy slid under the covers and wrapped his arms around me. His throttle remained on full, prodding my pregnant belly. His sac furred warm against my leg.

Men were always proud of their balls, proud to have balls. I was proud of Andy. Proud of the man he was, the dad he was. He was also a pilot. I married him

283

as a pilot, loved him as a pilot. Demanding he stop flying would cut off his balls—even if he *would* quit for me.

Andy flew high performance aircraft—whether I
wanted him to or not.

I loved the crinkles at the corners of his eyes—
laughter crinkles.

I loved the breadth of his shoulders.

I loved his sherry-colored eyes.

Flying very fast with skill was as much a part of him
as his eyes, his shoulders, and his hands. If I didn't take
the whole package—all his parts—we couldn't have a
life together.

My stomach hurt. I saw death so clearly. Death happened, but when it happened quickly, or unexpectedly
or younger than a full-life lived span I hated it. I asked
why. I tried to make sense of it. I tried to deny it. I railed
against the fates. I wanted my full measure of time with
those I cared for—and with those I knew and liked. I
even wanted a life-well-lived for others I hardly knew or
didn't know. Grief and regret were the debris from an
untimely death. Death hurt the ones left behind more
than the aviators who flew off to the great squadron in
the sky.

"Oh, baby." Andy's hand caressed my chest, from
one nipple to the other, ruching them both to hard
nubs. "I've thought of you all day."

I'd thought of him, too. Needed to think of him
and our life.

I wanted a life with him. He'd stuck with me
through my grief. I was stronger, better with him than
apart—we were both stronger together. He kept me

tucked under his wing; I would fly at his. Wingmen. I had to be part of the strength. I couldn't expect to always be safe. Life was not safe.

The alternative to being with him was a half-life and no love.

No Andy.

Don and Kathy didn't get happily ever after. But they got more than most. We don't get forever—we don't get perfect. I couldn't count on anything more than this moment—but needed to use this moment to make tomorrows better—to make me better, my children better, my marriage better. Life came without guarantees.

"I love you." I said. "I'll love you forever."

He tweaked my nose. "Even when I'm old and the hydraulics don't work?"

"Even when you're old." I smiled against his shoulder, biting lightly. "There are other ways to pleasure your wife."

"I thought Kathy said, 'There are other ways to satisfy your *husband*.'" He laughed. "But your version sounds good, too. Let's see if I can think of a few ways now."

And then he lit the afterburners and we flew a section takeoff.

He was a damn fine stick.

Chapter 23
Pressed Hams and Conga Lines

Early in the morning, four months later, Andy walked down our hall toward me in his flight suit, carrying his flight helmet bag.

How a baggy flight suit could be so sexy, I didn't understand, and didn't really care. He looked *good*.

"Shh," I told him. "Brooke's sleeping."

He nodded, then whispered, "I'm off to my first hop as a Snake. Don't know when I'll be done at the squadron."

Worry.

Fear.

Dread.

I loved him.

I could do this. "Will you call me when you land?"

"Sure."

Enveloped in a green Nomex hug, I breathed in. Tangy, spicy man. Yum.

"Andy?" I said as he walked through the front doorway.

"Yes?"

"Remember—as many landings as take offs."

Thumbs up. "Got it."

MARCIA SARGENT

I turned eagerly to the boxes piled in the family room and kitchen. Moving back to Mission Viejo—to the house we'd kept—made unpacking worth the hassle. I still loved my burnt orange shag.

All morning, Brookie and I alternated playing with Play-Doh and unpacking boxes. The boxes and newsprint occupied her attention best. Soon the whole family room had tunnels to rooms to tunnels. Honestly, I spent more time cutting doors and windows in cardboard sides than in taking out and putting away kitchen gear. Kathy would approve of my priorities. I'd call her later.

The phone rang. No one had our number, except Andy and the squadron. Too early for the hop to be over. Too soon for Andy's call. My heart paused in my chest. No. Not my Andy.

A crash. Brooke wailed. "Mommy!"

I pulled her out from under the cardboard house that had collapsed when she climbed on it. Holding her in my arms, I walked to the still ringing phone. Maybe they'd hang up.

Before I reached out and lifted the receiver, I knew. I knew it wasn't about an accident and Andy. I knew because the Marine Corps follows tradition and routine. If Andy's plane went down, men in uniform would knock on my door. They didn't call with a wife's bad news.

"Hello?"

Brooke's screams increased in volume. I couldn't hear the electronically transmitted voice for the high-pitched mayhem arrowing through my eardrums.

288

"Hold on. My little girl—" I switched the phone to my other ear.

Brooke switched to hiccups, then squirmed to get down.

I set her on the kitchen tiles. She scampered off to rebuild her home.

"Hello? Are you still there?"

"Is this Marcia, Snatch's wife?" A woman's voice.

"Yes."

"This is Diane, Fog's wife—from the Snakes."

Andy's new squadron, VMFA-323. My new squadron. "Hello. Sorry about the yelling. My daughter fell."

"Oh, I love baby girls."

"I like her better when she's not screaming."

Diane had the best laugh, like a little girl herself, but with musical trills. I pictured her about five foot nothing with long blonde hair. "I'm calling to invite you to the next wives' coffee."

A whole new set of women to meet. I felt—not nervous. A lot had changed since my first wives' coffee at Margaret Hanley's home.

Andy and I looked over the social roster the night before the coffee. He told me a bit about the guys and we matched their call signs to their wives. Thirty-six pilots and RIOs, thirty of them married, and I knew not one wife.

I looked forward to new friends. The exile to the desert left new grit all the way into my bones; some of it rubbed me raw to bleeding, some of it itched, most of it had strengthened my basic structure.

The doorbell rang,

"Mary!" My neighbor who lived around the corner. "Come in."

Mary showed her Midwest ties to German and Nordic blood in her thin blonde hair and pale blue eyes. "I saw the moving trucks yesterday on my way to work. Welcome back."

"I told you I'd be back. We kept the house. Want something to drink?"

"Sure."

We settled on sun tea. I doctored mine with a healthy portion of sugar, thought of Agile's baby Kellie drinking ice tea from a bottle, and deflected Mary's laugh at the amount I ladled into one glass. "It's why I'm so sweet."

We sat in the family room. I sat gently, hoping my pelvic floor would stay together until this new little one made its appearance. Pregnancy had almost as many charms as the desert.

She leaned forward. "I was angry with you when you moved to Twentynine Palms."

One thing about Mary, she never flinched from the truth however it reflected on her.

"I didn't have a choice. Why would I go to Twentynine Palms for a year and a half if I didn't have to? Have you ever been there?"

"But we had become such good friends. I hated you moving away."

"I know. You didn't speak to me for eight weeks before we left."

She smiled, ruefully. "I knew I'd miss you."

"The Marine Corps gave Andy orders. We had to go."

"I don't know how you stand it," she said. "I'd make Jim quit and fly a desk."

I changed the subject to talk about our children and her teaching and my pregnancy. Some other time, I'd tell her about Don and Beaufort. I knew she didn't want to hear it now. She wouldn't know what to say, so she'd say something like, 'I'd make Jim quit.' And then I'd be angry trying to explain the unexplainable.

The wives with husbands who flew in fighters shared certain realities; realities not understood by civilian wives.

I really hadn't wanted to move.

The Marine Corps excelled at being capricious. Just when a wife settled into a neighborhood, comfortable with the schools, the shopping, the neighbors, then orders arrived to somewhere else. Staying three years in one place on orders was to be appreciated. Returning to the same place where a family owned a house bordered on miraculous.

Mary could make her husband change jobs to stay where she wanted to be.

In the military, orders had to be followed. Once orders were cut, the aviator went. When we could, we went with them.

Our husbands might not be fighting in any war, only training, but on any given 'normal' day they could leave for work and not come home. Most of the time there wouldn't be a body to bury. If there were a body, the funeral would be with a closed casket. All the squad-

MARCIA SARGENT

ron wives I'd met—unless they had been married less than a year—knew at least one aviator who had not returned. Death was no stranger, even in peacetime.

Mary would never understand.

Our men loved to fly, and we loved the fliers.

———

The women clustered about in Diane's house, some perched on pillows, some sprawled on the rug, some on the sectional sofa and a few in chairs. Ferns and spider plants, a rubber plant behind the sofa. Cookies, tortilla chips and salsa. I loved southern Californian modernDiane walked in from the kitchen, her long blonde hair flowing past her ample bosom and wide waist. She might be five foot and not much in height, but there was a lot of her to go around, especially in front.

Duff would never have looked above her chin.

Diane's little-girl voice called out, "Who wants a margarita? The blender's ready."

Plenty of takers.

I loved being in a squadron again.

I'd had only one frozen margarita when I offered to have the next squadron party at my house, a potluck.

Bev, the CO's wife, patted my hand. "That's so sweet of y'all. You don't have to." She had the darkest brown eyes and a kind smile. "We can have it at our house. You *just* moved in."

"I have everything unpacked that I haven't hidden in the garage—"

Laughter.

———

292

Fog and Diane brought ribs and margaritas, with enough bottles of tequila and triple sec for happy hour at the O-Club. Fog towered over his plump pumpkin of a wife, but she pretty much ran the show. He just stood back and got out of the way. Smart man.

Lieutenants, one called Soup, another Spud, a Boomer, and a Captain called Okie, arrived with more beer, and more beer, and more beer.

Six-foot-five Taco with his Pancho Villa mustache trailing to his jaw, and his wife, Cis, brought seven-layer dip, a bottle of Mateus wine in a cool green bottle, a fruit salad and lemon bars.

"Taco." She put down the dip. "Behave tonight. I don't want to have to drive you home."

"Sure, baby." He swigged his beer, then grabbed her in a hug and whirled her around the kitchen nuzzling her neck under her long, dark brown hair.

At that moment, the CO arrived with his wife. I remembered the CO only too well. I'd seen his balls.

"No sex on the tiles!" Gazelle shouted to the nuzzler.

I'm sure Bev brought food as well, since she kept true to her South Carolina roots in graciousness and hospitality, but by the time they arrived, the margaritas had been blenderized, much beer had been guzzled, and little food had been eaten to soak up the alcohol, so I didn't notice what they carried in their hands.

"Darling! So good to have us at your house. Snatch said to be sure to come." High-pitched giggle. "I always come. Don't I dear?"

Bev punched his shoulder. "Behave. You're the CO. What will she think?"

Giggle. "Whatever she thinks won't be far from the truth. We met at the O-Club in El Toro a few years back."

"You didn't."

"I'm afraid I did. And weren't they a fine set of co-jones, darling?"

I shook my head, laughing.

Gazelle hugged me hello and whispered, "So sorry about your brother. He was a good man."

"He was. I miss him."

"Of course you do, darling. Of course you do." He patted my cheek.

He was a bad boy, but lovable.

I soon stood at the picture window drinking a Coke with lime and rum.

The pool was full of guy bodies, swimming, splashing, and cannonballing off the board. A group sat in the Jacuzzi swigging beers. A lieutenant waved me to join them in the steaming spa. No women. I needed to get that part of the party started. Having a pool party with all the women bone-dry seemed wrong.

"I think it's time I went in the pool."

A young man—Spud?—standing next to me, wiped his mouth from his last swallow of beer. "Uh, ma'am?"

So strange at twenty-six to be a ma'am. "Uh huh."

"The lieutenant waving at you to come in the Jacuzzi?"

"Uh huh?"

"Uh—his swim trunks went over the back wall five minutes ago."

"Oh. Thank you."

"You're welcome, ma'am."

I didn't go swimming. I joined Bev, Diane, and Cis in the living room, talking about what we would do to entertain ourselves when the guys went on deployment to Fallon. More guys went out to the pool. More wives and girlfriends joined us in the living room on the sofa and on the floor.

The new sofa was my pride and joy: a huge off-white cotton sectional with prehistoric type paintings of horses and long-horned oxen in light brown. It faced the TV, which happened to be on the wall facing the front door. We sat with our backs to the plate glass window, the back yard, the pool, and the boys.

Bev thought a video of all of us doing crazy things set to music would be fun for the squadron's return and Gazelle's birthday party. We had just started thinking of camera shots, like Bev in Gazelle's yellow Cadillac driving with the top down and a martini in hand, when a lieutenant's girlfriend sitting on the floor giggled and pointed to the backyard.

"Good idea. Some of us could be filmed in the Jacuzzi. I'll talk to Andy to see if there's a way to get bubbles without ruining the pool filter."

The lieutenant's girlfriend shook her head and giggled harder, covering her mouth to avoid showing her braces. She pointed again with the other hand. We turned to look, sure she had seen a naked someone.

Oh, she had.

Six someones.

Five someones who had already made a naked pyramid against my sliding glass door with their buttocks and balls firmly pressed against the glass, and a sixth, Taco, who grinned at his wife. He waved full frontal before stepping on the nearest back and boosting up to inelegantly climb the pile to the top.

"Goodness gracious. What will they think up next?" Bev stood up. "Come on, ladies. They're just clamoring for our attention and it's not good to give it to them." She walked regally into the family room, face averted from the pyramid display—and smiling.

We continued our planning in spite of the husbands who called their wives to come look, or to come swimming, or just banged on the glass.

The sliding door in the kitchen screeched open. Whispers and Gazelle's giggle.

"Be ready, y'all," Bev whispered. "No encouragement."

A male chorus da da dum-ed semi-musically through *The Stripper* song. The conga line snaked through the family room, giggling Gazelle in the lead, and every man of the squadron, stark naked, kicked to the side on each "DUM", uncaring about looking good at the field.

Taco definitely should have kept his clothes on.

I kept my eyes on their knees, mostly. The last in line, a major, had nothing on but a pair of cowboy boots. I checked his six.

That one would show well in or out of a flight suit.

A short time later, the boys reacquired their clothes. A few lieutenants headed to their cars clad in dripping wet jeans and shirts.

Bev and Gazelle both giggled out the door.

Cis nodded thanks and goodnight to me. "Come on, Taco. I'll drive you home."

Andy, fully clothed in dry shorts and a t-shirt, held me to his side, under his arm, close to his heart. His hand rested on the curve of my belly.

We were already home.

In Memoriam

1st Lt. Bernie Plassmeyer USMC—A-4E pilot lost over Vietnam, aviator not recovered

1st Lt. Timothy Octaaf Farasyn USMC—and his RIO crashed into Mt. Fuji, Japan

1st Lt. Phil Lahlum USMC; Capt. Mike Maher USMC—wing fell off over ocean, aviators not recovered

"Donut"—Capt. Willie Duncan USMC and 1st Lt. Jim Bassett USMC—crashed into ocean off California coast, aviators not recovered

Ernie Wadsworth—while CO of VMFA 314's wife

"Bullet"—Major Donald Stuart Jones USMC; "Razor"—Lt. Col. Fred Schober USMC; "Suitcase"—Major William J. Simpson USMC; "Kap"—1Lt Steven A. Kapitan USMC—killed 1980 in midair off coast of Beaufort, South Carolina, aviators not recovered

Former Marines and wives: 'Apple'—Doug Mott; Leo 'the RIO' Kraus; Judy Wiley; Kathy Walsh; 'Trigger'—Lt. Col. Bobby Rodgers USMC Ret.; Kathleen Conard Jones Barkley; 'Bash'—Lt.Gen. Duane Wills USMC Ret.; Joyce Dinnage; and my mom, Mary Jean Pearson Jones, 'buck' private in the Marine Corps 1944

MARCIA SARGENT

High Flight

Oh! I have slipped the surly bonds of Earth,
And danced the skies on laughter-silvered wings;
Sunward I've climbed, and joined the tumbling mirth
Of sun-split clouds—and done a hundred things
You have not dreamed of—wheeled and soared and swung
High in the sunlit silence. Hov'ring there
I've chased the shouting wind along, and flung
My eager craft through footless halls of air.

Up, up the long, delirious blue
I've topped the wind-swept heights with easy grace,
Where never lark, or ever eagle flew.
And, while with silent, lifting mind I've trod
The high untrespassed sanctity of space,
Put out my hand and touched the face of God.

John Gillespie Magee, Jr.

—Printed on the back page of the
memorial service booklet for:
Lt. Col. Fred Schober,
Major William J. Simpson
Major Donald S. Jones
1Lt Steven A. Kapitan
Beaufort, SC January 1980

ADDENDUM: THE

AVIATOR BRIEFS

Aviator Brief I
Call Signs

Call signs—military nicknames used in air-to-air combat to avoid revealing an aviator's identity to the enemy—served within the world of friendlies to identify members of the fraternity of airmen. Pilots always had a moniker, and RIOs—Radar Intercept Officers who navigated and worked the radios but didn't have a control stick to fly the airplane, poor bastards—often earned a name other than their own. Easily recognized were the self-bestowed call signs of pilots versus those invented out of the fruitful and irreverent brain of a fellow flyer. If the call sign sounded too normal or too cool, the pilot had probably given it to himself.

An ideal name like Burner incorporated an aviation term so those not in the know would think its genesis to be from afterburner—a part of a jet airplane that when lit makes the plane very loud and very fast. The way the name game is played, he could be very slow, very quiet, or have a tendency to pass gas with explosive consequences. Burner never said.

Pipperburn's call sign referred to something called the pipper. The pipper—predicted impact point—was the location where a bomb, missile, or bullet was expected to strike if fired. When an electronic aiming device was locked on an opponent, but not fired, it burned an imaginary hole in the opponent— and accomplished nothing. Pipperburn's youth, inexperience, and tendency to consume copious amounts of alcoholic beverages all precluded him from ever actually firing on any target—

whether an adversarial airplane or a female. He'd be expected to aim often, but never shoot.

Okie, of course, hailed from Oklahoma and had an accent and a hayseed outlook on life to prove it.

Slug must have reminded someone at some time of a big, slow thing.

Given names were common fodder for call sign generation: Swizzle's last name Cwaliscz, properly pronounced "Fahleash"—impossible to see and say, Donut's last name of Duncan, Bolt's last name of Leitner, Soup's last name of Campbell. J.C.'s first name and middle initial was John C., but he built his reputation doing stunts in and out of airplanes that made others say, "Jesus Christ!"

Snatch insisted his call sign meant 'to grab fast' and came from his ability to snatch victory from defeat in a dogfight. He never explained the inevitable laughter or its connection to a synonym for a female nether-part.

Aviator Brief II
Squadron Jobs—COs, XOs, Pilots and RIOs

The CO—the Commanding Officer—was the boss. He made command decisions, ruled the roost, and if he thought it important—it was important. Number one mantra for a squadron aviator: Don't make your CO look bad.

The XO—the Executive Officer—was the paper-pushing, attention-to-details, pain-in-the-ass who made sure the big vision of the CO was turned into reality. He did a lot of the admin work and in any court-martial, he was in charge of the details.

Snatch and I have had a running discussion for years on who was the CO and who was the XO of their family. I maintained he was the XO since he paid the bills and did the worry-work over the administration details; and I was the CO, making command decisions on the big picture like how many children we would have, what the rules were for the children, and where we would retire. He always snorted and shook his head after I reminded him of the qualifications, but he didn't really argue because he knew I was always right. Proof I am the CO.

The main job an officer had in the squadron was to be a pilot or RIO. Pilots were judged on their competency in the air, whether they were 'a good stick'. This ranking went on a scale from "a damn fine stick' to 'unsafe at any speed'. Pity the pilot in VMFA 314 known by the call sign Unsafe-At-Any-Speed. Pity him, but don't respect him—and if you're a RIO, try not to fly in his backseat.

RIOs lacked control in the air—except through the radio yelling at their front-seater to land before they ran out of fuel and through a RIO's capacity to command eject. They could decide to eject both seats if the pilot was incapacitated—or too stupid to realize he had reached the point of no return to controlled flight. Since some pilots would rather be dead than look bad at the field, that ability to make the decision to abandon a multi-million dollar airplane often rested on a RIO's realization that staying alive allowed for redemption, while a smoking hole in the ground did not.

The Ops O—Operations Officer—held a lot of power in the squadron because he wrote the flight schedule. Everything depended on getting as many hops—flying the planes—as possible.

The AMO—the Maintenance Officer, Aircraft Maintenance Officer—held a position of respect. As stated before: Everything depended on getting as many hops as possible. If planes were broken, they couldn't be flown. A good relationship with the man in charge of the troops who fixed the planes the pilots flew was therefore essential.

The Safety Officer's job also involved keeping planes flying—safely. The ASO—Aircraft Safety Officer—had done his job when there were no accident reports for the quarter, the year, or so many hours of planes in the air. Somehow, AMOs and ASOs had different ideas of how to accomplish this objective. A Safety Officer who micromanaged every little hydraulic fluid leak and stuck valve into a downed airplane created negative attitudes in the AMO, the pilots who wanted maximum hops, and the troops. An airplane taken off flight status meant a pilot and a RIO not flying it. It also meant the troops had to work longer hours repairing it. Colonel Mike Sullivan maintained, "If twelve aircraft takeoff down the runway everyday, nothing else matters." Corollary: When all the planes fly, the troops are happy—because when planes are in the air, they don't have to be fixed, loaded, unloaded, or fueled, and ordinance guys could lift weights and the maintenance guys could jaw-jack, shoot the breeze, and bullshit each other—what they liked to do when all the planes were in the air.

The Administration Officer worked for the XO doing all the grunt work of the picayune details of filling out all the paperwork a military bureaucracy can generate—and then taking the shit dished out when it wasn't done right. Admin was a thankless job even when the pilot liked the XO he worked for.

What was the worst job in the squadron? Call it the Voting Officer. The pilot holding that 'esteemed' position had to make sure everyone had absentee ballots if needed. Later, when drug tests came into vogue, the VO made sure guys peed in the bottle. Why was that the worst job? Well, part of an aviator's mystique and power was tied to the importance of the job he had in the squadron and the excellence in which he performed it. Absentee ballots and drug tests were completely non-essential to flying, with no opportunity for excellence. In fact, being excellent at getting your fellow pilots to pee in the bottle pissed them off in more ways than one.

Aviator Brief III
To Eject or Not to Eject

The Phantom F-4 came equipped with a Martin-Baker mkH7 ejection seat. Aviators fly planes. This is important to remember when discussing ejections. An aviator without a plane to fly becomes just a Marine, not a bad thing—but not as good, either. Ejections guaranteed a pilot would look bad at the field by abandoning a multi-million dollar piece of machinery to crash and burn.

Aviators did not want to eject. But plane wings could fall off; engines inhaled birds through the turbine blades—something known as FOD—Foreign Object Damage; or equipment could malfunction at a critical point in flight, creating an unrecoverable airplane. Those were regrettable, but not the pilot's fault. A pilot who ejected in these circumstances and survived received sympathy and joined the Lucky Bastard Club—an unofficial community, as well as the Martin Baker Tie Club—an official honor and tie given to all pilots who eject from a plane with the aid of a Martin-Baker seat. The count currently stands at seventy-two hundred pilots saved. Most of the time, ejection seats worked.

But too many things could go wrong with an ejection, not all of them dependent on the manufacture of the seat. First, the canopy had to be blown off. If not, the pilot or RIO would impact the thick plastic. The plastic would win. Then, an explosive had to explode under the seat to send it and the aviator up the rails, pulling ten to twelve G's. Elbows, knees, and shoulders needed to be tucked in or the force of the ejection would break, dislocate, or mangle. A rocket had to shoot the seat free of the plane. If the plane traveled at too high a rate of speed, the jet blast of air would hit the aviator like a brick wall. The jet blast would win. The parachute had to deploy properly and the aviator had to come down somewhere he could be recovered, preferably not in the fireball of his crashed bird. Pilots thought paratroopers crazy for jumping out of perfectly good airplanes. So there was a corollary to Rather Be Dead Than Look Bad At the Field: Airplanes Are Meant To Be Flown, Not Jumped Out Of.

If the afterburners wouldn't fly you out, there were three ways to eject from a fighter. The first required reaching up above the helmet with both hands, and grasping the face curtain—not an actual curtain, just a striped loop—then pulling down, putting the elbows in a safe position for launch. The second method required reaching between the legs and pulling up on the ejection handle, another striped loop.

The third method was not to eject. This has only been successful once. A pilot making a red-eye tracking run at the Yuma Proving Grounds made a very low pass. Too low a pass. He ran out of sky and bottomed out on the desert floor. Next thing he knew he sat amid the sage and scrub in his ejection seat, but without a plane surrounding him. It had disintegrated into pieces in the crash. He had not. Known as the immaculate ejection. Grins all around.

The worth of an ejection seat depends on circumstances. Shit happens. Machines fail. A lucky pilot who keeps his cool lives to fly another day.

Aviator Brief IV
Cross-countries, TADs, and Deployments

The number one job of an aviator was to log as many hours as possible flying the airplane. A cross-country was generally a weekend spent in the plane going somewhere and then coming back. If the pilot could get out Friday, he could land somewhere and spend the night; then fly somewhere else on Saturday and spend the night; then return on Sunday—three legs, more flying.

A TAD (Temporary Attached Duty) involved a longer period of time, sometimes with one aircrew—pilot and RIO, sometimes with more. Getting selected for the Navy's Top Gun school was TAD, so was Nellis Air Force Base called Red Flag where pilots flew against 'enemy' combatants to practice ACMs (Air Combat Maneuvers) There was another black (super-secret etc.) program near Nellis where American fighters flew against so-secret-I'm-gonna-have-to-kill-you-if-you-find-out-about-it something or somethings. Rumors were they had Soviet MIG fighters. How did wives know about any of this? They listened when the guys stopped talking, and usually they were listening before—when the guys had forgotten wives were present.

A deployment involved all or most of the squadron, officers and planes, often with troops to take care of the planes.

Some aviators went cross-country for the hours. Some went for the action—in the Officer's Clubs on far-flung bases, or in the bars well known for female players. Sometimes a female player would be single, but sometimes she'd be married and unhappy, or married and lonely—which qualified as unhappy. Aviators who were players flew planes by day and flew into any willing arms at night. They thought they contributed to the general wellbeing of the world—as long as their wives at home didn't find outThe advantage to playing around on cross-countries, TADs, or deployments involved the deniability factor to the wives waiting at home. Ideally, nothing had to be denied because wives discovered nothing. 'Gear down, rings off' had a corollary—'and mouth shut!'

Jack Proctor and Major Dawson, two pilot aficionados of happy hour at Tinker Air Force Base, took off from Beaufort, South Carolina late because of maintenance and fueling delays. Their objective: to reach Tinker Air Force Base in one leg with no refuel or they would miss the better-looking ladies. In Oklahoma, after all, good-looking O-club babes were a limited population.

When they took off, the blivot on the racks had been installed backwards, so the left main landing gear wouldn't fully retract. An unretracted landing gear slows down a plane and reduces miles to the tankful. Driven by a serious case of GetAboardItis—where getting there took precedence, overriding all safety considerations—they continued on anyway, following their heatseekers.

GetAboarditis came from the Navy aviator's imperative to get aboard the carrier. The option in the middle of an ocean was

314

a wet one—even if the ejection went well. Somehow, the mind-set transferred to all Navy and Marine aviators, even though many more places existed to set a plane down safely over dry land.

Twenty minutes from Tinker with fifteen minutes of gas, the pilot in the back seat kept saying, "Don't fuck it up. You'd better not fuck it up."

They made it on fumes.

No harm, no foul.

Aviator Brief V
By Any Other Name

Some pilots have more than one call sign—the one they have in the training command and later, the one they earn. One particular squadron CO probably had one he used all through his early years as a pilot, but that name changed forever after his first squadron AOM, All Officer's Meeting.

Picture the officers, pilots and RIOs, sitting in the ready room, eager to hear the words from their new CO. A lot of data could be surmised from the brief the CO gave straight out of the chocks. Would his words indicate he was a good stick, a stick-in-the-mud, or both? Would he operate a flying club— where his favorite guys got the majority of the hops—or would he be interested in keeping everybody up to speed, newbies and buddies alike? Would he be a micro-manager or a laissez faire, hands-off kind of leader? Would he be a screamer or silent and deadly when crossed?

So there they were, lounging in ready room chairs ratcheted to a reclining position, sitting in decommissioned ejection seats, perched on window ledges, with their morning cup of joe, or a cigarette, or both—and the new CO stalked in.

His speech went something like this: "Good morning, a—holes. Welcome to my f—ing squadron. You may not know much about me, but if you're f—ing pussies about my f—ing language, you can shove it up your a—-, and walk right out the g—damn door right now. I don't give a flying sh—t about your f—ing sensibilities and I won't be watching how I f—ing talk around you."

Except Col. Profane had filled in all the blanks, the air was blue, he went on for much longer, and the faces in the room reddened from laughter or transfixed by the level of skill required to incorporate that many body parts, bodily functions and irreverent verbs into one speech. Generally, a CO is expected to demonstrate a higher standard of behavior than a lowly lieutenant. In this case, the Colonel performed past all expectations. A lot can be forgiven a good stick or a great RIO. Excellence as an aviator in any arena is lauded.

History doesn't tell if any walked out of the ready room that day, but if they did, their call sign would forever be the equivalent of 'Pussy'.

By Any Other Name—Revisited

While stationed in BFE (Bum F-ing Egypt) Twentynine Palms, Snatch invited men home from the Expeditionary Air Field, the EAF, for a home-cooked meal. They spent most of their deployment living in tents in the heat, the dust, and with snakes—all to give them practice under real desert conditions. Their meals were C-Rations, C-Rats, food eaten when out in the field. No one considered these canned meals particularly appetizing. A home-cooked meal looked good, and the Marine officers who ate at Snatch's house were very appreciative.

But none showed their appreciation quite like Ray. He complimented Snatch on his incredibly gorgeous wife. He thanked the wife in a soft drawl for welcoming him to such a beautiful home. He commented on how lovely she looked and how charming their young children were. Then at dinner, with

318

each bite into his mouth he mmm-mm-ed and ohh-hhhed at the taste, the texture, and the excellent preparation. He said how lucky Snatch was to have married such a talented cook.

The rest of the conversation over dinner was a typical flyby of funny stories about funny aviators: aviators extracting themselves from situations with grins all around or situations immersing poor bastards in deep kimchi. Then someone at the far end of the table mentioned Col. Profane.

"Did you say something about Col. Profane?" Snatch's wife asked. "Who is he anyway? I've heard about him for a long time, but never met him."

Ray leaned forward to look the length of the table at her. "Why ma'am."

Chortles from around the table.

Ray ignored them. "You want to know who Col. Profane is?"

More snickers.

"That's me, ma'am. I've been real well-behaved tonight, haven't I?"

And he had been, and he was. Snatch's wife never heard a word of profanity from the Colonel that night or any other.

So, in the right company, with the right incentive—no matter how outrageous their behavior with each other—some members of the fraternity of pilots knew how to behave as officers and gentlemen.

Aviator Brief VI
The Ready Room

Before pilots or RIOs took off and slipped the surly bonds of earth, they met in the Ready Room to get their shit together with the other flight members.

First, they got the admin details out of the way: like when to walk to the plane, when to man-up—be in the plane ready to strap in—when to taxi and take-off.

Second, they had to brief the set-ups and engagements. Would the air combat maneuvers, ACMs, be on radar or visual? A radar set-up meant starting BVR—Beyond Visual Range—a visual set-up began much closer in.

Aviators then briefed where the planes would be the start of each engagement: defensive, neutral, or offensive. Different start parameters meant different tactics.

If 1v.1—one fighter against one other—in a defensive start, then the bogey had an advantage. The bogey—the bad guy—could come up on the fighter's ass or could have an angle of attack to shoot a virtual sidewinder missile for a virtual kill. Fox Two!

A neutral start began with bogey and fighter side by side, turning away 45 degrees in a butterfly maneuver before turning head on, so neither had an angle, neither had a position of advantage.

An offensive start gave the fighter an advantage—say at the six-o-clock ready to attack the bogey up the rear. Aviators preferred an advantage right from the git-go but they needed to

*practice offensive and defensive tactics so that in a real combat
situation they could get themselves out of tight spots, find the
bogey, and shoot it down—the job of the fighter pilot. As the
Red Baron said, "Anything else is nonsense."*

*The aviator's ready room brief also covered the ROEs—
Rules Of Engagement. Pilots needed the rules and expectations
for any hop to take away unpredictability—so they could come
back in their plane and without looking bad at the field. The
rules were like a good wingman, the pilot knew ahead of time
what the other aviator would do in any given situation.*

*One of the rules for pilots was 'right to right'—in any
potential nose to nose collision, each plane was to turn right,
veering away from disaster. Jet fighters went very fast. How
fast? Well, if an aviator told you the maximum speed, he'd have
to kill you. However, fighters routinely flew toward each other
at one thousand knots—1150 mph—of closure. Without prior
discussion, a pilot had a fifty-fifty chance of turning the wrong
way in a head-on confrontation. Bad odds for planes. Worse
for aviators.*

*Another ROE came about as a result of one aviator's ex-
cellence at finding the bogey. Randy Brinkley on an ACM—air
combat maneuver—centered the radar dot within a mile of the
intercept, pointing his plane at the same piece of sky as the bogey
and maintaining the collision bearing. A mile at a thousand to
twelve hundred knots of closure left little time to avoid a midair
collision. The pilot found the bogey all right—very quickly and
close enough to touch. Oops! Imperative in ACM and formation flying: 'no touch touch—however slight'. It takes very little
contact to make parts of planes fall off—often with catastrophic
results. The F-16 lost most of a wing, the pilot ejecting safely.
The F-4 ended up damaged, but flyable. The result? A new*

ROE that forbade centering the dot within a mile of the opponent.

The rules also mandated disengaging from and steering clear of planes out of control. Just as a weaving car on a road indicated the driver was non compos mentis—drunk out of his mind—and should be avoided at all cost, so aviators avoided the pilot who lost control of his plane for any reason. The out of control drunk wouldn't be looking out for other drivers; an out of control pilot didn't have the time or the ability to steer clear.

Pilots were also directed to knock off any air-to-air combat maneuvering at ten thousand feet AGL—Above Ground Level. Altitude saved planes and lives. A pilot who flew too low and ran out of sky ended up a smoking hole in the ground. No glory in that.

Aviator Brief VII
ROEs and the Edge

Marine aviators loved to push the envelope—especially if it would win them glory. In aeronautics, the envelope was the known limits for the safe performance of an aircraft. Test pilots had to test (or push) these limits to establish the exact capabilities of the plane, and where failure was likely to occur—to compare calculated performance limits with ones derived from experience.

ROEs for Marine aviators established the ground rules, but the main requirement for being a good stick involved knowing when to push to the edge of the rules and when the rules didn't apply. Marines were told what they couldn't do; Air Force pilots were told what they could. Air Force pilots flew by the book and had itemized checklists for all contingencies. True, they lost fewer planes on the average, but in a 1v.1 with a good Marine pilot, they were beat like a rug.

Any pilot experienced departure from controlled flight at some point. A smart pilot knew how to keep a departure from becoming a post-stall gyration. Only Dilberts continued to lose control until an oscillating spin required deploying the drag chute.

The rules also required verbatim memorization of spin procedures, so they could be accomplished automatically, without thought, while in extremis. Out of control? Neutralize everything or just let go and grab two nonessentials in the cockpit. Upright spin? Have to know which way the plane is spinning, then where to put the stick to reduce the angle. Inverted spin? Different G-forces, but a pilot still needed to know where to put the stick. Can't remember the spin procedures? Bend over and kiss your ass goodbye.

After briefing the Rules of Engagement, the pre-flight brief always covered a NATOPS—Naval Aviation Training Operation Procedures—question of the day. Every aviator was expected to know the answers found in the big blue NATOPS book. One question might be, "What is the hydraulic pressure supposed to be?" Know your plane, save your life.

The Emergency Question of the Day followed, such as, "What is the procedure in the event of the landing gear not extending? Know the procedures: save your life and your plane.

The brief almost finished, the guys would talk some more about the hop—the aviator's term for a flight—using the white board and/or stick models, planes—usually an F-4 and a MIG—on the ends of dowels to represent the good guy and the bogey. "You do this, and I'm going to be trying to do that."

Any questions?

Time to man-up.

Aviator Brief VIII
The Officer's Club

Any aviator worth his wings knew when to lock his pipper on the O Club, or Officer's Club, the predicted impact point of wild and crazy pilot life: Friday afternoon, squadron day done? Tuesday evening, date life slow? On a cross-country to someplace your mother had never heard of? Go to the O-Club and find fellow aviators with whom to drink beer, roll dice, and swap stories.

Happy Hour at the O-Club—a mandatory activity for all squadron aviators. The bonding benefits of alcohol were well-documented in male social organizations. Pilots needed time away from the airplanes to debrief and detour from the stress of flying high-performance aircraft. Happy Hour started on Fridays after the squadron shut down for the weekend, sometime between 1600 and 1630—4 to 4:30 pm. Wives and girlfriends joined their drunken other halves at the club as soon as the babysitters came, typically 1800 to 1900. Single women, looking to play, filled up the barstools and walls by 2100. In the days before a DUI would end their career, aviators without semi-sober wives at the O-Club just drove slowly on the way home and watched out for MPs, the Military Police. Or not so slowly. Donut discovered orange trees in 1976 cost $3000 to replace when he crashed into and knocked over a prime specimen on his way home from a raucous Happy Hour at the MCAS El Toro Club.

No one knew how to party better than Marine pilots—no one—and they partied best with alcohol and other aviators to compete against.

The lowest rung on the competition ladder was the FNG, the Fucking New Guy. An FNG could be a new 1st lieutenant, but usually an FNG was an Air Force puke, or a Navy pilot, or a ground Marine who hadn't spent time with aviators. It almost didn't even count to mess with their heads because they wanted to be one of the boys so badly they'd do anything to be accepted. Also, most of their brains were newly minted and/or not used to playing the game. What game? Any game.

The best games to play with FNGs were games that allowed the FNG to buy all the drinks and all the meals—for everyone. FNGs were never told all the rules. In fact, they weren't told any rules or strategy except the most basic—"In this game you roll the dice."

While playing Horse, a regular O-Club game, the object was to roll the best poker hand possible with five dice in two rolls. When the FNG chose dice to hold aside, the experienced O-Club aviator deployed the Iwakuni double-tooth-suck (open lips, put upper and lower front teeth together, and inhale briskly) to indicate the FNG had made a bad move—whether the move was bad or not—a strategy meant to cause much second-guessing and doubt. Every pilot knew, 'He who hesitated, lost'—in any case, he who lost bought the drinks.

The FNG was only told a rule when he broke one. "Bummer. You dropped the dice. You have to buy a round." "Double bummer. You didn't have the drinks by the time the game finished. You have to buy another round." "Well, damn. You lost the game. You get to buy lunch for everybody." At the Kingsville Training Command, that meant the FNG bought lunch for all ninety-nine other students and instructors.

328

Aviator Brief IX
Compromising Positions

Pilots and RIOs in the Phantoms needed each other. Each had their tasks to accomplish. Each watched out for the bogey and other bad things heading their way. Pilots have saved RIO's lives with spiffy flying. Backseaters have saved their pilots' asses by seeing what they couldn't, or command-ejecting both when the front-seater wanted to save his reputation and/ or the plane more than his life. But RIOs all have a story of a pilot determined to fuck it all up.

Mike Fagan was a RF-4 backseater flying with his CO as pilot. They climbed in formation from Navy Dallas, Love Field, under IFR—Instrument Flight Rules—in big thick thunderstorm clouds. Formation flying in thunderstorms is difficult, so hard to do even the best pilots 'squeeze the plastic'—whiten their knuckles around the plastic control stick. In IFR formation flying, one plane takes the lead, flying instruments only. The wingman has to keep in parade position—slightly back off the wing of the lead plane while keeping it in sight. The planes were buffeted about, in and out of thick clouds. The CO drifted a little too far from the lead plane, and lost sight.

At that point, the smart thing to do would be to take a 45-degree turn away, radio call, "Lost sight," hold the heading and rejoin above the cloud cover. Instead, the CO tried a shad-

ow rejoin—joining up on a shadow he thought might be the other airplane in the clouds—a definite no-no by all formation flying wisdom. He collided with and damaged the stabilator on the tail of the lead aircraft. The contact, not-so-slight, disintegrated their own radome—the fiberglass nose of the plane covering the radar—that was sucked into the jet intake, FODing their own engine—FOD, Foreign Object Damage—very bad for turning turbine blades.

A pilot with good judgment would shut down the affected engine to avoid a fire and evaluate if the plane was flyable. If it wasn't, then a smart pilot would slow down the plane for a safer ejection. A sharp pilot knew to yell, "Eject! Eject! Eject!" because the RIO is the first to leave the plane via ejection. By the time the third "Eject!" left the pilot's lips, the canopy would have been jettisoned and the RIO would be up the rails, well warned and in a safe position for sudden departure from his flying machine.

None of that happened.

Mike Fagan, the backseater, knew he had a good fifteen minutes after take-off before he had any necessary task to perform. So he brought out his flight maps for later, kicked back mentally, and had just opened up the latest Hustler magazine to the centerfold spread when he heard a thump, followed shortly by a cough. He didn't know it was the sound of shit hitting the fan—the radome parts hitting the blades of the turbine and the subsequent engine deceleration. He didn't know and he had no time to think about it. Within half a second, and without warning from his pilot, the canopy blasted into the jet stream, maps and magazines sucked out in the vortex. Immediately, he was exposed to a driving thunderstorm with no mask or visor—he had been looking at the pictures, fergodsake! A half second later

330

the seat gun exploded him up the rails and out into blinding rain, cracking lightning, and hailstones.

The plane landed in an empty schoolyard—thank the good Lord for Sundays. The wheel chocks punched three feet deep in a driveway. Mike Fagan and the pilot landed on a golf course, an empty golf course because of the sheets of rain, wind, and lightning flashes. Mike never recovered his Hustler magazine, though his sense of humor did help him recover his temper—eventually.

Donut, a RIO, had a face curtain on his living room wall, courtesy of Unsafe-At-Any-Speed's command decision that it was safe to fly with the air-refueling probe door tied down with safety wire. In the Yuma landing pattern, the jury-rigged door popped open, the fueling probe flailed out into the windstream, and then ripped off. It punctured one of the fuselage fuel cells, which caught fire. The F-4, in an extremely short period of time, transformed from flying machine to flaming death trap. However, the Martin-Baker ejection seat performed as advertised. Donut had a new tie and a new wall decoration. Not good. RIOs hated to fly with hamburgers.

Aviator Brief X
Unflappable.

Some wives were hysterical most of their days, others were known for their calm demeanor under the most unusual of circumstances. Fish's wife owned the descriptor unflappable—rightly so. One day she answered the doorbell in her southern California home to find a man standing on the doorstep wearing a Lone Ranger mask—and nothing else.

She swung the door wider, turned, and yelled up the stairs, "Honey, it's for you! It's Rob!"

She never did admit how she knew the CO with his face covered and totally, starkers naked.

Aviator Brief XI
Flappable.

The runway for jets at Marine Corps Air Station Yuma ran parallel to the runway for prop planes. The target area for practice bombing was almost perpendicular to both. Snatch took off and his wingmen followed shortly thereafter. The lieutenants in the second and third jets had been told to join up as quickly as possible. Lieutenants want to please the senior officers and don't always engage their brains before trying to do so. So they took an early right turn, gear up, immediately after takeoff—right in front of a C-117 holding short, ready to take off in the other direction. An F-4 in take-off afterburner is loud and violently vibrates anything it passes close to—rattling the plane on the ground and probably soiling the C-117's pilots' underwear. Didn't help some general sat in the C-117.

Someone complained. Someone always complained. They called the squadron—because the VW on the F-4—the designated tail design for the Black Knight squadron—had been front and center in the windscreens of the startled prop guys. The XO, Hanley, got the call. Remember, deflecting flack away from the CO remained his main job . He stomped into the Ops office and demanded to know who was in the air.

"Why, Snatch is." The Ops Officer didn't mention the lieutenant.

After their ACM over the water, fuel low, the birds returned. The XO met Snatch's plane on the flightline even before the engines had been shut down. Rumplestiltskin had noth-

ing on Hanley for getting purplish-red in the face and hopping up and down and stamping his foot. "You're grounded! You're grounded for weeks!" The veins on his neck looked ready to explode.

Snatch had no idea why or what had the XO fuming. He'd taken off first and had been miles away when the lieutenants spooked the props. But he knew better than to argue. He let the bulldog chew on his ear and snarl and snap on the way back to the ready room.

Hanley grabbed the Ops O and stabbed a forefinger at his face. "Snatch is off flying for the next three weeks! Maybe longer!"

The Ops O blanched. "If Snatch doesn't fly, we don't have enough pilots to fly the hops to get the required hours."

"We don't?"

"Nope."

"Oh." The XO paused, regrouped, and retreated. "Snatch, you're back on the schedule."

Aviator Brief XII
Yen Rolls and Sweet Cake

One O-Club competition, known as the Yen Roll, began on base while stationed overseas—in Japan. Usually later in a drunken evening than earlier, someone collected the yen. Typically, they anteed up 3000 to 5000 yen per aviator, about 10 to 15 dollars. Starting with a number—often the squadron number—say 232, the aviators took turns rolling five dice. Each ace rolled subtracted from the original number.

The aviator who rolled the last ace, grabbed the money and hai-yakued to change out of his flight suit and make for the bars and girls in the ville. The lucky aviator had to spend the yen as fast as he could in places unlikely to be discovered—if found by any squadron-mate or -mates, he had to split the remaining funds. $300 US could buy a real good time in Japan in the late 60's and early 70's. Half that, half as good a time. Find the bogey and shoot it down was a time-honored tradition in air-to-air combat. Not surprising the fly boys figured a way to play it on the ground.

Aviators also competed at the O-club for the attention of women. Some—the players—competed for women who were players. Some just competed for the hell of it. Sometimes a lowly lieutenant or Captain took a bullet for their senior officer. At Tinker AFB's O-Club, a mother and daughter act looked for action with rich, handsome officers or any aviator. The mother's age and looks placed her in the more than slightly gunned-over category. The XO—a thirty-something, not-so-rich-or-handsome major—took for his own the sweet and tender twenty-something daughter and stuck the twenty-something 1st lieutenant with the mother. Not cool, but hey—he was an FNG. Hopefully, the lieutenant earned some extra flight hours for being a good wingman.

Aviators loved drinking and swapping stories over beer and laughter, but creating stories was even better than telling stories. Naval aviators considered the O-Club their frat house and a perfect venue for competition in outrageous behavior.

Bullet and Snatch, while stationed at Iwakuni, Japan as young lieutenants, deployed to Naha, Okinawa with a bunch of other young lieutenants. That evening, as they all drank in the Air Force O-Club, the base CO's daughter celebrated her Sweet Sixteen birthday party in an adjacent room. The centerpiece of the party, a multi-tiered cake for two-hundred guests, drew the less-than-sober aviators' attention. They pooled their funds to pay Worm, the youngest of them—whose first name really was Dick—to stick his dick in the cake. The 1st lieutenant looked at the hundred dollars they scraped up and shook his head. He might be young, drunk, and stupid, but not THAT drunk and stupid.

Instead, he walked into the room, backed up against the wall, took a running start, and bisected the cake with a full hai-karate chop. Cake flew everywhere. The AP, Air Police, arrived quickly and hauled his ass off to the base jail. By eight the next morning, the Red Devil's Squadron Commander walked into the Naha Air Force base's CO's office to apologize.

What happened to the lieutenant? What could you do to a lieutenant? He promised never to do that again and returned to Iwakuni, one hundred dollars richer.

338

Aviator Brief XIII
Fear and the Aviator

Aviators avoided even thinking about fear. Belief in invulnerability was essential to performance in situations where weak dick pilots and the lesser folks of the universe crashed and burned. Pilots trained to make automatic the choices keeping them in controlled flight. RIOs trained to be an extra set of eyes and ears, and brain for their pilots who held the control stick but might not have total SA—situational awareness.

Sometimes events happened so far out of normal that fear tapped a skeletal finger on even the bravest aviator's shoulder. On a hop—out near San Clemente Island—Doug Farmer, a RIO in VMFA 531, hadn't been able to keep his front-seater from getting disoriented in the clouds and departing controlled flight, so they both had to eject.

Doug soon floated alone in his little survival raft on a glassy sea off the California coast, his pilot nowhere to be seen. Through the tendrils of fog and mist, he noticed the waters roiling quite close to his raft. Something huge and dark appeared out of the depths and rapidly approached the surface. A black conning tower of a submarine erupted out of the ocean next to him, rocking him with the wash. Rising higher and higher, thirty feet out of the water, it loomed very, very dark and very, very big—with no markings on it to indicate its national affiliation.

Doug Farmer had a lemur.

Lemurs typically happened when a pilot got thumped—one fighter came underneath the second plane, then swooped up right before the victim's radome—the front pointy end of a fighter. The jetwash of the first aircraft thrashed the victim's plane, resulting in a physical thump. Getting thumped sent a cold shot of piss to the heart.

It wasn't another pilot fucking with him, but in this confrontation with a submarine, Doug Farmer's heart stuttered.

Men came out on the deck, but didn't speak. They threw him a line and waved him toward the boat.

At the time, high tension existed between the Soviets and the United States, with the Soviets known to patrol the waters off California. Why wouldn't the crew talk to him? The only explanation—they spoke Russian and he'd soon be spending years in a Siberian gulag.

Fear sloshed in his raft. He did not take the line. He did not paddle closer. He did not say anything either. Name, Rank, Serial Number, he reminded himself.

Détente.

Whoop. Whoop. Whoop. Coming closer.

A helo appeared overhead, US squadron markings clearly painted on its sides and belly. Rescue divers jumped into the water, waving at the sub crew before helping winch Farmer aboard the copter for a ride back to terra firma, terra cognita, California. The sub disappeared again below the waters of the Pacific.

Turned out the sub was a boomer—our nuclear super-secret-stay-underwater-for-two months-at-time-and-never-let-anyone-know-where-you-are-so-you-can-launch-missiles-at-the-enemy submarine. But the call had gone out 'Plane Down' and they'd been very close to where Doug's locator beacon had been

340

pinging. The captain of the sub broke protocol just to surface. Obligated to check in case he needed medical attention, they weren't going to talk to him. Not even to assure him they weren't bogeys.

Fear turned into a great story at the O-Club. Looking good at the field.

Aviator Brief XIV
Loss of Consciousness

―――――――――――――――――

A necessary piece of an aviator's equipment while flying a high performance aircraft was a G-suit worn over the flight suit. The aviator inflated the G-suit by connecting it to the bleed air from the turbine engine. It prevented the blood in the brain from pooling in the toes. Brains do not work well without a blood supply; they black out, experiencing LOC—loss of consciousness. Hard to keep a plane under pilot's control if the pilot has 'checked out' or 'taken a nap'. When pulling G's—increasing the pull of gravity from earth normal to up to 10 times earth normal—the valve in the suit connection sensed the onset of G, opened, and the bleed air filled the suit, pressing air bladders in the torso and legs to keep the blood from the extremities. A pilot helped this evolution by grunting, holding air in his lungs, and bearing down—all actions reminiscent of taking a dump. Not romantic, but neither was crashing and burning.

Mike Flood, an FNG lieutenant known as Flash, was flying a 1v.1 ACM hop, which called for a neutral start engagement. As the two F-4s arrowed straight toward each other, radome toward radome, Flash—trying to look good at the field and impress the lead plane's veteran pilot, Fog—made a high G bat turn at the pass—a very quick, instantaneous turn—to the left, but it was too high G a turn, at least a G or two above his G tolerance. Neither Flash nor the G-suit could compensate quickly enough. Flash checked his six—looked behind the plane—over his left shoulder and promptly 'took a nap'.

MARCIA SARGENT

The airplane came off the turn doing odd things, like rolling over and falling out of the sky. Steamboat Willie, Flash's RIO, tried to get his pilot on the ICS—the Intercom System. No response. The plane continued doing weird things, departing from controlled flight. Steamboat Willie saw the pilot's head flopping to either side. He called out, "Mike? Mike!" As the plane pointed nose down, passing 10,000 feet above sea level, speeding toward the center of the earth, the wise backseater called, "Eject! Eject! Eject!" turned the T-handle, and command-ejected both of them. From all reports, Flash didn't come to until he floated in his chute, about to hit the water, with absolutely no clue where he was or how he got there.

Turned out to be one of the first documented cases of sudden loss of consciousness. Not documented before this because, in most other suspected incidents, the pilot, the plane, and the RIO hadn't survived. As part of the accident investigation, they put Flash in a centrifuge, spun him up to a certain amount of G-force, had him look back over his shoulder and he blacked out. When he came to after they stopped the centrifuge, he had no idea where he was or how he had gotten there. In the interest of scientific inquiry—and maybe to fuck with the young pilot—the investigators had the centrifuge cranked up twice more. Flash turned his head and it was, "Say sayonara, baby" all over again. The video was a cult hit at squadron parties for weeks afterward.

On the day of the accident, once the helo had plucked the crew out of the water and flown them to Miramar, after determining both were safe and uninjured, Snatch called Flash's nineteen year-old wife. Squadron protocol dictated contacting the wife or next of kin before the wrong story came from unreliable sources—i.e. Other wives.

344

She answered the phone.

"Now, Mrs. Flood, Mike's been involved in an aircraft accident and had to eject over water. I called to tell you he's okay and uninjured."

A pause.

Snatch was sure she's going to cry, panic, or faint following the words 'accident' and 'eject'—all normal and justified reactions to the survival of an ejection by a loved one. Wives tended to be hysterical when reminded how dangerous their husbands' jobs were. "The helo's picked him up and they're bringing him back to Miramar. He'll call you himself as soon as he can."

"Oh. Okay." Her voice burbled bright and bubbly. "Tell him I'll be at the beach."

Unconscious and Unconscious's unconscious wife.

Aviator Brief XV
Swim Quals and Sea Monsters

Trigger dreaded swim quals. Raised in inland Texas, comfortable on horseback, roping calves, and comfortable training pilots from his rear seat in the airplane, he could barely manage to keep his head above water even in a pair of swim trunks, much less in a flight suit, g-suit, seat harness and flight boots.

Pilots and RIOs were required to pass a swim qualification—recreating what they'd have to do if they ejected over water and their life raft failed to inflate properly. Aviators had to jump into the practice pool fully clothed, take off their flight boots, and tread water for a period of time without drowning. Since the military invested a lot of time and money on aviators by the time they got to swim quals, there were rescue divers in scuba gear in the pool watching to save any who might be in trouble.

Taking off his boots required the longest time with Trigger's face underwater, so he thought he'd outwit the hardest part by loosening the laces until they barely stayed on his feet on the pool deck.

When ordered, the aviators jumped in. Unfortunately, leather became sodden and sticky when wet. Trigger tried to remove his boots without submerging, only gasping on the sur-

face, his lower lip barely clear, while tugging frantically. He must have struggled too much. The ever-helpful rescue diver on the bottom of the pool came up and helpfully tugged on the boot as well, pulling Trigger's lower lip and head under. He gasped in a lungful of chlorinated water. He clawed his way to the surface.

He did not pass that round. Rumor had it he took three tries before barely succeeding.

Trigger was even less fond of the parachute drop. A motorboat would tow the aviator up in the air over the ocean—think Acapulco parasailing—and then disconnect the parachute and aviator from the towrope. The aviator would then float to the sea, and into the sea, where he'd practice disentangling or cutting himself from his parachute without drowning.

As much as Trigger disliked the intimate contact with water, he feared what lurked beneath the surface more. He knew, just before his toes touched the water, a great white's open maw filled with razor sharp teeth waited. He called the parachute drop, 'Trolling for Sharks'.

Aviator Brief XVI
Command Sympathy

A well-run squadron was like a family, with the CO the tough yet benevolent father figure watching over his aviators. Personal troubles at home could affect performance in the air. A pilot might be taken off flight status temporarily for a death in the family, financial problems, a separation, or a pending divorce—anything with the potential to divert concentration. The CO had an obligation to evaluate how each aviator handled stressful situations and the likely impact on his ability to fly safely.

Jack Hartman got called into his CO's office. The CO invited him in, told him to take a seat, and make himself comfortable. He offered Jack a donut out of a pink bakery box. Jack chose one and sat back, waiting to see what the CO wanted.

The CO hemmed and hawed, then in a roundabout way suggested everyone went through tough times and there was no shame in it. The CO said, "I hope you know you can always come to me to talk about anything troubling you."

"Sure, CO." Puzzled, Jack figured the boss needed to feel needed. He took a bite of the donut.

Silence.

The CO said, "So tell me about what's troubling you."

Jack didn't know what to say. He took another bite of the donut and mumbled, "I don't have anything troubling me."

"You're not going through marital problems?"

"Nope."

The red-faced CO stood up, grabbed the half-eaten donut out of Jack's hand, and kicked him out of the office.

No troubles? No donut.

Jack unknowingly broke the number one rule. Never make the CO look bad at the field.

Aviator Brief XVII
No Guts, No Glory

On a day of such crappy weather even the seagulls stayed grounded on the grass between the runways, Colonel Sullivan turned for takeoff from Runway 7 at MCAS El Toro. Pushing forward the throttle and kicking in the afterburner, he lifted off from the surly bonds of earth into a flock of seagulls startled by the decibels of an F-4 turbine.

Three hundred seagulls funneled into a jet engine were a problem of compressibility. Blood and feathers, guts and bones don't pack well into the relatively small space of a Phantom's engine.

With one turbine destroyed and unsure of the damage to the other, the colonel looked at the land near the base. If the jet stopped being able to fight gravity and he had to jump out, the hunk of steel and explosive jet fuel would twist and burn into homes, schools and/or stores. Not a good option.

Good pilots make good decisions in the worst of circumstances. He pointed his radome south and flew the crippled bird with its many mangled birds to Yuma, Arizona, where he managed to land safely.

The CO of the squadron appreciated the decision to divert, preventing a potential public relations disaster. He also appreciated the skill of the pilot in preserving a valuable piece of machinery. Engines could be replaced. A plane crashed and burned was unrecoverable.

Yuma, the day Col. Sullivan landed, had a high of 105-degrees. Yuma registered 105-degrees the next day, too. The plane, with its multiple bird strike, FODded engine, sat on the flight line in the heat for two days.

Then the maintenance officer, Snatch, flew to the desert to inspect the extent of the damage to the engine.

The guys in Yuma working on the tarmac were happy to see him. A wide area had been cleared around the colonel's aircraft. No one wanted near the miasma of gull guts rotting in the gutted turbine blades. Neither did the hapless maintenance officer.

Snatch got the guts. Col. Sullivan the glory.

Aviator Brief XVIII
Formal Corps Traditions

Most formal occasions in the aviation community, such as the Marine Corps Ball, had wives and girlfriends present— in recognition of the women's civilizing effect on flyboys. Women also enjoyed dressing up more than the men. Formal clothes for women were slinky and comfortable, once they removed the killer heels. Formal wear for the aviator was stiff, starched, and tight on the collar—the complete opposite of a flight suit. Short of taking off the jacket and unbuttoning the collar, no relief was to be found from the constriction. No relief from the restriction of socializing with generals and colonels, either.

Once in awhile, Corps tradition presented a formal occasion with no women. At Basic School, Mess Night for each class became an institution. Beforehand, company XOs admonished new lieutenants about such taboos as loosening a tight collar or imbibing to the point of passing out at the dinner table. Several minutes of the lecture explained the requirement for bladder control and the planning needed to accomplish it. They cautioned that the bugle call "last call for the head" just prior to marching into dinner might be the most important musical accompaniment of the night. The requirement to remain at the table once dinner had begun was absolute.

At Mess Night, the band played and Marine officers marched in adhering rigidly to custom and tradition. They ate and drank their way through a multi-course dinner. Stewards filled wine glasses when appropriate, and the serving and removal of courses evolved with the panache of the Sunset Parade at 8th and I. Cigars appeared and the President of the Mess lit the smoking lamp. With the last toast, "to the Corps!" all felt proud to be a Marine. Mess Night reached its climax at the bar: lieutenants, captains, majors and colonels holding snifters of brandy. An evening to remember.

A pre-cruise dinner at NAS Lemoore evolved into a night to remember in a different way. Two Navy squadrons hosted two Marine squadrons and the other Navy squadrons that were part of CAG-11—Carrier Air Group 11. Meant to be a bonding time for the squadrons who would be sharing the confines of a ship for six months, it was put together as a Navy version of a Mess Night.

All had progressed as it should up to the meat course. Then, as someone at the head table spoke at the microphone, a lone roll arced high overhead, followed by a return barrage of rolls, some buttered lavishly. Before long, heavy artillery in the form of fully loaded potatoes launched. By the end of the evening, the rolls and potatoes were the least of it.

The El Toro based Marine squadrons saddled up and departed in the squadron jets by ten hundred hours the next morning—aviators breaking the 'twelve hours from bottle to throttle' rule.

The Lemoore base CO did not see the damage until early afternoon. He pulled in the MAG-11 CO, who dragged in the A-7 COs, who burned up the phone lines pulling in all their

*squadron officers. The Marines from El Toro did not fly back in
to help clean up. Their absence was duly noted.*

*Shortly afterward an official message arrived at MCAS
El Toro addressed to the two Marine squadrons:*

MARCIA SARGENT

```
** ** ** ** ** ** ** ** ** ** ** ** ** ** **
* U N C L A S S I F I E D*
** ** ** ** ** ** ** ** ** ** ** ** ** ** **
PT 02 00        085 1517 06


RT TU ZY UW R HH GG O4 18 0851 M -U UU U- -R
UW JG FA 1S
ZNR UU UU U
FM ATKRON TWO SEVEN
TO RUW JG FA/VMFA THREE TWO THREE
RUW JG FA/VMFA FIVE THREE ONE
ZEN/COMLAT WING PAC LE MOORE CA
RUWJGFA/MAG ELEVEN
INFO RUWDVAA/COM CA RA IR WING FOURTEEN
RUWJOHA/ATKRON ONE NINE SIX
RUWOAA/CA RA EW RON ONE ONE THREE
BT
UNCLAS //NO 17 10//
```

RETURN DINING ENGAGEMENT
1.   THE OFFICERS OF VA-27 AND VA-97 ACCEPT
     WITH PLEASURE THE UNSTATED INVITA-
     TION FROM SNAKE ONE AND GHOST ONE
     TO A RETURN DINNER ENGAGEMENT AT
     THE MCAS EL TORO OFFICERS CLUB.
2.   REQUEST DINNER MENU AS FOLLOWS:
     12 DOZEN LIGHTLY BAKED POTATOES
     WITH SOUR CREAM
     48 BASKETS OF SOFT ROLLS

356

48 ONE LITER CARAFES WINE (CHEAP, RED ONLY)

4 FIRE EXTINGUISHERS

3. REQUEST FRANGIBLE RESTROOM FIXTURES

4. ANTICIPATE THE REQUIREMENTS OF 8 STEAMOVAC DO-IT-YOURSELF RUG CLEANING UNITS TO BE EMPLOYED AT DISCRETION OF SNAKE ONE/GHOST ONE FOLLOWING FESTIVITIES.

5. VA-27 AND VA-97 SEND

The Marine squadrons got the message. The COs of VMFA-531 and VMFA-323 held closed-door sessions with their officers. Significant "voluntary contributions" in the thousands of dollars were extracted and forwarded to NAS Lemoore.

Aviator Brief XIX
Flying At Any Cost

Maintenance officers appreciated pilots who got a plane home to be worked on. If it could be flown safely—fly it. Some weak dick pilots and RIOs downed their ride for every little hydraulic fuel leak. Phantoms were elderly planes—they all leaked a little bit. Get some balls, fergodssake.

An FNG lieutenant in VMFA 314 didn't like causing trouble for his AMO—Aircraft Maintenance Officer. So, on a refueling stop in Yuma, one leg away from home base, frustrated when the F-4 wouldn't accept external electrical power from the starter, he decided to try a non-standard procedure, principally used for testing the RAT—ram air turbine, in order to get going.

In the non-standard procedure, high-pressure air is directed at the RAT, which spins into operation, providing power. The lieutenant deployed the RAT, and standing on the wing, held the nozzle of the hose from his Wells Air Starting Unit.

The pilot intended to guide high-pressure air from the hose across the blades of the RAT. The RAT would spin and produce enough power to light off his fighter.

Fast-moving air charged through the hose to the nozzle.

Unfortunately, back-pressure on the hose caused it to thrash about wildly. The hapless lieutenant, flying twenty to thirty feet in the air, whipped back and forth, held on as long as he could before being tossed to the concrete below.

Medical personnel needed over a hundred stitches to close up the deep three-inch gash on the lieutenant's arm.

He lived to make general—and to be a credit to the Marine Corps.

Ignorance was temporary, unless it proved fatal.

Aviator Brief XX
Quick Change

One A-4 squadron must hold the record for the most Changes of Command in the shortest period of time—three in six months. Generally, a CO's tenure lasted from a year to two years. Getting fired short of a year required fucking up enough that the Group CO announced he had 'lost confidence in the ability of the squadron CO to lead.' Some men spoke seriously of falling on their swords when faced with such a scenario. They'd rather be dead than look bad.

The first hapless CO flew into Lemoore NAS. Wanting to show the Navy that the Marines had the right stuff, he brought his flight of four overhead in a flashy, yet frowned upon, fan break-where all the planes rolled together toward the runway. Unfortunately, in concentrating on looking good, the CO neglected to deploy his landing gear before touching the aircraft down on the runway. The plane ground to a halt in a shower of sparks and crunched plane parts.

A Change of Command Ceremony was hastily arranged with a band and printed programs.

The new CO of the squadron, Tim Dineen, a good stick and a good guy, flew a plane with a high time engine which should have been in overhaul. Engines were required to be reworked every certain numbers of hours. A ten-percent flex was built-in just in case a plane was on a cross-country when the maximum threshold had been reached. Col. Dineen flew a plane well past the flex hours, and then ran out of luck when the over-the-maximum-threshold engine quit, he had to eject, and then was ejected from his command.

They held the Change of Command ceremony the next morning in the Group CO's office, without a marching band or printed programs, presided over by the frown of the Group Commander, and with the outgoing CO conspicuously absent. Did Duke Lind, the brand new CO, feel any need to knock wood, cross his fingers, or light a candle in the base chapel?

Duke had been on the schedule to fly well before the emergency change in squadron leadership. What better way to celebrate, or mourn the ouster of a friend, than to launch into the sky? The flight of two prepared to take off on their briefed, low-level navigation mission. Unfortunately, Duke's plane did not cooperate in the celebration. It broke in the chocks seriously enough that Duke and the plane were grounded.

The FNG pilot in the other plane asked if he could continue, flying the briefed mission solo. Duke saw no reason both should suffer from his bad luck. He cautioned the new lieutenant, on the radio, to stay above 5000 feet—although the original brief had been down to 1300 feet above ground level.

Perhaps the radio was broken, too.

The FNG lieutenant returned and landed—miraculously—at MCAS El Toro in an A-4 that had its canopy and tail sawn almost in half by 90 to 100 feet of high tension wire. No ceremony was held for Duke's ouster.

His tenure as a CO? Six hours.

Aviator Brief XXI
Dark Waters

A pilot flying out of Iwakuni, Japan had a night hop over the Sea of Japan. Next thing he knew he was being picked up out the freezing water by SAR—Search and Rescue. He remembered nothing of a crash or ejection, but his plane had disappeared. Pilots hate mysteries. What they don't know can, and often has, killed them or others. With any accident, there is an Accident Investigation to figure out the cause of the mishap.

In an unusual step, they had the pilot hypnotized. Under hypnosis, he remembered going to join up on lights below him, but instead of his wingman's lights, they must have been reflections on the water. His plane flew into the sea before he realized he needed to eject. He came to, in absolute Stygian darkness, in a cockpit filling with icy water. He tried to manually open the canopy, but the pressure outside wouldn't allow it. The ejection handle wouldn't have helped; the water would have held the canopy on and he'd have been rocketed into the plexiglass. So he waited in the black cold until the cockpit filled, then he opened the canopy and swam up to the surface, one hundred feet above the plane. He kept his cool to live to fly another day.

What could go wrong, would go wrong, and ejections were no exception. Jack Hartman on the USS Saratoga was on the catapult to launch. The bridle connecting his jet to the cat broke on one side and the catapult flung him and the plane from zero to two hundred miles per hour in six seconds—twisted sideways with one wing forward. He knew the plane would never fly, so he ejected successfully. His plane crashed in front of the carrier. He floated down to the sea surface directly in front of the bow of the ship going twenty-five knots. The aircraft carrier ran over him. The last thing he remembered while underwater was the sound of the screws, with blades twice the size of a Volkswagen. No one could figure out how he was spat out by the wash without the parachute or parachute cords tangling in the blades.

It wasn't always enough to be good—sometimes an aviator had to be lucky.

Aviator Brief XXII
Flight Procedures

1. *Strap in*
2. *Pull the ejection seat pins*
   a. *Done by the plane captain. 11 to 12 pins. Shows them to pilot between his/her fingers to make sure all are out. Seat won't fire if they're in.*
3. *Put away map bag and any other gear*
4. *Check switch positions*
5. *Make sure ICS is on (Inter-Cockpit System—mike with RIO)*
6. *Give two-finger start up hand signal.*
7. *Plane Captain checks plane to make sure all the flight surfaces work and there are no leaks*
8. *Taxi out*
9. *Take off*
   a. *Both planes roll—release the brakes—at the same time*
   b. *Execute section take-off so flight clearance can be made for both*
   c. *Put in burner*
   d. *Communicate with hand signals to other pilot*
10. *No touch-touch*
11. *Avoid clouds full of rocks*

Aviator Brief XXIII
Landing

---

1. *Take turns coming into the break to land.*
2. *Open canopy with canopy lever when entering fuel pits; in case of fire, get out quickly.*
3. *Hot refuel.*
4. *Taxi to flightline.*
5. *Wait while plane captain chocks airplane.*
6. *Wait until plane captain signals, 'Cut engine'*
7. *Cut engine.*
8. *Get face curtain pin out of pin bag and put it in to 'safe' seat.*
9. *Climb out of plane and on to deck.*

Aviator Brief XXIV
Aviator Credos

When in the air:
1. *Be prepared for the unexpected*
2. *Know where your wingman is at all times*
3. *Watch out for bogeys*
4. *Find the bad guys and shoot them down*
5. *Have as many landings as take offs*
6. *Remember—if it was easy, anyone could do it*

Acknowledgements

Writing a book is a daunting, sometimes lonely task. Thank you to all my writing critique groups. Wing Wife would never have turned out so well without your discerning eyes. Particular thanks to Chris Simon, Debby Gaal, Michele Khoury, Kimberly Keilbach, Pam Bennett, Joanne Wilshin, Judy Whitmore, Dennis Phinney, Mary Gulesarian, Janet Simcic, and Linda Williamson for keeping me on the write track. Thank you to my instructors and mentors: to Lou Ann Nelson--without her and her classes at UCI Extension I would never have written any book, to my gentle and discerning Pirates leader John Daniel at the Santa Barbara Writers Conference, to Laura Taylor, and especially to Lisa Lenard-Cook who convinced me I wrote a memoir and gave me unending friendship along with her good advice.

Thank you to all the fine men and women of the United States Marine Corps, active duty, retired, and particularly those who served with my husband and my brother. The time I spent with you and yours was the most fun I've ever had—and what wasn't fun taught me about life, death and the reasons we don't go through this world alone. Here's a shout out to the regular grunts: the pilots and RIOs get all the glory, but the troops keep them in the air and back for safe landings through thorough maintenance, safe fuel handling, and general attention to details. Semper fidelis.

Most of all I want to thank my husband Andy for his love. He believed in me when I didn't believe in myself. Our life is more a controlled crash than a smooth cat launch but he stays on my wing. Furthermore, without Snatch's technical expertise, the authenticity of this memoir would be much less apparent. I listened to the flyboys, but he flew with them.

Everything in Wing Wife happened to me or to people my husband and I knew. Some names have been changed to protect the guilty and the time frame of some events has been changed for story flow. But as the guys used to say when they remembered mishaps and misadventures over beers, "You couldn't make this stuff up!"

Any mistakes I made are all my own.

Marcia Jean Jones Sargent
Laguna Beach 2010

About the Author

A Marine fighter pilot's wife from 1975 until 1987, Marcia observed and interacted with military aviators and their spouses when they still had a great time and damned the consequences. When her husband "Snatch" retired back to Southern California, she issued imperatives in her elementary school classrooms and worked as a social studies and language arts mentor for Saddleback Unified School District. A University of California-Irvine Writing Fellow, she wrote the Interact (Social Studies School Service) simulations CHINA and EGYPT and two YA fantasy/adventure books.

When not writing, Marcia now walks the sand in Laguna Beach with her husband and a golden retriever named Sir Lancelot. Her cat named Snicklefritz and an African Grey parrot, Princess Aurora, wait at home since they do not like immersion in salt water.

Visit her website http://www.marciajsargent.com to find out more about her writing, see photos of people and places and planes, and to read her blog.

Made in the USA
Charleston, SC
15 November 2010